T0367515

# FALLING INTO DARKNESS

## ALEX DIAZ

authorHOUSE®

*AuthorHouse™*
*1663 Liberty Drive*
*Bloomington, IN 47403*
*www.authorhouse.com*
*Phone: 1-800-839-8640*

*Published by AuthorHouse 8/27/2014*

*ISBN: 978-1-4969-3660-8 (sc)*
*ISBN: 978-1-4969-3659-2 (e)*

*Library of Congress Control Number: 2014915271*

*Any people depicted in stock imagery provided by Thinkstock are models,
and such images are being used for illustrative purposes only.
Certain stock imagery © Thinkstock.*

*This book is printed on acid-free paper.*

*Because of the dynamic nature of the Internet, any web addresses or
links contained in this book may have changed since publication and
may no longer be valid. The views expressed in this work are solely those
of the author and do not necessarily reflect the views of the publisher,
and the publisher hereby disclaims any responsibility for them.*

# DEDICATION

To all those who read this book, thank you, no really thanks. I don't know what would happen if none of you did.

To Lori, who inspired me to be a writer.

To my toilet, who's been taking my crap ever since I was able to sit on her.

To Funny Pics and my CoC clan, told you I would include you all here.

And finally to Joslyn. To the one who gave me a reason to keep waking up each morning, to the one who stop me getting the deep cuts on my wrist. You really are the best I can ask for, and more than I could have ever wished for. And I'm sorry for making you feel the way you do about me now, guess we couldn't have our happy ending. Please know this book is for you and no matter what, I will always love you.

# CONTENTS

# CHAPTER ONE

## DARK SIDE OF COLONY EDO 1

### FIVE HUNDRED THOUSAND LIGHT-YEARS FROM EARTH

There was something in the air along with the smoke, the ash, the fire, and the sulfur. It felt like a painful agony. It hurt me knowing that the city was wounded but that the pain did not bother me. The clouds did not want the suns to show on this forsaken piece of rock that was called a planet. No, they preferred it gloomy and melancholy. Fitting, given how the town was reported to the government of Earth. Hands in my pockets, I continued to gaze upon the scene. It appeared that every building was burned to the ground, burning, or scorched with hellfire. I tiptoed inside a building that had been the old police justice building in happier times. Since the Japanese people had first inhabited this side of the planet all those years ago, the houses were built out of wood, with thatched roofs and the most up-to-date holographic communicators and electronic equipment from the interstellar market. They had funded their expedition, so they could build their colony as they saw fit.

There were enough burned bodies in the building to make an undertaker feel as if Death were watching him work. I took a good whiff of that sweet smell and stepped back, covering my face with my sleeve. I had read a book about those who had faced the ovens in the camps, and they talked about that sweet smell, as did every soldier who described the burned carcass of his friend or enemy. In my seven years of service, I had smelled that scent as well. This massacre seemed fitting to the horrors of the times. In the middle of the building was a hole the size of a quarter. It was easy to see, for the floor was red, and the hole was black. An ember rose from the hole and died out in the air. I moistened my lips with my tongue. It was almost skin melting hot which in turn reminded me of an inferno in there. Sweat beaded on my forehead, reflecting the heat, my fatigue, and the unmistakable feeling of dread. *That hole is not supposed to be there,* I thought, as more embers erupted from the gap in the ground. I looked around the ruined offices at the remains of monitors, projectors, and data collectors of such advance craftmanship. It was strange to see such familiar objects in an unfamiliar and darkened state. I took about fifteen steps toward the hole and fell into an even larger trap hole.

The darkness into which I fell was paradoxically very chilling. I had tried to grab on to something to avoid falling in, but this was a very cleanly dug hole. The blood inside my head rushed upward, then downward, and then to each side before going upward once again. The fall would have been painful if not for the fact that the ground was very soft, like a combination of sand and mud. There was a tunnel in front of me and behind me, a corridor. The putrid smell of burning bodies seared my nose and made my eyes water. I hated that odor more than ever, mostly because my breathing had speeded up, and my hands had begun to sweat more.

The source was down there. I stood up, startled by a faint noise, as I reached shakily for my two knives, which I guarded closely in the scabbards at my back. An eerie silence answered the noise. I turned around and put one knife in the wall of the hole that had trapped me. I then used my other knife as support and started my way up. There was another presence in this pit, and it sensed me, uttering an ear-shattering screech, which told me it was time to get to the surface. I had heard that screech before on a desolate planet when I was working on an escort mission for a scientist. I did not want to face it again, and I began climbing faster. My knives pierced the dirt as easily as they would butter, but the soil was as sturdy as ice.

While I was climbing, I didn't even make it five feet up before I noticed holes that others had probably used to help them climb. The dark wall had more secrets to share. Boot marks, and what seemed to be finger marks, littered the wall. One of my knives stabbed a hand and then my other one stabbed a leg. I yelped but regained my balance without falling. It seems that other victims had the same ideas as I did about escaping, but they didn't have anything to help them climb up. Whatever had stabbed them made a burned entry wound in their bodies and left them pinned to the wall of the hole. It saddened me and made me desperate not to share the same fate as these poor people. The temperature suddenly flared up, bringing a sulfurous smell to the room, and I knew that whatever had killed these people was beneath me. Its wail pierced the silence and if any surviving wildlife lay close, ran for its life.

*What to do? My knives will melt if I stab it, and I need them. I can't run away. I need to kill it. Containment. Remember containment. Keep the mission. What to do, damn it!* I argued with myself, trying to form a plan.

I reached the top of the hole and spotted a ceremonial katana. Although my two knives gave me more power and speed, their drawbacks were having to get close and personal just to harm my attacker. The unearthly creature was coming up the hole faster than I had. Seeing no choice, I grabbed the katana, and when the creature popped its head out of its trap, I was able to see my hunter. The mouth was where a normal human mouth would be, but instead of being horizontal, it was vertical. The torso was somewhat humanoid, but its arms were blades that glowed red with a light that emitted intense heat and energy. The lower half of its body was something that resembled a centipede, but it gave off a dark light that cast a shadow against the other shadows. Its eyes seemed to care about nothing, and, what was worse was that the creature looked hungry.

A scorcher, from the planet Corpus V. A creature from the other side of life. A half second later, I pulled the katana for one last duty, hoping it was *its* last duty, not *mine*. A quick slash to the head decapitated the creature but also melted my weapon, leaving a burn mark on my hands. This alien beast fell to its grave in the hole that was the resting place of its victims. I rubbed my eyes and sighed with some relief. *That shouldn't have worked,* I thought.

*I should be dead, scorched, mutilated, and probably eaten.* My breaths, which had been racing with the quickened pace of my heart, finally slowed.

"Evelyn ..." the glass and electronic transmitter sent out my words.

"This is Evelyn. Talk to me. Are there any survivors?" a voice that sounded like honey replied.

"No, not here, and that's not what's worrying me. A fully grown scorcher did this. A fully grown, fed, and angered scorcher did this. Something that isn't supposed to be out of a quarantined planet did this," I said to her as something caught my eye.

I walked toward a pile of rubble and a pool of a dark liquid. A little hand beneath the rubble seemed to reach for something. I crouched down and picked up what remained of the child's teddy bear. I couldn't speak or react but could only stare.

"So you think someone brought it here?" Evelyn asked cautiously.

"I don't know what to think about that, but how did one scorcher get into a colony and massacre every man, woman, and child? Let's start with that," I said coldly as I stood up and took off my jacket, which was on fire.

"You really don't care about them, do you? All you care about is the mission! Don't you care about other people anymore?" she hissed at me.

I knew what I had to say to please her.

"I care about you, sis," I replied, holding both hands up.

"But you're different now. Just send the pictures," she spat at me over the radio.

"You really don't like me anymore, do you? I'm sorry I'm cynical and apathetic at times." I took out a recording drone from my jacket, and it flew around as it sent pictures from this little hell to the servers on Earth.

It did occur to me that these last few years I'd said less, worked more, and started disconnecting with reality to an unhealthy degree. Evelyn always complained that I slept and ate so little. The bags under my eyes proved that.

"I don't like what you've become. I'm sorry," she replied sadly.

"That's all right."

"How can you not care?"

"A man who fights monsters will eventually become one," I said, quoting an old dead man.

"Those aren't your words," she replied. "You still aren't a monster … Do you care about anyone else?" she asked bitterly, but of course she knew the answer.

"That's a story for another time, but don't worry. I'll tell you someday," I lied. Somehow that false promise would come true.

I pulled up my sleeve and strapped my watch and touchpad to my arm. I pressed the camera option and put on my glasses. The lenses would take pictures and audio, recording events from a first-person perspective. I turned and took pictures of the mounds of ashes that could still be identified as people. Some were holding guns in a futile attempt to kill the creature. I took one picture of a family of three huddled in a corner, the father trying to shield his family.

As I paused over this horrific scene, which looked the same as the scientific camp that I guarded five years ago on

Corpus V, a memory from the past returned. It was always in my nightmares—the first time I saw those blue and black eyes. The way they glowed in the dark yet seemed to cast a shadow on the darkness. Of all the creatures in the universe, scorchers were the quietest killers and the loudest murderers. They could kill an entire generation without making a sound, but murder peace with the screams of their victims. The drone I released earlier was ascending over the town to scan it.

"I am alive when these people are not. I see victory when these people cannot see. I walk through and around death, but not with it. It is because of these dead that many will live. It is the dead who allow them to live."

"Who said that?"

"You met the man who said that. And now he is one who joined his words by also dying."

"Maybe you should come up with your own sayings."

"I will, sis."

I left the police justice building and entered the orphanage next door. The sky was orange-red, and the fires still burned, as if in Dante's Inferno. In entering the orphanage, I almost slipped on some ashes. I stopped to see them, hoping there were no bones in those ashes, begging that they were not children's ashes, but I was saluted only by grief as the things that I had hoped were not there appeared hidden beneath. I clenched my teeth and bit my lip and kept biting until I started bleeding. I couldn't be hurting myself here on a mission; self-caused pain is never good. I abhor it and don't even wish it on those who do me harm.

The entire room was black and burned, and it was

almost impossible to think that humans used to live here. The smell of burned electronics was pitiful. It wasn't the first time I had been in an orphanage, and how I dreaded returning to one! It was the first time, however, that I could leave of my free will, without my sister. I knew that upstairs was a sight no one would want to see—no one with a sensible mind. But everyone, from all sides of space, must know what happened. I took my first step on those charred stairs in the middle of the room and could almost hear the sound of children. This made me wish I could stop imagining things. I went up the stairs and turned down the corridor to the left, where the infirmary was. I heard a faint lullaby—a faint, eerie, disembodied version of "Twinkle, Twinkle Little Star." I reached for my sidearm, a black, metallic, long-barreled .454 Dark Hammer pistol, and drew it out of its holster. I seized the handle of the door, which was locked. Next to the door was an electronic keypad that was illuminated by a red light. I stepped back and kicked the door down. I heard crying when I entered and saw a sight that made me smile. I might dislike adults, but not children. Inside the untouched room were two nurses and four babies and a lot of blue. Blue walls, blue cribs, blue monitoring devices, and a blue and white nursing station. I might not have been able to speak Japanese, but I put my index finger to my lips, motioning them to be quiet and to follow me quickly. They reacted by blinking and walking backward. They feared me. I took my identification patch, and it projected to them the standard message in Japanese.

"I am United Galactic Federation Defense Agent Gerald. This is an emergency. I was sent from Earth to assist, contain, and extract. Please follow me and do not be afraid. I will not harm you," the patch relayed in Japanese. The nurses spoke to each other and seemed to trust me after that.

They seized the four babies, one in each hand, and I grabbed a bag, which I filled with baby supplies. I ran through the rest of the orphanage, yelling "Hello" or the traditional "Hey." No one answered. I took the scope from my jacket pocket and aimed it at the drone scanning the city. The silver tube emitted beams and communicated with the drone. When the drone finished scanning the city, only seven live forms came up on the monitor—one male, two females, and four babies—and it even showed us in the damaged orphanage. We went outside, and the nurses held the babies tightly and closed their eyes. I took more pictures of the city, the cars, the pedestrians. All burned. What level of hell was this? This was no longer a beautiful, thriving city. It was worse than Hiroshima and Nagasaki when the bombs were dropped on them. At least those victims never saw it coming. No, their stallion was silver and flying, their angel of death did its job quickly and painlessly, so long as they were in the immidiate blast zone.. I wanted to say something to them, something that would have, something that might have ... anything.

I sent the pictures to Evelyn. I made sure to send the picture of the survivors first. I heard a sigh of relief over the radio. She then must have looked at the next picture, for I heard her gag and almost vomit. I heard typing and crying. So many dead but none responsible for this crime I felt horrible for making her cry.

A gust of wind made me turn. The temperature

dropped. A quiet rustling passed behind me. That gut feeling had returned.

As if threatened, whatever wildlife was nearby stopped making any sounds. The silence could be heard, and it was heard loudly—loudly enough to make the grass stop growing and for the ruins to hold their breath. My eyes darted to the side as I looked for the intruder into the ghastly peace. My breathing slowed down, and I heard more and more. I turned to the nurses and pointed to the police justice building, which housed the corpse of the scorcher. I headed to the building, hoping that whatever was out there would follow me so I could capture it. But nothing showed up. I dismissed my paranoia and decided to learn more about my defeated attacker.

Directing some of my attention toward the door in case that ghostly presence appeared to us, I took my data compressor out of my pocket and ordered it to give me more information on scorchers. I knew that scorchers, who inhabited a mostly volcanic world, were creatures resembling demons. Their gray and tan skin was resistant to extreme heat and fire and tough enough to protect them from the sharp, jagged, rocky surface of their home world. Adult scorchers were considered fully grown when they were six feet tall. Their razor-sharp, hand-like blades were able to cut flesh, and scorchers could make traps very easily, thanks to the heat their "hands" exuded. I hated these things.

"Your transport is here." Evelyn's words broke my concentration. "Also, a cleanup crew is on site. The survivors are going to another facility."

"All right, Evelyn. See you in a bit after I clear my head."

"There has never been a bigger jerk than you. You know that."

"Eh. Hey, Evy, tell the cleanup crew to keep an eye out. Something was watching me, and I don't know what it was."

"Think it was another scorcher?"

"No, it was something else. I have a bad feeling about it." I took the communication device off my head and looked at the pink sky. The smoke rising from this once sleepy settlement seemed to mock its peaceful past. A falling star dropped from the heavens.

I changed my mind about it being a falling star when it stopped falling and shot back up into the atmosphere. It was a ship. And it was unlike any I had seen before.

# CHAPTER TWO

## UGF COMBAT TRAINING FACILITY

The bell rang, and the crowd roared with noise. Two guys dragged my defeated opponent from the circular arena. I grabbed the wooden sword from my right hand and took off my black shirt with my left. The damn thing was drenched in sweat from the last thirty matches. My obsolete dog tags dangled around my neck. An opponent from the crowd appeared. He was in his twenties and wore protective gear. I had no gear on because it restricts mobility, and you don't wear it in real combat.

He pulled out his sword and held it like a samurai. I held mine at my side. Another bell rang, and my opponent ran toward me. He swung at my head with his sword. I blocked with my sword and pushed him back when I pushed his sword away. Taking the opportunity, I hit his legs with my sword and knocked him off balance. He whimpered, and I hesitated. I was about to deliver the winning blow when he attacked from the ground, knocking my sword out of my hand. It landed on the floor to our left. He rolled on his back to his feet and returned to his stance.

A worthy opponent. All sounds of weights and fitness machinery stopped as the others swarmed to see this match. The green circle on the floor that held this match was soon glowing brighter.

"Come on, finish it. Do it!"

My taunt worked. He looked around and spotted my wooden sword on the ground. This gave him the courage to lunge toward me. He raised his sword over his head and prepared to strike me. I grabbed his arms and kneed him in the stomach. I then grabbed him and threw him across the mat. Using my foot, I kicked my sword into the air and caught it. He was kneeling and using his sword to help himself up. He looked at me and released a war cry. That sent my blood rushing through my veins, and a crooked smile grew on my face.

We ran toward each other and met halfway. I threw my sword over his head and then quickly slid under his feet, catching my sword as it went over him. My back was to his back, and I had the sword in my hand, its wooden blade aimed at his back. With a quick movement of my left hand, I hit the butt of the sword, and the blade hit his back.

The bell rang, and everyone cheered or booed. People started to hand each other betting money, and those lucky ones kept clapping and cheering. The commotion died down, however, as the crowd parted to make way for someone. My opponent took off his helmet and held it under his arm. He was sweating profusely. I offered my hand because he was a good opponent. He shook my hand and walked away, his hands over his ribs. It made me regret hurting him, and I felt as though I should have been easier on him. One of his friends helped him walk to the lockers and the armory. I heard footsteps walking up the arena. They sounded like the standard-issue high heels that the UGF gives to women in uniform. I turned and saw my sister Evelyn walking toward me. She was wearing her UGF uniform, which consisted of a black skirt, an olive-green, button-up shirt, and a black beret. In her hands were tablets and documents. She looked at those whom I had defeated, and where still sitting on the sidelines and placed a neatly folded towel next to my wet shirt. It was strange to see her in such a formal uniform—as pale as I was and now sporting bright pink hair. Last year her hair had been black like mine, but a few months later she had come home with it colored bright blue.

"Hello there! Are you my next challenger?" I joked, which possibily aggrivated her.

She in turn grabbed her standard-issue electro-rod from her belt holster. It was a black titanium shock rod that was about fourteen inches long and was able to stop a heart or jump-start it. She hit my left arm, and I winced in pain. The settings must have been on low, or I would have been on the floor, thrashing like a fish out of water.

"I won," she said calmly with that smirk of hers—a smile that I had probably taught her earlier in our lives.

The crowd went back to working out or sparring in their own arenas. Evelyn made a face—one that always stops me from hitting her back. She approached me with her arms extended and wrapped them around my scarred and sticky body. I returned the kind expression, which she paid back by going to my locker and retrieving my clothes and blue pack.

"Oh, I'm sorry, Gerry. I have to stay late. There's trouble on one planet. Could be technical, too early to say. I'm so sorry. Here, take the keys to the car." She tried to make it up to me by giving me the keys.

"And let you take the train? Are you crazy? No. I'm not letting you do that. I'll be fine." I smiled at her and sighed.

She hugged me again and turned to go to her post. I decided to take a shower there and then go home.

### ***TRAIN THOUGHTS***

The man left the military base with his blue pack and walked toward the hovering, wheelless buses. They would take him to a station where he would take a bus toward the downtown area.

He noticed he was the only one in the grey metal bus. There was no driver because the bus was operated with AI systems. The man sat down at the end and put his head down and his pack to one side. Feeling nostalgic, he pulled a picture out of his dark-green jacket. It was an old picture, taken many years ago, many light-years away, on a holographic cube that preserved his happiness and sanity. It helped calm his troubled mind.

The bus began moving forward on the empty road. Back to the city. His wet hair dripped occasionally onto the picture. He simply wiped off the drops of water and recited the names of the people in the picture. How cruel life was. Cruel to all people. He thought of the two nurses, loyal to their infants to the end. Luckily, it wasn't their end. Just the end of about two thousand inhabitants. Of eight hundred and thirty-six children. Life was cruel, but the strong must be able to take it. And the strong also had to help those who could not.

The bus had passed into the limits of the huge city. The towering buildings appeared to be at home among the trees and the bushes that the government had planted. He hated going to the city by bus. And for good reasons.

The bus stopped inside the station. He stood up and put the glass cube that projected the picture back into his pocket. He got off the bus and walked into the waiting platform for the train. A woman stood in the glass and metal booth, he never really bothered to paid her much attention, she could have been real, she could have been a hologram, either way from the little attention he does pay, it's never the same woman. From behind the glass, her automated voice greeted him and asked him which ticket he wanted. He asked for the one that would take him to the downtown, midlevel section of town. To pay for the ticket, the man put on his enhancement glasses and approached the retinal scanner. It analyzed his credit storage and completed the transaction. Only then was he allowed to pass through the metal doors and onto the train. It wasn't as crowded as it sometimes was, for which he was grateful.

A group of young people–barely adults—was laughing and yelling about things that others would have considered simply stupid.

The group appeared to be two men and two women, all heavily inked with tattoos that could move, light up, and emit sound. Piercings lined their faces, ears, and other places where a human should not be pierced. Were people really dying to protect abominations like them? Abominations who dressed in clothing that was considered a style yet was so generic that the style promoted nonsense and stupidity as the symbols and words etched on them. A few rare individuals had old twentieth-century-style suits. Others had jackets over simple shirts and pants.

Individuality was becoming less and less common in a society where everyone seemed to be trying to stand out. The man sat at a distance from the others. He was thinking of a quote that he had once heard.

The train sped down its track as the passengers occasionally started conversations with one another. The train traveled at over five hundred miles an hour and might reach the next station in five minutes, as it passed skyscrapers, corporations, and living quarters.

When the train stopped, some couples and more idiots got on. The man was the only one who got off. He passed an unmanned police drone holding a rifle and guarding the people and the peace.

Something was bothering the man. The more he looked around, the more desperation he felt. Almost everywhere he looked, there were people holding hands. People holding each other tightly. Couples kissing. And that sight saddened him. It made him feel desolate and despairing. It tortured him. As hard-hearted as he was, and as angry as he looked, he actually longed for someone. Just as Frankenstein's creature needed a companion, he needed one as well. He did not want to feel alone in an ugly world. Why do we need someone? He could not confess it to anyone, not even to his sister. He was afraid, though. He was afraid of having someone. He did not know how to behave or even what to do or say with other people. He was afraid of having someone and then losing her. He had lost people before, but not someone he cared for or called his; that scared him, it changed him.

"Hey, baby killer, stop!" a voice shouted from behind him in the crowd.

Gerald turned around and looked for its source.

"How many kids did you kill today?" the officer asked harshly.

Gerald glanced at his data compressor and back at the officer. It was not uncommon for citizens and police officers to feel resentment and hatred toward soldiers and government agents, who had license to use deadly force.

"Well, none today, but if you don't shut up, that could change," Gerald replied.

"You think you can do what you want and get away with it, huh, baby killer?" the officer said, spitting on the ground. A crowd of people stopped to see this embarrassing display.

"Basically. Hey, does it anger you that the government prefers us over you? The people who train harder and stay behind to watch over the government and yet are ridiculed by the government and the people you are sworn to protect?" Gerald taunted him.

"You bastard," the cop said, enraged. He got out his energyzer stick—a rod stronger than the military-issued one—and was about to strike Gerald when a hand stopped him.

A fully armed United Galactic Federation regular, who would normally patrol the cities, along with police officers and drones, was intervening.

"What the hell do you think you're doing?" the regular asked, throwing the police officer's hand down. "This man risked his ass for you, and that's how you treat him. You people know no respect!" the African American soldier exclaimed, looking around and shifting his rifle around on its strap.

"Is there a problem, citizens of the UGF?" A drone approached from the crowd. Its green metal parts whizzed and turned. The drone was six feet tall and carried a plasma rifle attached to its power supply.

Above all law, drones were judge, jury, and executioners. Cold, yet accurate, they had made courts disappear overnight.

"No, there is none, Unit six-two." the police officer said.

"Acknowledge. Disperse, then," the drone said in its harsh, monotonous voice.

The whole crowd, including the police officer, moved on.

"These things keep on happening. Too many mobs. Good thing is we stick together. Right, sir?" the regular asked Gerald.

"That's the way it works for us."

"You're a captain, ain't you, sir?" the soldier asked.

"Was. Now I'm just a Defense Force agent." Gerald answered.

"In our book, you still are. Now, sir, you should get moving, I still got my rounds to complete."

"Roger that, sergeant," Gerald answered, looking at the man's patch.

"Just be careful sir, these people are ungrateful."

"We the unwilling, led by the unqualified, to kill the unfortunate, die for the ungrateful," Gerald remarked.

The regular smiled. His mood was very cheerful because he had saved one of his associates. It was true. All soldiers had their support. The men saluted each other before walking away, one to his duty, the other to kill time.

Before the men parted, they both placed a good number of credits in a homeless man's hand.

# CHAPTER THREE

## UGF (UNITED GALACTIC FEDERATION) HEADQUARTERS, EARTH

As Ryan Kayre, a wrinkly old commander and, director of the United Galactic Federation Defense Force, sat in his decorated office, he began to enjoy the rare moment of silence. Being director of the UGFDF meant sacrificing peace and quiet. But at the moment all operations were running smoothly, and all colonies were fine, except Edo One and a planet controlled by the Helena Kingdom. A simple loss of communications due to solar interference, the tech guys said. Nothing to worry about, they thought. Well, that translated into: it was their problem, then. He hoped they were right, and he could sit down for a while. The director whirled around in his rolling chair a bit and decided to drink something from his secret stash. Edo One was the world's government higher-ups' problem, not his anymore.

*Well, might as well relax,* he thought, taking a glass and a bottle from his hidden compartment. He had started to relax too soon, for he heard five sets of footsteps approaching his office. Ryan sat up straight and looked at the door. Instead of knocking for permission to come in, four Helena Council Guards entered his office and stood in pairs on the opposite wall. Behind the guards was a chairman from Helena. The man had dark skin; he was bald and wearing a black suit; and his sweat was bleeding through his clothing..

"Well?" asked Ryan, hoping the council member would leave quickly so he could recover his moment of peace.

"We have a problem," the councilor replied, trying desperately not to overwhelm the officer with his worry. He was shocked that the director continued to look annoyed.

"I can see that. Now, the way to solve this problem is for you and your four goons to leave my office and come back in one hour," the director suggested, hoping that maybe the councilor would postpone his work.

"You've probably noticed that communication with the Helenac kingdom is down," the councilor pointed out. "Well, we have suspicions that there is something disrupting comms with the planet."

The sound of an alarm suddenly blasted out of the speakers, killing the silence.

"All stations report to duty. Repeat, all stations report to duty. Director, you are needed in the war room. This is not a drill. Repeat, this is not a drill. Goliaths and possible scorchers have been spotted in Helena," a female voice said in an English accent through the PA system.

The director's left eye began to twitch rapidly. This was getting worse than he cared to think about. The one time he could have had a little solitude, an issue had to arise to force him to work. *This must be how a superhero feels,* the wrinkly director thought. He sat up and shut his data compressor. *This is going to be a long night.* He had wanted quiet, but the director knew he had work to do now.

"Councilor, shut the door. There is something we need to talk about," the commander said before telling him of the situation on Edo One and getting the file of his best agent,but his most hated one. He would have to bother his friend, who he knew would argue and consider not doing not doing what he is ordered to

# CHAPTER FOUR

## AFTERMATH FROM ANOTHER PERSPECTIVE

A man was sitting in a pub drinking a dark pint. His dark hair covered the scar on his left green eye—a souvenir from his last mission in his military days. His head was down, and he appeared to be sleeping, until he stood up and looked around. He had that same feeling on Edo One and on the bus.

"I have a bad feeling about this," he said aloud as he took out his wallet and put a tip near his unfinished pint. He stood up and left the pub for his second train.

*This is why I hate my life now. If I'm not on a mission, I'm here boring myself to death,* he thought as he boarded the train. Each day was almost the same. He patrolled a world that was deemed in trouble and he would then return and go to the pub before heading home and washing his clothes. That always bothered him, but today something else also bothered him. It was a feeling of something to come—something that would bring change—but he couldn't figure out what type of change. That and a freaking sense of paranoia.

No one imagined how the future would look. Could

anyone in the Victorian era have imagined that a city such as Washington DC would look like a city of the gods? Could they have imagined that the buildings replaced houses? Could they have imagined that the city's forty-two layers would rival the height of Mt. Everest? The communication, the transportation was the most advanced accommodations in stock all over for the civilian markets. There weren't any fuel-consuming cars. All cars were sold back to their dealers, who sold them for spares to make new hovercars. Not flying cars, but hovercars, inventors said. With the spare metal, the government bought the auto industry and used it to make a monorail system that expanded across the entire Earth. When the planet's population surged over ten billion, it was decided to establish outerworld colonies to combat overpopulation. As a result there were no wars for resources and no overpopulation—a first for humanity. During the first decade, new discoveries aided the human races, the first being a new world that had the most fertile land in the entire galaxy—the planet Yuni. However dark events and another world war ended up eventually uniting all of humanity in peace.

The train stopped near the man's destination. He got off, walked through an alley, and took a left. He went down the street in the cool August night. The sky was dark and almost crystal-clear, and the stars ... it's funny that he had never noticed how beautiful the stars looked. And the moon ... breathtaking.

# CHAPTER FIVE

## VISITOR

**S**omething was off about me noticing the stars and moon. I would never notice that. I wouldn't care about that ... but they were so beautiful, the stars. I kept walking toward home. The sign saying Space Rose Living Apartments was what distinguished it from the other apartment buildings. I entered and went up in the elevator. When I walked into my apartment, I was surprised to see that I had company, and the darkness did not cloak them as well as they thought.

"Hello, sir."

"Hello, Agent Grey. I hope we are not intruding," Director Kayre said, emerging from the shadows.

"Well, I wasn't expecting any company, Director. How can I be of service?" I asked as I took off my jacket and hung it on my coat rack. Four Helena Council guards accompanying a Helena Chairman also made themselves known.

"Good evening, Agent. My name is Councilor Nathan Wright. I regret to inform you ... We, the United Galactic Federation, have a problem. For the past four days we have been out of communication with the Helenac kingdom. Yesterday we sent a team to make contact with the planet. Of the ten ships we sent, none have returned. I fear a plague has come down on my home world. An evil has landed on my beautiful world, and I fear for the life of my king, for the princess, for the spirit of Helena." He had a deep voice that took me by surprise.

One guard straightened his shirt and rubbed his head. Another glanced at me nervously after seeing my holster and two knife scabbards, although he calmed down when he saw that they were empty. The other two were looking out the windows to make sure nothing was out of the ordinary. The director sat down on my kitchen table and took out his flask. I soon knocked him off the table by smacking his back.

"So let me get this straight. Helena, the biggest exporter in rare elements and power cells, is not responding to our calls. We lost 250 guys to see what was going on, and we have not heard from them? And what do you want with me?" I put my feet up on the table as rudely as possible.

"You are the best agent and the best soldier in the whole agency. You survived the attack on the Russian colony, the biohazard disaster in the Chinese colony, the Remen incident, the rebellion on Kepler, the discovery of the scorchers ..." The director paused and looked toward the floor, avoiding my gaze. "The Battle of Clo, I mean basically any bloody conflict we have had, you were there."

"Yeah, spare me the ass kissing." What a lovely way to put it.

"Honestly, if I didn't know you were gonna say that,

I'da asked someone else if they'd do the bloody job." Ryan smirked.

"So you want me to go and check on the planet?" I asked.

Not even back from Edo five hours, and I was to be sent back to the field.

"No," the Councilor and the director said in unison.

"No?" I repeated, surprised. *What was the purpose of this mission, then, if … Oh, the royal family.* "You want me to rescue the king and his family."

The chairman chuckled at my cleverness. The director looked quite pleased with my being able to solve it that quickly.

"I'm a defense agent. I'm no longer military. Go ask them."

"Not if I have a say in that, Gerald," he said in a mocking tone. "You still didn't finish your second five-year agreement. You want me to ask for military personnel? I'll reinstate your ass back into the machine, and you'll become another piece. So there is no way of saying no." The director always got what he wanted.

"As you are aware, the constitutional monarchy of the Kingdom of Helena does not have a military—only a small police force. We believe the interference might be caused by a jammer. We believe that the reason no ships are leaving is that a layer of its atmosphere is covered with an EMP dust that might have already settled. However, we are afraid something else is down there," the lead guard said.

He stared at me, his blue eyes looking deep into my green ones.

"Scorchers?" I asked, my voice quivering.

Words failed me after hearing that as the thought of those red eyes burned in my mind. When one scorcher was in a city, it razed a peaceful town and butchered almost all of its inhabitances in a few hours . If there were multiple scorchers running around a whole planet, that would not end well. The councilor's next word turned things from annoyingly bad, however, into terribly worse.

"Worse." His eyes darkened. "We believe that the reason no ships can leave the planet might be ... Goliaths."

That last word hit me in the stomach like a baseball bat. The defiant attitude that protected me from kindness by not allowing me to share it, jumped out of me, abandoned me, and left me to rot.

"When do I leave?" I asked, my mouth open and my knees trembling.

This had become serious. A Goliath was no joke. These reptilian creatures could grow to towering heights. Some called them Godzilla, but the official name was Goliath. But what terrified me was that there weren't supposed to be any Goliaths left. The last one was abandoned to die on its planet, with all of humanity watching.

"We have a transport waiting for us downstairs," one of the guards said.

"Well, hurry up! We're wasting time," I replied, grabbing my jacket.

This was bad. Very bad. A Goliath could raze an entire a planet if it was awake or infuriated. Hell, it would level the whole place just for fun.

All seven of us started down the stairs to the waiting hovercar, inconspicuously parked in the street. The olive-green vehicle had armored plating and tinted windows that I was willing to bet Evelyn's money were able to withstand a bullet bigger than a carrot.

"Gerald, you seem to be in a hurry. You seem to care for once. Did something change?" The director chuckled as he got into the armored car.

"I feel changed. I don't know how, and I can't explain it."

"Well, hopefully this 'change' will still bring you back alive."

*I hope not,* I thought to myself as I looked out the window.

The rest of us got into the car, and the bald-headed Helena council guard started to drive to the UGF headquarters spaceport. The towering buildings of Earth seemed to block the horizon.

Using the major highways and overpasses, we saw the old Lincoln memorial and the expanded White House, which served as the home of the Prime Minister of Earth. Since, during this four-year term, the prime minister was of American descent, the White House seemed an appropriate place for that politician to live. It didn't matter to me, since I hadn't voted for my fellow countryman. I had voted for the Russian one, and I still considered it a shame that she had lost.

"Councilor, what if the royal family is dead?" I asked as we passed two cemeteries where the casualties of old wars were buried.

"Take out the Goliaths. Avenge them. Kill those who are responsible for their deaths." There was a fire in his eyes as he answered. Talk about devotion ...

"Councilor, I don't believe you are authorized to give

such orders to him. I also don't think he can easily kill the Goliaths. Gerald, if they are dead, your new objective would be to take out the jamming device and get as many people as you can to the evacuation points we will - I'm also afraid this might be related to those damn coward terrorists. Remember that terrorist cell?" the director asked.

"You mean those self-appointed saviors?" I chuckled, which made him smile. I knew who he was talking about—the "Libertas."

Such a foul taste those syllables left in my mouth! I hated myself for wasting my time by even saying their name. Terrorists are cowards. They claim to be heroes, but are like diseased garbage that seemed to breed with a mutated dog from Chernobyl. They have no honor; they have no courage. Only death awaits them. A war has been going on with their revolting kind for more than a few centuries. It brought me no pleasure to remember how the old governments destroyed an entire race just to quash terrorism. Two and a half billion killed. An entire desert landscape became even more uninhabitable.

"Yeah, those guys. Driver, could you drive faster, but not like you are trying to kill us?"

"What about them?" I asked the director.

"Last week we raided one of their bases. We found it empty, but the place still had some equipment and intel. It mentioned a credit transfer for a transportation service. We also found a speech talking about liberating Helena, Kepler and a few other planets, plus maps, blueprints of key buildings, basically the works."

"Is that why you said to kill those responsible, Councilor?"

"Just do your job, Gerald," the director replied.

The operation was bigger than I thought. As we arrived at the base, I could see that everyone was mobilizing. Medical crews—angels of life, as they were nicknamed— were taking their supplies from metallic boxes that vehicles brought from underground storage units. Soldiers in dark, olive-green uniforms who were wearing lighter green and with black and tan helmets, were grabbing ammunition and supplies while awaiting their orders. It seemed that everyone was getting on a ship to head to an orbiting carrier. The pride of the Earth's Navy. Built out of newly discovered space metal, with improved weapons. The carrier was only a few years old, yet it was considered a veteran. I could imagine the officers on the bridge in Earth's orbit, planning and preparing for their soldiers.

"This must be the first action they've had in months," I commented.

"Yeah, for most of them it is. All right, Gerald, here's what's gonna happen. We're gonna stop in Hangar Three. There, you're gonna get your new equipment and your new, standard-issue armor. We're reinstating you with same rank, pay, and privileges. You'll then board an F/A/C/ Hyperion and rendezvous with the Navy's station in the Havoc system. From there, you'll switch ships to Helena," the director said to me.

"How much longer before the Navy bombards the planet with battle suns?" Battle suns were a new weapon that could easily kill Goliaths—but also every other living thing—without damaging infrastructure. He sighed and looked at the holographic clock on his wrist.

"How long, Director?" I repeated.

"You need to extract the royal family and anyone else

you can, quickly." He had avoided my question, and my brow furrowed with annoyance, I hated when he stalled on important subjects.

"How long?" I repeated as the car stopped in front of the gates, and the guards let us through.

The director ignored me and got out of the car. I followed him.

"Damn it! Hhow long before they kill every damn luckless bastard who gets left behind!" I exclaimed, holding on to his collar. The director was a very short person—several inches shorter than I was—and he walked around with a charisma and an aura that made people stand up straight and salute him, whether military or not.

"Forty-eight hours," he responded blankly, grabbing my hands to make me release him.

My blood boiled. Not because of those who were going to be left behind. No, it angered me because that left me less than twenty-one hours to rescue the family and get the mission done.

The chairman looked surprised and dumbfounded. He was shocked that not all of his people were going to be saved, which was probably something either the director should have told him or I should have not mentioned. This was news to him, but protocol to me.

"Councilor, Darwin once stated that nature favored those fittest for survival. Those who are going to be left behind apparently aren't the fittest," I said, storming off to Hanger Three. The chairman fell to his knees, with his eyes to the ground. I knew the director stood straight and watched me walk away. I knew he offered his hand to the downed councilor. This was cold reality.

# CHAPTER SIX

## HERR DOCTOR

The entire facility was on full alert, and I was almost crushed by the crowds. The seventy-five-hundred-thousand-acre facility had its own training area, living space, and offices apart from the federal space station and weapons facility. Tall buildings with the federal seal marked what their purpose was. Altogether over half a million people worked, lived, or were at the facility at any given time. Hangar Three was a short walk from the parking lot. The car didn't stop at the parking lot, however, so it took me twenty minutes to get there.

As I approached the hanger, two guards whose rifles would have had me spilling my guts with a single bullet, stopped me and asked me for identification. I reached into the pocket of my jacket and took out my glasses. These glasses allowed an iris scanner to analyze my eye more effectively, and to anazyle my credit storage. The LCD screen confirmed two things—first, that the director was right about my being reinstated into the military, and second, that I had the right of access to the area. When the guards had done their duty, I was allowed to pass.

The hanger could no longer keep its secrets from me, as it had in the past.

Men and women working on experimental weapons, engines, and computers were absorbed by their projects and paid no attention to me. The only one who did was not wearing a white coat. He motioned me to a work station that was completly void of any projects, possibily the only one in the hanger or laboratory.

"Herr Grey, it is a pleasure," said a man with an accent thicker and richer than the imitation German beer that was sold in non-Earth stations. A man in his late sixties dressed in a very conservative manner, appeared carrying three metal cases. He set down the three cases and fixed his yellow bowtie. He extended his hand as one gentleman would do to greet another. Seeing no way out, I humored this amusing man by firmly shaking his hand twice. He straightened his light-gray vest and opened the smallest container on the table in front of us.

"Well, Herr Grey, it is my pleasure to present to you this weapon. Although it's small, it carries quite the punch. This weapon was very hard to make. It is a hybrid of a pistol and a high-powered rifle. It's called Dark Punch." He smiled to himself as he handed me the strange pistol. I checked the chamber by pulling on it and was surprised to see a .44 round in it. The gun was mostly red but had a few white spots and many black ones—urban camouflage. The funny little man handed me a magazine that was fully loaded, and it seemed to weigh no more than the cartridges.

"Now you'll notice that the gun is very light, probably no heavier than your current pistol. However, its penetration power can rip through approximately four unarmed people or kill one Goliath spawn. This weapon has the first ever suppressor, making it virtually noiseless, and attached to the suppressor is a grip for extra comfort and control. Well? What do you think?" he asked, quite pleased with himself, as he combed his perfectly trimmed white beard with his fingers while I held on to my torso.

"I think I might never give it back," I replied as I inspected the weapon. The German man then handed me a holster for my new weapon. After that, he passed me new magazines and boxes with ammunition for the weapon, which I put in the third metal container, the largest of the three. I had not looked at the contents, but since it was not full, I decided to put everything in it. He then put the second container on the table and opened it. It was a weapons container.

"When I heard about the terrible beast on this poor planet I had to get my best gun for the job. So here are your new rifle and knives. The beautiful part about them is that the knives are extremely resistant to heat, allowing you, Herr Grey, to stab scorchers with ease. The rifle has two brand-new features. This weapon can accept all types of ammunition, thanks to its hybrid chamber, and it can charge shots for more power. Theoretically, with the charged shots you can penetrate walls. I've called this gun Klein Waffen or Hornet-396." He handed me the rifle, and the most interesting thing about the rifle—other than that it displayed what round it was on the receiver—was the sight, which caught my eye.

"I think I forgot to ask you what your name is, sir," I asked as I looked into the clear panel of the sight and flipped the backup iron sight on the side.

"My name? My name ... it has been a long time since someone has asked me that. I have been too busy to remember that. And mostly everyone just calls me Doctor," he said, taking off his glasses and using his shirt to clean them. "I've asked to be called Herr Doctor, but we all know that is not my name." He looked at me, and I noticed his blue eyes. The eyes of a hurt, exhausted, man. For a moment the gentleman in front of me looked familiar. His weak, gentle smile tried to hide that familiarity.

"You look familiar, Doctor. Have we met before? ... No, we have never met. My mistake." I stood there, my mind twisting between cosmoses, trying to recognize the man. Finally I said, "You're the man who made the Battle Stars. You are the soldier who fought the off the entire rebellion at Hera planet."

His smile faded as he thought of that time. He dropped his gaze and put his glasses on. He looked at his hand as a reminder of what had happened there, and I suspected that he saw the blood he had had on his hands at that time—a reminder of what he had been. A person he no longer wished to be. Why had I reminded him of that? Hera was his nightmare, a wound that I had opened up and poured salt in.

"That was a long time ago, but those acts were not as grand as your future ones will be, my boy. Now this," he said, dragging out the last of the metal containers in which I had stored my ammo and other supplies he deemed fit to send me off with. "I wish I could have seen you wear it. However, we have run out of time.This, my boy, is your new uniform. And ammunition as well, just to prepare you, son."

"Really? You wanted to see me wear it?"

"No, why would I? Why would I want to see you wearing a uniform everyone else is wearing." He chuckled lightheartly

A guard came up and looked at the doctor. He held a key for a hovercar. This was my ride to the ship.

"Here, the guard will take you to the launch bay." He dropped the last container. I grabbed the cold, green crate and my new weapons.

"The sight on the Hornet is made out of Prometheus tears. The sight will automatically find targets, and you can increase and decrease the zoom on it, and it will do whatever a Promethean's eye can do. Take care of it, my boy. It is the only one of its kind. Just link it up with your helmet."

"I will, Doctor," I replied respectfully. I turned around and had started walking toward the guard waiting to take me to the airfield when I remembered one more thing about the old man.

"Doctor," I said as he turned, "it wasn't your fault. The attack on Munich two could not have been avoided. You did everything you could in that city, but your wife and daughter cou ... It wasn't your fault, Colonel."

I stared into that man's eyes, and I had an epiphany. This man, was me. A more suppressed, hurt version of me. His eyes revealed that deep abyss, a perfect darkness. This was the man we all knew. We had all given some for the effort, and he had seen more than his share of those who gave all. But we weren't there, we weren't there, we just weren't there to understand or even help him.

It dawned on me that this might be my end. The end was always a possibility, but I didn't fear the death of my physical self, but the end of my sanity, for the great rivers of despair flow through one at every moment.

"I tried, Captain. I wish I could have stopped it. I tried, to no avail," he said, straightening his vest and turning away. I kept walking to the gray metal door. The guard walked to a doorless hovercar, which looked like a golf cart, and from the distance, I turned to see the old man again. He sat on a bench looking into the distance, seeing his past again, and a quiet sob broke from him. No one saw him but me, and I saw a broken future image of what I could become. We both had lost so many, and the difference between us was how we dealt with—and hid— those feelings, the darkness, and the empty shadows.

I walked toward the car carrying my boxes. The guard and I both hopped on and sped to the airfield. Soldiers were putting supplies into the ships. Specialists were loading bombers.

"So which ship is the one we're taking?" I asked the guard, whom I noticed was from special forces.

"We? Sorry to burst your bubble, sir, but it's only you. I'm just here to take you to the Hyperion and back," he replied, swerving to the left to avoid the marching soldiers.

"Well, how far is it?" I asked.

"Not that far. Just at the end of these rows," he replied and then fell silent. I knew he wanted to ask something else, for he opened his mouth and quickly closed it.

"You want to ask me something, don't you?" I inquired with a blank expression.

"Would you answer, sir?"

"Yeah, what is it?" I responded, looking at my scope.

"What do you mean about the doctor and Munich two? Did something happen to him there?"

I spat on the tarmac, which was now useless, since the ships took off and landed VTOL style.

"About twenty-five years ago, the colony of Munich two was attacked by rebel forces. The colonel led the counterforce to put down the rebels without telling anyone that his family was there. He did a pretty good job, but the rebels got desperate. They took control of the only Prometheus alive and set it loose on the city. Killed over two-thirds of the civilians, including his wife and daughter. Sad story. He caught the Prometheus alive. Who knows what he did with it," I replied, remembering the story on the news.

"What's a Prometheus? I've heard of them—but then nothing. Never saw pictures, or even a single sketch."

"A Prometheus is this one race that we really don't understand. Only one has been found. And that's the one that was in Munich two, and the same one we put in a bunker fifteen hundred feet below ground. What we do know is that its eyes can see in four dimensions—five, if you count abstract space. Its eyes can see through materials and heat signatures and total darkness. If I didn't hold that much respect for the Colonel, I would consider it the greatest creature in the universe"

"So your rifle sight, it can do all that cause it's made of the same stuff?" he asked.

"No idea," I said, shifting the rifle on my lap.

We arrived at the Hyperion, and there was a big surprise waiting for me. A noncombat military woman was there, holding a thin, very long rectangular box. The two pilots stood there talking with the woman.

# CHAPTER SEVEN

## THREAT

The hovercar approached the Hyperion. I stepped outside and waved the driver off after grabbing the case. I turned and faced the three people awaiting me. One pilot appeared to be Korean, and the other was from South Africa, as his patch showed its flag. The Korean was attempting to flirt with the woman, which was humorous, since she kept cutting him off. She finally shut him up by running up to me and giving me a hug.

"Happy Birthday, Gerald!" Evelyn exclaimed in her honey-sweet voice as she wrapped her arms around me.

"What?" I exclaimed, racking my brain to try to remember my own birthday. "Oh, didn't I have one last year?" I complained.

"Oh shut up, I got you something," she said.

"Is it hookers?" I teased with a smirk.

She punched my shoulder and said, "No it's something else."

"And like that, you lost me."

"Oh shut up, you jerk," she said, handing me the long, heavy box. I looked at her and then opened the box. In it

45

lay a black sword. I was unable to say anything because it was a spectacular display of modern craftsmanship combined with ancient weaponry.

She hugged me again and buried her head on my chest. For the first time in years, I was glad she was there with me. I was content to see her and content that she had given me the sword—happy that she had done something for me and showed me that she cared.

"Happy birthday, big brother," she said.

"Thank you, sis, it's amazing." As I put it back in its box, I asked, "How much did it cost?"

"I can't tell you that. Your old squad helped with that." She brushed her hair out of her eyes. It's been over three months since I last thought about them ... or visited them.

"Sir," the South African said, "We better get going."

Evelyn hugged me one last time, giving me a quick kiss on the cheek.

"Come back alive, big brother. Next time I see you, I promise to have you a cake."

"I can't promise I'll come back alive," I said, looking at the ground with a sly smile. "That's a horrible thing to say," she said. "Bye, big brother, I love you. Make me proud."

"You know what they say—suicide is a way to tell God, 'You can't fire me, I quit.'"

As I laughed, her smile disappeared. It was my sick humor, but sometimes I went too far. These jokes just don't cut it sometimes.

"Yeah, yeah, see ya, Evelyn. I'll call you later." I said as she left the launch pad. She turned around smiled as she waved good-bye. She blew me a kiss and began smiling.

I got on the cargo bay of the Hyperion. The back of the ship was open, with the door down. I noticed that the ship was fitted with two rows of cytostasis beds, sitting in an upright position. I put the case and the sword on the seats facing the devices and took out my holographic watch. In the time it took me to leave home and get on the ship, about two hours had passed. The power was turned on, and the cargo door closed. I heard talking in the cockpit and started to buckle up.

"All right, captain, we're cleared for takeoff," the Korean pilot said on the loudspeaker.

Before sitting down, I placed the container the doctor gave me on the yellow magnetic holding mat. The yellow tile on the floor of the ship was a powerful electromagnet that was used to hold metal objects into place. It locked on, and I held on for my dear insanity—the only thing I actually cared to worry about now.

The engine was deafening—a screeching, roaring monster that pushed us upward as we started our ascent into the heavens. The ship leaned back, as it was going to ascend at an even faster speed than it achieved horizontally. The ship plunged forward at speeds that would have made a bullet jealous as we broke through the sound barrier. We rose higher, our speed increasing at a tremendous rate. I'll admit that the first time I got on a ship, my stomach decided to punish me. A few hundred rides later, my stomach forgave me and stood still. All in all, this ship was one of the fastest transport, attack, and fighter ships in the galaxy.

We started to shake as we neared the atmosphere. The gravity was a lot weaker now, and proof of this was that trash, debris, and little objects began to float around.

"All right, Captain, now I'm going to put the coordinates into the computer. When we leave the outer atmosphere, I'll punch it to the Havoc station," the Korean said.

"Thanks. Like I haven't been on a ship before," I interrupted sarcastically.

"We're out of the atmosphere in two minutes," the South African added.

I buckled up, pulling the seat belt tight and locking it into place. Going faster than a light-year a second could give a nasty whiplash when artificial gravity was activated. Exactly two minutes later, the ship catapulted out of the Earth's atmohspere. I laid the Hornet on its stand and stood up.

If I was going to be waiting for ten hours, I might as well put myself in cryo-sleep. I had stopped sleeping well and couldn't fall asleep naturally anymore. Doctors said it was stress and too many problems. I took off my restraint and got into a cryo-chamber. I turned on the chamber and set it for nine hours. The liquid screen was lined with gray metal and had an electronic touch screen for setting up the sleep.

I did want a dreamless sleep. Dreams usually meant nightmares for me. Nightmares never meant my imagination drifting off into space. No, for me it meant memories of the past and my past actions ... the haunting voices of those I had shot. In order to help you fall asleep, the cryo-chamber introduces a mixture of chemicals into the body. Some are to make you happy, some are to help you remember, some to erase the past, and the rest are just needed for that sad, sweet sleep. I buckled up inside the chamber and closed it, releasing the air inside. I adjusted the controls, and just before I hit the sleep button, the communications device crackled to life, and if it wasn't the Korean. I saw him clearly on the monitor in my chamber.

"What do you want?" I asked him impatiently.

"Uh, Captain, can I ask you something?" he asked nervously.

"No," I said casually.

Ignoring my response, he asked, "Is, uh, your ..."

I quickly pressed the red button, which released me from reality.

A blue woman, surrounded by a blue glow, appeared in the darkness. She was nobody, just a computer program, to help with any difficulty—or so I thought. She smiled and waved at me. Following standard procedure, I returned the wave. I then blacked out into the darkness of my mind. To be more precise, I fell into that darkness. It. Did. However. Take. Time. For. My. Consciousness. To. Stop ...

### ... NINE HOURS LATER ...

I saw the green light from the pod. My sleep time was up. I punched the red button that would open the pod and let new, drug-free air enter the chamber. When I left the pod, my head still felt as heavy as lead. My stomach grumbled, and the sweat on my skin started to feel cold. A tiny drone came up and cleaned up the waste products I had just vomitted.

I sat down and let my head recover from that mess of feelings that spun around and around inside. My vision cleared, and I stood up and looked for my container. As I made my way to it, I grabbed my rifle and the weird pistol, which were on the gun rack on the side of the ship. Inside the main container were four more green metal rectangular containers that had 6.59 caseless rounds. Underneath were another two boxes, but when I opened the first one, it had a familiar pistol, my black pistol, Dark Hammer—the ebony .454 pistol that was as dangerous to me as to the enemy, since the recoil could knock me out if I wasn't careful. The other box had ten ten-round magazines, which were useful for me. I put those aside and found a cleaning kit for the weapons. Even deeper into the container was a uniform for me from Herr Doctor. It was a standard-issue dark, olive-green battle dress uniform with a black T-shirt, a web belt, and a dark, projectile-resistant vest that could hold my supplies, along with many patches for the uniform, sheaths for my knives and my sword, slings for my rifle, and many other attachments, gear, and even food rations. The large container also contained boots, as well as a helmet and metal exoskeleton bioorganic armor and amplifier parts.

It was all new, standard-issue UGF infantry uniform and equipment, upgraded compared to what I had used before retiring from the military, yet exactly the same. The vest had an armor plate on the chest, and there were little pouches for shotgun shells on the right chest. There were also grey armor knee and elbow pads built into the pants and shirt that could have been taken off and put back on with the straps, as well as three external pouches for ammunition that would be attached to the vest, along with a flashlight and a few light probes that attached to my belt and added more protection. The helmet was dark-tan and a similar shade of olive-green, and it had retractable gold and green lenses—the first for day use and the second for night use.

The exoskeleton was lightweight armor that allowed the user to move faster, jump higher, and have 250 percent more strength than the average personThe armor and the exoskeleton also had sensors that would indicate my vitals. Blue was normal, and red meant that my heartbeat was irregular, indicating that I was dying or severely wounded. Black meant dead, I thought.

I took off my jacket, my shirt, and my old pants and felt the coldness of space inside the ship. Putting on the black shirt and soon the green pants and buttoned up shirt made the cold go away. Then came the fun part, I put on the light vest and attached the chest piece to it. My heart beat soon activated the sensors, and a white-hot piercing sensation stabbed me on the back as the sensors turned blue. I attached the pouches to my vest, clipped on sheaths, holsters, a sling for my rifle, patches, rank, and name onto myself. When the patches were strapped on, voice activation was needed to put text onto the blank patches, I rather I prepared myself manually, a machine was not magical enough to kindly and gently put everything on me. I needed to put my helmet on so the voice commands would be recognized, so that is what I did. Because of the coldness of space, my socked feet were cold, and that had to change. With them soon covered in boots, I then needed to don the exoskeleton parts.

A long, straight plate that resembled a black spinal cord had to be connected to the back part of my vest. I placed it over my spine, the sensors soon recognized that it needed to connect and my horrible hunch was corrected while two dozen screws tightened to the vest. Two plates that resembled thin, flat metal bones had attached themselves to my arm, expanded, and connected themselves with the spinal piece of the armor, all automatically that it actually did seem magical because they floated onto me. The attachment of the leg armor was not so much fun, since the nerve connections were enough to knock someone out, and I hoped that my grunts and yelps of pain were not loud enough for the pilots to hear. I looked toward the door, expecting to see the pilots rush out to see what was going on, but luckily nothing happened. I quickly put on fingerless gloves that could be extended to cover my fingers if I needed them to.

I sat down and took my rifle apart. The barrel was extremely dirty. *Too much test firing,* I thought as I grabbed the cleaning kit and got to work. It took me a while but eventually the Hornet and my weird pistol were clean. I checked my black .454 pistol, which I humorously decided to name Virgil. After cleaning the pistol, I found a black device that resembled a thin stone with an opening to sharpen both my blades and my sword. While I was sharpening my sword, the Korean came into the cargo bay.

"Hey, Captain," he said.

"'Sup?" I responded, continuing to sharpen the sword. He looked confident. I liked that, but I wasn't going to give him advice or reassure him that he was going to be safe. At least I thought that was what he was going to ask me.

"Is your sister single?"

I stood up and held the side of the now-sharpened sword against his throat. My blood heated to the boiling point, and my teeth were clenched. There was a line you don't cross with sisters. I might mess with her too much, might make her mad, but I've always protected her. I wasn't going to let some military pilot do anything with her because he might ... most likely ... surely ... would die in a mission and leave her alone and hurt.

"Choose your next words carefully," I cautioned.

"I want to take her on a date," he said, staring at the blade. His eyes lost their look of confidence, and I saw dread in them.

"Captain, we are nearing the Havoc station," the South African pilot said. "We will arrive in two minutes."

While I was distracted, the Korean grabbed his knife and used it to push the sword away from his throat. He then used his other hand to grab my arm and lift it higher than his head. His knife circled, heading toward my neck. I was not expecting that, and it caught me by surprise. With the knife in my back, and I thrust it toward his neck and kept it there. He dropped his knife and looked me in the eyes. He had courage, I'll give him that, but now there was a glimmer of fear in his eyes. The ship stopped, and I put my rifle on the strap and let it hang from my back. I put my pistols in my holsters and my blades in their scabbard. The container still had the ammunition, magazines, and other equipment that was coming with me.

"Captain," the South African said from the cockpit. "Welcome to the Havoc station."

# CHAPTER EIGHT

## CONTINGENCY

The cargo doors opened, and a bright light invaded the gloomy cargo bay. I turned around and quickly got off the ship, where I was greeted by a waiting officer. I looked at the Korean and said to him, "You have courage. You think quickly. That's good. However, as long as you're in the military, I can't let you near her. Let me make it simple. You have to quit if you want to do anything with her. Or just stay away from her."

He looked at the floor, mumbled something, and turned around to sit on the Hyperion's bench.

"Well, you seem to be having grand time, Captain," the officer said. "Come now, your ship is waiting for you."

He gestured toward the only other ship in the hangar. The Havoc station was a sight that made you marvel at the creativity and engineering that science can achieve. This was my third time there, and I looked at the walls and marveled at the complexion and the dark beauty of the station. There are, to my knowledge, about three million men and women working and maintaining it as it orbited around the nuclear gas giant, Havoc. The planet offered an unlimited supply of fuel for the station's every need, including the ships.

The station was at the crossroads of human colonies on the midpoint of the Milky Way. Stretching four miles across and two miles wide, the hangar made an ancient seaborne aircraft carrier look small. The port had landing pads for any ship to land. I couldn't stay and marvel at the station. I had to go. I didn't feel that down about having to leave so soon; people could work here their entire lives and not see every part of this station, or so I had been told.

"We have a contingency plan, in the event that a planet is under attack like this. Come, let's walk." We walked, and he gestured in the direction of a container near the ship that was being armed. We walked closer and saw that it had more supplies, which made me happy, considering that I would need to carry them until my mission was complete.

"So, the embassy on Helena has a platoon of special forces. Chances are they're holed up in the bunker, so when you knock out the jammer, go get our boys. They're armed, and they'll help you extract the king and his men," the officer said. He wore a wrinkly uniform and had an optimistic air about him.

"That doesn't seem so bad. Might as well let them do the work."

"Here, the director and the council want to know where you are, so we can extract you once you fulfill your mission," he said, giving me a wrist receiver. I put it on, and the red light started to glow. It was a green shell that contained the wiring for intergalactic communication and Big Brother surveillance.

"Now, here is your map of the planet. Luckily for you, you just need to go to the main city. The rest of the cities will be worked out by the council." He gave me another tablet that could be attached to my wrist, only this one was interesting. It had a dark screen that showed the mapping of the station. I swiped one option, and the map turned 3D.

"Sir, does the king have a transmitting device that I can use to track him?" I asked, hopeful that this would make the mission easier.

"Yes, but we can't detect it. Too much interference. You need to get on the ground to find it."

Two men then appeared from a door in the hangar. They were carrying a box of about three feet by four feet that did not look like military issue. It appeared to be way too heavy for such a small box. They looked at me and then at the officer and continued to sneak onto the Hyperion. They entered, and one poked his head out the cargo bay. Then they exited the craft and began refueling the ship while arguing about something.

"Agent, Agent, erhm Captain, did you hear me?" the officer asked.

"Huh?" I said as I turned to him.

"I said, if you were paying attention, that once you destroy the jamming device, you hit the button on your tracker to contact us. If something goes wrong with your transmitter, hit the green button to have us lock on the map when we orbit the planet."

I looked at the transmitter and tried to think of ways to get rid of it. I hated that they were always keeping

Alex Diaz

watch on me as if I were some teenager who couldn't be trusted.

"During the trip to Helena, the signal won't reach you, will it?" I asked.

"No, that is correct," he replied, looking at his watch. "Now listen carefully. You have only thirty hours to reach Helena and complete your mission. Knock out the jammer and find the royal family. Your map has a built-in sensor. The more it jams, the closer you are."

I had turned and started walking away when the officer spoke.

"Oh, I almost forgot. Here," he said, throwing to me a box that I thought contained cigars. I realized I was wrong when I felt its weight. I opened the mysterious box and was surprised to see seven long cartridges. Each cartridge was about two inches thick and ten inches long. I pulled out a cartridge and put it on the straps used for shotgun shells. The case was about seven inches, and the bullet extended three inches further. The glass tip housed blue matter that hovered inside.

"These are experimental high-explosive antiship rounds. In case you're wondering how to load them on your rifle, here," he said, putting his hand out for the rifle. I took it off my back and handed it to him. On the butt of the rifle was a hatch that he slid off.

"These rounds can punch through even the toughest enemy tank armor and take out a crowd of people."

He inserted the round and told me to close the hatch and press the trigger three times.

"First one registers the round, second one charges

it, third one hits the kill switch," he said, looking down with a smile.

He opened the hatch, and the cartridge ejected. He handed the rifle and cartridge back to me and also gave me a Coke. Unbelievable company. Founded in the eighteen hundreds, and it was still around.

"Good luck, Agent. You have fifteen hours after arriving on the planet to find a ship to evacuate. We will bomb the planet, regardless of who is there."

"Understood, sir," I said, saluting him. He put his hand on my shoulder and looked at the two pilots near the Hyperion.

"Here's a tip: don't let them drink anything. That ship is a prototype, and they are unpredictable when they are drinking."

"Understood, sir," I said, confused. *Drinking what?* I thought.

"No, really—nothing. Those passive-aggressive bastards somehow get drinks. Do not, under any circumstances, let them drink," he warned me again.

I grabbed my rifle and container and walked to the Hyperion, which had a little bat riding a drag-racing car drawn on its side with the word "Dragula" written on it.

When I boarded the Hyperion, I almost vomited at the smell. Unfortunately, the door closed behind me, and I was stuck in a ship that smelled like vomit, alcohol, and urine.

# CHAPTER NINE

## PYRRHIC VICTORY

I put my container on the magnetic lock and quickly put myself in the cryo-chamber. Without looking, I set the timer to nine hours and hit the button, which brought me back to the dark void of unconsciousness.

The blue woman came back and walked closer to me. She circled my paralyzed body. I then realized my foolishness. In my attempt to avoid the horrid smell, I had forgotten to set the no-dream option.

My breath intensified, my palms sweated. I could feel my eyes widen. Even in this virtuality, every feeling was too real for it to be false. The woman kept circling me, smiling darkly, or so I thought. This was the first time I had actually paid attention to her. She was beautiful in a sense. Midtwenties and in shape: she looked like the perfect woman. I felt her getting close to me and whispering. She put her arms around me from behind.

"What do you want to relieve? A dream or an event from the past?" she whispered. I could swear she was smiling, as though she knew this was a pain for me. I couldn't go back to the past—anywhere but there. The surface of the sun would have been a better option than the past.

From the corner of my eye, I could see that she was smiling. She looked at me, smiled again, and rested her head on my shoulder. Then she shifted her arms, putting them around my waist.

"Back," I strained, clenching my teeth, and fighting the paralyzing feeling.

"Back? Oh, you mean like the past? All right, let's choose that," she said happily.

"No!" I croaked. Why did it hurt me to talk? Why did it pain me?

"Clo? Planet Clo? Oh, that happened two years, eight months, seventeen days and five hours ago. Hmmm. It looks like you're trying to block that memory. Why is that? Let's go there and find out," she said, letting me go and spinning in front of me, giving me a light kiss on the cheek.

Before I knew it, I was in a void that was darker than that of a black hole.

## PLANET CLO: TWO YEARS, EIGHT MONTHS, SEVENTEEN DAYS, AND FIVE HOURS AGO . . .

I was back in an old Hyperion, wearing an older military uniform, which had a black urban BDU and metal plates. This uniform had a weak exoskeleton and even weaker armor. I dreaded this day. It was what had caused me to be who I am right now. A harsh, apathetic, rude man.

My squad was my group of friends, my family, my brothers. *Again I will see them killed. Again they will die in front of me*. I looked at one member as I lost control of my body and automatically repeated the actions I had already committed here, the first was by putting my helmet on, and giving him an encouraging smile. There was a silence, the type of silence that forever resounds so loudly in one's memory.

"Movement on buildings at starboard side," the pilot said. "We're dropping you off in seven hundred meters."

"All right! Listen up!" I yelled through the helmet's microphone. "Hostile rebels are in the area, and our job is to make sure they don't take the city's downtown area. We got to hold out until—"

The alarmed sounded, and everyone turned to see the light hanging from the ceiling. Someone was trying to lock on to us with an antiship weapon.

"Driver, get us the hell out of here!" one of my squad members yelled.

"Don't worry, that lock is why I'm here. I got it," the copilot said, trying to jam the signal.

"Thirty seconds," the pilot announced.

"All right, let's get ready," I said, chambering my rifle. I could only repeat what I had done, even if I knew the end result. Out the corner of my eye, I spotted the blue A.I. sitting on one of the seats of the ship, looking pretty worried and not smiling anymore.

"All right, we're at the square," the pilot, said, referring to the town square. The hangar doors opened, and I held on to the gravity handle, which dropped me and my captain down first. The city square was massive. The buildings were all at least six stories high, and a few were ten to twelve. I moved to secure the area, while the rest of the squad descended from the gravity handle.

When the squad surrounded the area, the Hyperion took off.

"Set up a perimeter around the square. I want MG and AT troops facing the main route. I want two of you on the flank, two on each side, and the rest watch the rooftops and hold on to this square with your own lives," my captain said.

"What about our drones and you know, tanks and support, sir?" someone asked.

"They'll be on their way. They will be here only for a while before needing to return to base to refuel and rearm, so don't depend on them," the captain responded.

The A.I. was just sitting on a bench, sitting peacefully in the midst of a tense operation. She was just looking pretty, and completly unaware of what was to come.

We all moved into position and got ready, but nothing happened. The birds chirped their songs, and the leaves rustled. A silence overtook this place. We looked around and around and back to our original spot.

I looked through the sight of my rifle and saw something fall on the rifle itself. I looked up and saw clouds in the sky. More flakes began to fall, and we could all see our breath in the air. An hour later we lit a fire to keep warm and cook our rations. Even though it was a dream, I was reliving the tiniest details—every feeling, every action ... except I knew the end.

Later on the captain and I began to argue about the brain. I wished later on that we hadn't argued about it and had paid more attention to what was going on around us.

"The brain is not a parasite, Gerald," he said, reading a report from his wrist communicator.

"It's a theory. Look, maybe it ain't all a parasite, maybe just a part of it."

"Which part would that be?"

"The newly developed one."

"The one for higher-order thinking? Yeah, you are out of your mind," he said, chuckling.

"The brain named itself. You also know you can't kill yourself easily. Your brain is smart enough to stop you or to keep on going if you try. If it loses contact with its host, it dies," I countered.

"Look, as your good friend and commanding officer, I'm ordering you to drop this," the captain said, flashing the scar on his lip. It always made him look as though he were smiling with half his face.

He walked away to check on the other troops.

One of my squad members, Secret, came up to me.

"Hey, Lieutenant. I need to ask for some advice."

"Shoot," I said, rubbing my hands to keep them warm. The hologram was shivering at this point.

"It's about Proctor. His weight is getting out of hand, and so is his blood pressure. How do I tell him to take care of himself?" Proctor was his brother, and he was letting himself go. Even with all the countless advances in medicine, if a person does not attempt to heal himself, all that medicine and all those procedures go to waste.

"I'm his superior officer. I'll deal with it," I answered, chuckling.

I walked over to the fire, where the A.I. woman was trying to stay warm, if that was even possible. I saw Proctor and noticed that he was cooking meat for a sandwich. He slowly put the meat on the bun and started eating it. It made me feel strange, seeing the man eat. A weird sensation that almost made me want to wait for him to finish.

He looked at me and put the sandwich to the side.

"Lieutenant," he said.

"Proctor, I need to talk to you." I was so relieved that he stopped eating in front of me.

"What is it, sir?" he asked.

"Look, we all worry about you. We are all brothers. Brothers in arms are brothers for life," I started. Everyone else got closer to hear what I was telling him.

"We take care of each other in all ways, and we'll look after each other, so look at us and then at you, and notice you shou—" I paused, looking at him incredulously. "*Stop eating, you fat piece of lard!*" I yelled. The entire squad cracked up.

"Jeez! Then you ask why you have high blood pressure? Look at you. Stop it!" Even Proctor started laughing at this point. We all sat back in our positions and listened to the firefights and the occasional thermobaric bombs the Hyperion was dropping.

A beep in everyone's helmet alerted us of an incoming message, and everyone held on to his helmet to hear the transmission.

"To all United Galactic Federation troops, this is Forward Command. We are taking heavy casualties. If this keeps up, we might need to pull out. We have already lost over 37 percent of available fighting force. Stand by for orders."

"Jeez, 37 percent. Don't they teach the brass how to

keep the troops alive and win?" the captain commented, pulling out his synthetic smoking device.

"Dunno, Captain. Looks like we're expendable," someone answered.

"Well, we've been here for about two months. If this fighting keeps up, we're as good as dead," someone else added.

"If this snow keeps up, might as well freeze with the MAIDs and ships, eh, Lieutenant?" Secret asked.

MAID—the Mechanical Armored Infantry Division. This was the crown jewel of the military. Mechanized suits that were essentially walking tanks piloted by special and talented tank drivers.

"Well, if you're feeling cold, go get us coats," I ordered.

"You kidding? We can't run with those on," someone argued.

The coats were actually not that bad, but they were knee length and tight enough to restrict our movement. Secret went to a metallic crate, kicked it open, and started to pass out coats to everyone. He went around the fountain, cursing about the stupid coat. An explosion in the distance brought down a towering skyscraper. The channel carried more transmissions, and more ships were descending from the carriers.

"Hey, Captain! Where do you think these guys get their equipment?" I asked.

"Hell should I know. We're on the other side of the universe, far from the border or any weapons factory, so no damn clue," he answered, taking another whiff from his smoking device.

The hologram was staring at the buildings, and I knew what was going to happen now. A crackling in the distance made me get her head and push it behind the cover of the fountain. This was the first time I had control of my body in this nightmare.

Within a minute the first bullet hit a few inches from Secret. More bullets flew past everyone else. A rocket buzzed, destroying the fountain, and shrapnel and rock sprayed everywhere. One man flew over his barricade. It was Brain, the medic. His blood started to flow onto the snow. That was casualty number one. Eight more to go.

"Brain's hit! Someone cover me!" Secret yelled, jumping over his cover to get to Brain. I saw movement of bodies sprinting on the rooftops and started shooting in that direction. I saw a rebel drop and I kept that area suppressed. I always remembered the small, hurried breaths I took. The slowing of time, the projectiles hissed and snap around me. The spray of water from the fountain behind me, the tiny pieces of concrete that would hit me when they exploded. The dirt that covered my visor when the ground took a bullet in front of me. Chaos brings out the tiny details that we remember, but it also brings out what kind of people we are.

"Secret, you got him yet?" the captain asked, firing another round into a building. In the dark it was easier to see the flash of their weapons, but that applied to us as well.

Secret got Brain in time and, hoisting him over his shoulders, was walking to cover. The A.I. was cowering behind the destroyed fountain, her hands covering her ears, screaming. I broke a bit, and I was sorry that she was here with me. I wanted to yell and to grab her and hug her while begging for forgiveness. Secret brought Brain over to me, and I checked his pulse. Gone. Nothing. He'd left us.

I looked up at Secret and shook my head. At the sight of my face, he began to clench his teeth. He stood up angrily and shot at the building from which the rocket had been shot. A round left one of the buildings and made its way toward his neck. He plopped down and began to flop like a fish out of water, trying to hold his blood in with his hands.

"Secret!" Proctor yelled, abandoning his post. He ran up to his brother, grabbed his head, and cradled it.

"Gerald!"

I turned to see who had called me. It was the captain.

"Get on the comms. I want those buildings gone, and get me some evac for Brain and Secret."

"On it, sir." I grabbed my transmitter and called it in. I was behind a wall that was taking the many bullets around me. Many pieces of metal were flying all over, too— shards of light in the darkness around us.

"They're everywhere!" someone yelled. I couldn't believe it then, and I couldn't believe that I was living it again now. Two more of my squad members were hit and were bleeding out. One had been hit in the stomach, the other in the head. The snow began changing to a crimson color. The captain took the rocket launcher and fired it at a room filled with rebels. The room lit up with fire, and five rebels were wiped out, all thanks to the captain.

Proctor, having momentarily recovered, stood up and fired wildly.

"Sit down, you idiot!" a squad member yelled. But Proctor ignored him and kept shouting and cursing in Russian, with the mad hope of killing the one who had killed his brother. I had never seen anything like it—the tears in his eyes, and his pure rage over losing his loved one, his brother, whom no one could replace.

He was gunned down after a minute, gunned down like a dog. He went down with a smile on his face, a sure sign that he had killed someone—not the one responsible, but someone. Only five of us were still alive. The rebels came out of the buildings and charged at us. The captain then spoke his famous last words.

"Hold on to this square. Hold on to it with your very lives," he said before a rocket evaporated him completely. One rebel jumped over the cover and shot another soldier in the back. I turned over and gunned him down.

"I'm out!" a squad member yelled.

"Here, last mag," someone else said, throwing him his last magazine.

Three more rounds and I would need to resort to my pistol. Of course in a few seconds my dreamself would remember the heavy machine gun facing the main road. I was in command of two soldiers, and I called them over, telling them about my plan, which they understood. Using themselves as decoys, they brought on suppressing fire, while I stood up and, by sheer luck, was missed by every bullet. I jumped over the bodies, ruins, craters, and debris and picked up the heavy gun, aiming it at the remaining rebels. The weapon roared to life, and I gunned down the rebels as they charged, trying to overrun my position.

The Hyperions flew by and destroyed the buildings.

By now, however, it was just an aesthetic—a simple touch of chaos and untimeliness. The fastest vehicle in the universe—the one thing that could have rescued people—was too slow to save them.

"Secure the landing zone," I ordered as I moved back to the bench where the A.I. had been sitting, shivering, and cowering. For another time, I was given control of my body.

"What happens to them? What happened here? Why did you want to be brought here?" she muttered. Tears came down my face. I started shaking and she put her arms around me.

"One of the rebels has a bomb on his chest, and he detonates it when they are close. This city was in a state of rebellion over a religious conflict or some other idiotic thing. Four billion lives were lost here." An explosion detonated behind me, and the shock wave rocked me as the ocean rocks a ship. My dream self took over and as I stood up and turned around.

"No!" A secondary explosion ripped through the air, and I received a gash under my eye.

I got on my knees and kept yelling that word. My fist hit the ground and kept hitting it. Two burned bodies had replaced my friends and those who were supposed to be under my watch. In a way, I had sent those men to their deaths. Men with families, spouses, and friends.

"Ghost three-two, this is angel two-one. Is the landing zone clear?" the transmission in the helmet said.

"Angel two-one, LZ is clear," I answered with dread in my voice.

"How many casualties?" the pilot asked.

"Everyone else," I answered.

"We'll get you out of here soon."

"Thanks."

There I stood, waiting for the ship that would rescue me. The hologram crept closer to me. My helmet brought me a new transmission.

"Ghost three-two, this is Forward Command, we're pulling the plug on this world. We need you to get yourself and any surviving members of your outfit out of the square and into the following coordinates. We're pulling out of here, and that Hyperion is getting redirected."

"No, no, no! You cannot be doing that!" I spat. "I just lost my entire squad, and you're telling me we're pulling out? Do you know what that means? It means they died for nothing!"

"Orders are orders, and these are the orders I'm supposed to give. I'm sorry."

"Worthless bastards!" I yelled, throwing my helmet to the ground. I was given control of my body as the hologram stood in front of me and put her hands on my shoulders. We both kneeled as the sharp knife of dread stabbed me over and over. This was the longest day in my memory. She caressed my face with her blue fingers. Her expression was full of sympathy and remorse.

I was holding back tears. It all crumbling in front of me. The entire square was a quiet, destroyed graveyard. The buildings were razed, and fires and corpses littered their ruins. More buildings were brought down, more fires danced, more rivers of blood flowed, and the enemy cheered and charged.

The hologram kissed my forehead with her blue lips

as my body reconstructed my actions from the past. The dog tags of my team members were soon in my hand and then in one of my pouches. Their ammunition was also stuffed in there. Before leaving, however, I stood each of their rifles on end in the mud and dirt, helmets on top. This was my last good-bye to them.

My walk to the extraction point led me to other friendly troops, but our route was filled with rebel fighters, demolished buildings, and dangers that we needed to face. At one point, I found myself in control of my body, leading the hologram by the hand out of a rebel-infested building, firing a pistol with my other hand. The stairs were destroyed, debris covered the floor, the walls were riddled with holes. It was strange that I was holding her hand even though she was never there. The city was a battlefield for retreating soldiers, and I was saving a hologram.

At times she sang. In one of her songs, she just repeated the same things over and over again—the same phrase, but in a beautiful, melancholic voice. It went,

> Hush, little soldier, my soldier.
> Wait to die with me, hold your breath
> for me, mmhhmhhmmhhmm hhmm.
> One day we'll be free, but today is bloody.
> I'll be waiting to see you with me.

At other times she sang,

> You are my sunshine, my only sunshine.
> You make me happy when skies are gray.

You'll never know, dear, how much I love you.
Please don't take my sunshine away.

I wanted to talk to the hologram, but there were times I was not in control and could only relive the past. But the emotional buildup of my feelings was staggering. It could break at any moment, of course I couldn't since that wasn't what happened, also I couldn't control my body thanks to hologram. The hologram knew this. At one point in the fighting between me, the rest of the UGF soldiers, and the rebels, the hologram was separated from the group by a large piece of debris. When we were reunited, she hugged me and grabbed my hands, stopped the whole world and walked me to a rooftop, and she began to spin us on the rooftops on that winter day.

"Let's get married," she suggested.

"What?" I said, chuckling. I couldn't believe my ears.

"Just you and me. Right here, right now. No one needs to know," she said.

I decided to humor her.

"All right. Yeah, I take you as my wife." I smiled at her.

She hugged me, and we made our way back to the surviving soldiers.

I eventually made my way to the extraction point with the hologram. Just me and her. The war had gotten to the others, and they shared the fate of Ghost three-two. Ryan was there, watching me and waiting for the rest of Ghost three-two. But it was only me, and he knew that when I gave him the dog tags of all those who had fallen. He put his hand on my shoulder as I held on to the hologram's hand and began to show signs of breaking. We had to abandon this world. We had lost too many lives, but we eventually forced this world to surrender when we starved it out with a blockade. We knew that this victory had come at too great a cost and was too bitter for us to go back as champions. It was a beautiful Pyrrhic victory. On the ride to the fleet, I held the hologram's hand and didn't let her go. I felt an emotion for that hologram that I had married. I felt ridiculous—like a clown and a creep.

# CHAPTER TEN

## BACK TO DARKNESS

I was back in the darkness, with the A.I. I sat down and began to sob uncontrollably. She sat next to me and hugged me. Oh, the irony! I finally show my true colors, and the one who is there to witness it and to comfort me is a hologram. A program with no emotions. She held me and continued singing the songs she had sung before. The melody calmed me down.

I was actually getting comfortable with the A.I. It made me curious who had designed her.

"Where were you created?" I asked her.

"My creator and model was the princess of Helena. She ... we are really smart," she replied with a beautiful, quirky smile.

"Wait, why did you say 'we'?"

"She programmed me with her personality and her emotions," she replied blankly, staring at her extended hand.

Okay, maybe she did have feelings, but this was way too coincidental, for my mission was in Helena, and I had already met the princess. Sort of.

"She's ... both of you are in trouble. The kingdom is under attack. She is at risk."

Her blue eyes widened, and her smile disappeared quicker than the hopes of doomed humans.

"You should know—I have a way to connect my memories with her. She built it in case someone like you came. That way we would both have you in mind forever."

"Wait, what?" I stammered, putting my hand on her face.

We both stood up, and she stared into my eyes. Her face was the only extremely detailed feature she had. It was strange that I was still bleeding from the shrapnel of the dream. It was strange that I was still in my old uniform. It was strange that I was still my younger self, my old self. The darkness taunted us; yet it welcomed me even deeper. But I knew what it was. This darkness wasn't just a void-filler, it was my own imagination and topics at which even Friedrich Nietzsche would cringe. Yet, the only light was being emitted by me and the hologram. I held on to her as my greed and my demons began to stir from the darkness. I held her close. I would not let anything happen to her. She only smiled at my gesture. I wanted to ask her what her name was.

"Hey, can I ask you—"

"Your time is up in a few seconds, but she will remember you," she said, pushing me to a slow fall. She kissed me, but it was a fake kiss, for she was a program, and I was flesh and blood.

I think I married a princess. And I never got to ask her, her name.

# CHAPTER ELEVEN

## DRAGULA

"Hey, you all right, man?" one of the pilots asked me. Both of the pilots were standing in front of me and watching my every move.

I threw up the chemicals that were in my body. I then smelled the air again and threw up what was in my stomach.

"Ahh, he's fine. It's just the smell," one barely managed.

He took out a flask and drank from it. He had a Russian accent, which matched his Russian drink.

"You sure?" the other pilot asked. He didn't seem to have an accent, but my money would bet he was Mexican, not that it mattered anyways.

He opened the box that he sneaked in from the Havoc station and started drinking from a bottle containing a yellow substance.

"Who ... who's driving ... the ship?" I asked, seeing double.

The men looked at each other and then toward me and back at each other. That started the argument.

"It was your turn to drive the bloody ship, Emanuel."

"Hey, I drove it from Havoc to here, Dimitry. Don't try to make me do everything."

"Don't pin this on me, Emanuel, like every time we go out and drink, you always want me to pay."

"Well, maybe if you helped out a little, like refueling or driving the ship, maybe I wouldn't ask you to pay."

"Hey, I help out a lot. Like if it wasn't for me, we would have both gotten shot down in Enda."

"We did get shot down in Enda. You were too sober to drive, and you didn't want me to take the damn stick."

"You idiot, that was in Chasper, and we didn't get shot down; we crashed. And if I remember correctly, I dragged you out of the crash site."

This was sort of amusing, so I let it keep going. They spat these things at each other until they started yelling in either Russian or Spanish. I opened my metal container and started to put my rounds into my magazines. The two pilots kept screaming and arguing like starving lions over a piece of meat. They then took out their swords and began dueling like pirates for control of a ship.

After I completed loading the tenth magazine in my Hornet, they took out their sidearms and began threatening to blow each other's brains out.

"Whoa! Both of you! Calm down. Jeez, shouldn't both of you be driving this ship?" I intervened, my role as peacekeeper commencing.

"He's right. Dimitry, after you." Emanuel pitched his eyes up.

"Very funny," Dimitry answered, entering the cockpit.

Both men drank from their containers, and I noticed

that they stumbled and were barely able to walk. This must have been the most frightening ride in a Hyperion. If only I had listened to the officer on Havoc.

I kept loading the magazines into all my weapons until a half hour later, the PA system buzzed with life.

"Sad man, we are in the Helenac atmosphere," the Russian said, burping between words.

This planet was in the Goldilocks zone. Its mass, atmosphere, and gravitational pull were identical to Earth's. The only difference was that its rotation and slant were the opposite of Earth's.

Finally, it was only a matter of time before they landed.

I looked at my right wrist, which held my map, a device I could probably have upgraded. I also noticed that it had a clock and a timer with about twenty hours left on it. That reminded me of the tracking device on my other arm. It would take a while until it gave my position to command. I put it on the bench after ripping off the band and, with the butt of the Hornet, smashed it to bits. Then I swiped it to the floor with my left arm.

"Hey, sad man, I pity you. Therefore I will play some music," the Russian man mumbled through the PA system.

As if on cue, a piercing screech penetrated my ears and sent me to the ground dropping everything I was holding. The noise continued until screaming began and knocked everyone down.

"I think band is called White Rob," the man screamed over the PA system.

"What?" I yelled, putting my hands over my ears purely for cosmetic effect.

"Agent," Emanuel's expression and words spoke over the music "come to the cockpit and tell me what is that?"

His worried voice and his ability to talk over the music made me jump to my feet and into the cockpit. Emanuel pointed at the towering, dark, red-eyed monster. Dimitry rubbed his eyes, took another gulp from his flask, and looked at the creature once more. My jaw dropped as I saw it. The behemoth of walking gray flesh, seemed to be dropping oval objects. It then occurred to me those were eggs.

"Are you drinking and flying?" I asked Dimitry, looking at the fully grown Goliath.

"Is your rank above major?" he croaked.

"No, it's captain," I answered, noticing the Goliath turning around and looking at us.

Dimitry chuckled insanely before looking at the alien and beginning to sob at the sight of its aura.

"How loud is the music? Can we hear it, or are you using the outside speakers?" I asked as I began loading all my equipment in the remaining packs in a sloppy manner.

"Outside," Emanuel replied, quivering.

"Why do you have it on outside? This was supposed to be a covert mission!" I yelled at their stupidity.

"Emanuel, help him into a paraglider and open cargo door. We are not landing Dragula," Dimitry ordered.

The Goliath turned around and roared a sound that would have made the devil run for cover. It grabbed some of its eggs, which would hatch into spawn to throw at us. Even from the distance, the protective glass of the ship vibrated, the glass around the monster broke, and we held our ears, like cowards in war.

"Go! Now!" Dimitry yelled. Emanuel took off his seat belts, and we both ran to the other end of the ship. I took off my helmet to pack the last of my headgear, which consisted of my face cloth, goggles, and headset, and then the helmet. Emanuel put the paraglider over my sword, which was sheathed on my back. I quickly adjusted the paraglider to my settings and size and got my metal container—no time to put anything in it. The song was still blaring when the collision alarm sounded. Emanuel and I stared at that light and hurried to save our lives. My whole body was shaking, and my head began to spin.

"Hold on!" Dimitry yelled. Both Emanuel and I grabbed on to something that was attached to the ship.

The altimeter counted 18,556 and dropping. The cargo door opened, and I looked at Emanuel. I grabbed his bottle and took a sip of liquid courage before spitting out the burning liquid.

"That's a hell of a drop," I yelled.

"Yeah, well, that's you, not me," he shouted.

"What kind of a song is this?" The collision warning was on again, and he began to try to push me off the ship.

"Well, it's named after the ship. Now *hasta luego*," Emanuel said, kicking me and the container of the ship. As I fell, I heard Dimitry either singing or proclaiming the same thing the song said.

"Devil on your back," Emanuel yelled before he started screaming.

I was about two hundred feet falling down when a massive heat ball exploded behind me. The sound burst my eardrum. With the explosion behind me, however,

I didn't turn around. I didn't want to know what had happened.

I fell. Oh, how I fell. It was a rich feeling. I felt like I had all the time in the world to think. I thought as tears rolled out of my eyes. They came out for no reason, other than to lubricate my eyes. My shallow breath made me feel at peace. I closed my eyes and felt as if I were at home in my bed, on the verge of falling asleep but awakened by the feeling that I was falling, then waking up in a familiar place and realizing that everything was fine, everything was all right, that it was just a dream.

The timer on the paraglider brought me back to current reality. A push to the button on the strap had extended two wings and had brought out a thruster that quickly activated. I was holding on to the container for dear life. All my remaining ammunition and equipment was in there. I couldn't lose it until I put it away properly in my packs.

To descend gracefully into the massive city of stone and metal, to a city of buildings that did not come from Earth, to a new world, to a new people, made me glad to say that not many people had had the opportunity to do that. The wings took me next to a building that the Goliath must have hit, since water was spilling from its side. One building had a garden on its roof, with flowers and trees. This city was not like Earth's, Kepler's, Mars's or any other city in any of the worlds I had been to.

The wrist map soon began to ring an alarm, making me realize that the jammer must have been close, but the glider on my back needed to land me safely to avoid the shock of such a precipitous drop. From a distance, I could see an alley in a suburban neighborhood. Two Goliath spawn, newly hatched, about five and half feet tall, with claws that could tear a tank to pieces, were at my apparent landing spot. I tried to land somewhere else, but my fate was sealed. I was to face the creatures. I was about ten feet over them when the idea of dropping the container on one of them and landing on the other occurred to me. Taking a deep breath, I let go of the box, and it landed with enough force that the sick sound of breaking bones as it landed on the Goliath's neck made me cringe. Blood smeared the walls of the alley. The other Goliath turned to see its fallen brother and began to screech. I landed on the creature and pushed it onto a wooden fence that was behind it. The push broke a piece of wood and ran the creature through.

The Goliath was impaled on the fence post through the chest, and it started to ooze a dark, moon-blue blood. It made a soft growl like that of a dying wolf. I stood over it and heard its dying sounds. One of the last of its kind, and it was at my feet, dying, and in agony. But contrary to what you might expect, this did not make me feel superior to it. To see it bleed, to see it dying, to see it cry out in pain, made me feel like the monster. Finally, I had had enough of its suffering and decided to put it out of its misery. I pulled out my sword and, with one quick jab at its head, I put it down. The black metallic wings retracted into the backpack at this time and I kept it on, not knowing whether or not I would need it later on. The thrusters began to refuel from the air around me.

The spawn had pale skin, which, if the creature matured, turned gray. Its sunken eyes were its most disturbing feature. Its exterior was black, but its interior was gold and crimson, which seemed to reflect my past and look deep into me and my soul.

I was glad it could no longer see.

# CHAPTER TWELVE

## EMPTY

I cleaned the dark-blue blood off my sword with grass. With my sword sheathed, I took out my weird pistol and chambered it with a quick pull of the slide. It was afternoon, and the sky was setting, but it left a beautiful pink color in the sky.

I kicked the container open with my foot and grabbed my magazines and organized them in my ammo pouches. I had 615 bullets both for the pistol Herr Doctor gave me and and 1,541 bullets for my Hornet. I put the .454 pistol ammo into pouches hanging from my belt and a pouch on my thigh. I then slipped the pistol itself into the holster on my back. All that was left was the hybrid pistol, which had the words "Offense Weapon" etched into its side. That was put into my leg holster while its magazines were placed on the pouches near the holster and back.

I was now ready to search the city for its king and take him and his family to safety. Or so I thought, because my stomach loves to talk to me in the worst of times.

"Not now."

My stomach responded louder. *I should listen to it.*

*I haven't eaten since the ride before Edo. Two and a half days ago.*

"Not now. How about I get to a secure location?" I asked it, and it agreed with me.

I grabbed two preprepared food packets and put them in my remaining pouches. Then I took the flashlight and a handful of light strobes, my wrist rope, a landing beacon, a NOVA grenade and a regular air-burst fragmentation one, a water pack, and other essential equipment and placed it all in my packs.

The container was now useless to me, although it had been helpful with the spawn. I started to walk away, rifle at the ready, out of the alley and into the empty street. The Helenac nation had no large aerial forces to evacuate the citizens, but something could not let any ship leave the planet anyways, and there were no civilians anywhere. Crouching behind a car helped me think. This wasn't right. If no one could leave, then where was everyone?

Palm trees lined the street, and at one intersection there was a downed civilian transport ship which downed a few of the trees. I ran to the ship to see whether anyone had survived or whether there were any bodies, but it was all empty. Smeared with blood, but empty.

I walked to the plaza, where I made my first discovery of people. I found the bodies of a squad of police officers and one Goliath spawn. There were at least three pairs of Goliath footprints. There was also a crowd of human footprints, and it appeared that the police went down trying to give the civilians time to escape.

"Noble," I muttered as I put on the black face cloth and continued to look at the deceased and their wounds—rips and tears at the neck and impalement in their stomachs. Not pretty deaths. But, then again, none are, and neither is the smell.

Despite all this, in my mind it was honorable. Yet I really didn't believe in an honorable death; it was just that the UGF had spent countless hours drilling that into my mind. They died in battle—as all UGF forces wanted to go—yet none needed to die this way. I would die for the mission if needed, because as long as this was a mission, then my life just meant that little, or so my combat manual said.

I kept walking, following the sounds of ghosts in the empty city. At a distance, near the heart of the city, the monstrous Goliath reigned. At the midpoint in this darkening hour, I entered a luxurious apartment building and looked out the windows. I secured the site, breaking down nearly every door with ease, thanks to the exoskeleton suit, and I saw that, like the city, the building was empty. Even the panic rooms were devoid of life.

I made my way to find a room for me. Of all the rooms in the building, I wanted a suite. The first suite I took wasn't a presidential suite, but it sure was more than anything I could afford, for it had a massive hover bed, a bar, a hot tub and other expensive luxuries that I never could have afforded unless I had borrowed Evelyn's paycheck. I then realized who was staying in the room. It was in evidence all over the papers and the computer that I found. The room was rented to a very bad, egotistical, foul-mouthed, insupportable, intolerable, conceited, boastful, idiotic "musician."".

His bad music, lifestyle, and syntax and his disgusting

personality left me sitting on his rented bed panting with anger. The bed, however, felt as if it were made of clouds. I really should stop following the life of celebrities I hated on the news.

I personally prefer music that has real instruments or incredibly good vocals and lyrics.

My stomach then talked to me again, reminding me I was hungry.

Without remorse and hoping to teach this bad artist a lesson, I grabbed his clothes and papers and laptop—hell, anything that was his I put in a pile and lit it on fire. I then grabbed one of my food packs and cooked it with a press of the pack and a chuckle.

It was August—a long and dark one. I waited for my meal to cook—a nice, if tiny, steak and mashed potatoes, just like home. The musician's junk burned and burned, as did my hate for him. It occurred to me that I shouldn't be hating people, the hologram would not have liked that. I needed to be nicer to others.

# CHAPTER THIRTEEN

## SEEN

I kept the fire controlled, since I didn't want to damage the building and cause unnecessary physical damage. I added to the fire things like papers, the occasional article of clothing, and awards that the musician had received—which surprised me, since I had not the faintest idea how he deserved to get any.

I was eating my food with the fire to my left and the window to the right. I decided to camp out here until daylight when I would start looking for the jammer. Planning ahead was a smart idea, in order to reduce the risk of danger and meeting up with the Goliath and any spawn.

I took a bite of my steak and realized how far away I was from the downtown. How far away I was from the monster. How far I was from Edo, from Clo, from Earth. How far away from my wife who was in virtual reality and not even in this physical world. Would the physical self be the same as the virtual one? I looked across the horizon of this abandoned city, hoping for an answer.

How had life in this city been before this disaster? It had been only three days since the whole situation began. I sat down and thought about things for about an hour, until something down below caught my eye. Seeing movement kicked my reflexes into top gear, and I tripped on my way to the window.

In an alleyway I saw someone or something running. I aimed my rifle in that direction, and my sight had six red squares in one area. I looked at the sight and then through it once more. I shifted it to the right, and more squares appeared on the screen. Something grew inside me— something that weighed my stomach down. I couldn't close my eyes at this sight.

Herr Doctor's words about the scope's ability to perceive enemies echoed in my head. I was surrounded.

I noticed that the Goliaths' footsteps in the distance had stopped. Actually, they had sounded louder a while ago before they disappeared.

It made me nervous, and I reached for more paper to throw in the fire. I had turned to put it in the fire when another glow lit the room. Everything stopped—my breathing, my motion; even the fire seemed to stop. Rifle at the ready, I slowly turned around. I moved one foot, then the other, until I no longer had my back against the window.

A massive eye was staring at me, blocking my view to the outside. It was black, gold, and crimson. I had never seen it so close. It had no eyelashes and no mark; it was the purest eye of this size that I had ever encountered. The eye looked into mine and stared at my very soul and reflected on my past. I knew whose eye that was. It was the Goliath's.

I turned around and sprinted for the door. All the while I aimed my gun at the window, the trigger pulled, leaving only rounds to greet the beast. It took over ten bullets for the glass to break, and the rest penetrated the eye in a sickening plop.

The Goliath roared in pain. Its massive roar shook the entire apartment. I tackled the door, and my weight shattered it, leaving me on the ground. I made myself stand up and keep on going. I was high up in this building, which was probably one hundred-something stories. Growls and screeches were a sign the spawn were here too.

"Damn it!" My cage was set now.

They were coming up the stairs, running toward me. Luckily they were still many floors under me. Luck abandoned me, however, as the fully grown Goliath recovered and shook the building. The reverberations threw me off balance, and I collapsed to the floor again.

The spawn picked up their pace and were closing in on me.

"Well, damn!" I said.

It did not take any special gift to see that this was trouble. At that point the Goliath's fist broke through the building as though it were a hot blade and the building was butter. The top part of the building began to tilt and fall, with me still in it.

A huge roar erupted from the monster and traveled deep through my ears as I tried to pick myself up.

"Stop! Stop it! Damn it, shut up, just stop it!" Blood began to flow from my ears and nose at this point because of the vibrations caused by the roaring. I began to feel as though I were floating as I tried to clean the blood from my nose. The creature hit the building once more, and it slowly started to fall on its side.

My gaze fell to the center of the room, where it was possible to see the lobby because of the honeycomb design of the building. The Goliath had cut the upper portion of the building. It miraculously saved its children, but left me to die by leaving me on the part of the building that would tip over. How model like of a parent.

I pulled myself to a point close to the edge of the broken building. I kept descending, falling, dropping. As I fell, the spawn, hundreds of them by the looks of it, cast their sunken eyes toward me, and my eyes were cast on them. I stared into their eyes and realized how evil they appeared. They were trying to kill me, a man with a sister to maintain, a house to pay for. My sister was the reason I couldn't really die. The suicide jokes were only jokes. I would never forgive myself if I died here, and in my head a scene of Evelyn crying over my death was looping over and over. A painful thing for her to imagine. But the stars in the sky would soon witness that that would not be, for my survival would be ensured, if only to prevent the melancholy of my sister if anything were to happen to me here at the hands of these monsters.

As the building continued to collapse, about a dozen spawn jumped in with me.

"Just ... why?" I asked, cleaning the blood from my headset.

Who, in his right mind, would jump in, knowing he would be ending his own life? They must have been very determined to kill me.

The broken section of the building slowly began to spiral forward, and I took the opportunity to move to the outside of the broken building to the open air. I kept moving and walking on the windows, and I waited. The broken section slanted to a forty-five-degree angle.

I slid down the broken section. The spawn saw me through the windows and screeched their five hearts out. Like lightning, I replied to the screaming by pulling my Dark Hammer from its holster and shooting at the window of the other building, which I was about to crash into. Without faltering, I fired off an entire magazine, but I only cracked the window, though I did weaken it significantly. I then broke it with my boots and slid down the building into the other building, safe and sound. The only thing that seemed appropriate was to laugh and to check every piece of my body to make sure it was all right. To show the Goliath that it had failed in killing me, I turned around and bowed at the doomed spawn that were falling to their deaths in the collapsing building. On my descent, I breathed a sigh of relief at my stupid luck. As I replaced the magazines of my rifle and pistol, it had not sunk in that survival was mine. The Goliath was still across from me.

It took me about less than a minute before jumping my way down the last steps. Fortunately for me, the ruined section of the building was in between the hotel and the other building.

I heard something that sounded like a hatch closing behind me, and I turned and aimed my rifle toward where I had heard the sound. Unable to investigate because the monster began to screech, I went outside and looked for the Goliath. The beast was walking with its eye bleeding, thanks to me. It neared the ruins and saw its dead spawn.

For the third time, it roared at me, but this was a roar

of pure rage. I had to cover my ears and scream to prevent more hearing damage.

I hated when it did that, and it made me want to kill more of its spawn. To teach it a lesson, I grabbed the experimental bullet and loaded it in my Hornet. With a quick seal to the hatch and three pulls of the trigger, payback was mine.

Once, twice, three times! The bullet left the barrel of my rifle at an incredible speed. A half second later, fire and shrapnel hit its face. Its massive body tumbled forward, then back, and finally into the hotel. The Goliath was furious.

In its blind rage, it smashed the building with its massive, claw like hands, its spawn still inside. Debris came down, as did chunks of metal, fire, and flesh. I chuckled and spun one 180 degrees down the street. I knew that the creature hated me. It and its spawn would look to kill me. Now things got interesting.

# CHAPTER FOURTEEN

## STRAY

After the encounter of the Goliath, I picked up my pace and laughed as I hurried down the street. It would be a while before my foe recovered. At least now it was out of the downtown area. I was sure the jammer was there.

I went down a main road and found it full of abandoned cars. Some had bloodstains on them but many had baby seats and that made me stop to look at them. I hoped the people were all right. I jumped onto the hood of one of the cars and looked around for a vehicle to drive downtown.

Every vehicle must have been disabled because they were all stranded, having hit a tree, a building, or another car. Damn these electric cars. They could have used ethanol or hydrogen, but no, they used electricity, and this was the consequence.

I trekked closer to the downtown area and continued to remove the blood on my nose and ears. More ships were crashed on the road, on buildings, and on trees. Each building was more ruined than the last.

I checked my wrist, and the map showed that the

signal was getting stronger. I needed to destroy the jammer to view my map better. It was nighttime already, and the streets were dark.

I got tired of walking on the roofs of cars, so I jumped onto the sidewalk. The fires provided very little light to the ghost town, and it was the stars that lit my way. I had to steal a glance at them. Turning to see that the Goliath was about three miles away from me, recovering from our little encounter, I stared at the little stars. I sure loved that creature. Maybe if I had a chance I would go back and give it a hug, if it didn't kill me first. I checked the map on my wrist and saw that the jamming signal was even stronger now. Strong enough to tell me that I was closer.

There was something wrong in the air. It was too quiet and too hot. My nerves pricked up, and I imagined noises of little dark creatures behind walls.

"Stop it, you idiot," I told myself.

The doctors had told me that my condition was PTSD and that psychological trauma had caused me to have a mistrust in everything—or at least that's what they thought. They really weren't sure. I kept walking down the sidewalk and on my right I passed a school—something I wish I attended. I mean, I received an education, but not in school.

As I crossed a street, I saw the downed remains of a police ship in the middle of the intersection. I checked and found that the cargo door was open, and an entire SWAT team was dead inside. Both pilots in the cockpit were also dead, but they had not died the same way. One had died from the impact of the crash, as his head had hit between the monitors and the controls, and his blood was pooling on them. The other had survived the crash, but he had died from a gunshot wound to the head. A well-placed, professional shot had ended this man's life, and his brains were splattered all over. I saw this and ran back to the breached door at the back. The police officers here were riddled with bullets, and none of them were even wounded by the spawn. A downed cruiser and an entire squad of police officers shot to death? This meant I was getting closer, and things were going to get more serious. The buildings had a menacing look to them. The windows, however, looked all the same, with their steel-gray reflections.

I kept walking until I reached a skyscraper that had housed the stock exchange. It was tall enough that if a jamming device was placed on top, it could disrupt communications with the outside. I pointed my rifle at the building's two massive glass doors.

My wrist map was going bonkers, and I could tell I was in the right place. As I entered I noticed that thefloor was littered with papers, and machines were spilling coffee, tea, water, and other beverages. Some of the window screens had bullet holes in them, and occasionally I found a body, bloodstains, or, very rarely, a Goliath body. The scene did not look right—it was as if the blood and bodies had been added after the building was abandoned. In the middle of the room I stopped, lowered my rifle, and looked around. There was an eerie ringing in my ears caused by the white noise of the monitors that had not shut off from the electromagnetic pulse. At the edge of the massive room were the stairs and elevators. With the power out, I had no choice but to get my lazy ass up to the roof by climbing the stairs.

"Well, I needed the workout anyway," I snorted.

# CHAPTER FIFTEEN

## COMPANY

About forty minutes, two breaks, and having vomited up my meal, I reached the top of the stairs. I sat down against the door and rested before opening it and moving in to destroy the jammer.

"I need ... to do more ... cardiovascular ..." My wheezing didn't even sound like me; it resembled a dying cat.

A screech pierced the air. Spawn, they came at the worst of times. I had time to destroy the jamming device but didn't have a single idea about how to get out of the building.

"I can't use the stairs. Can't use the elevator. Don't have a rope long enough to jump down to a different building. Ah ... the paraglider."

I was glad I still had it on. My tiring trip up the stairs seemed to have given me hope that I would have plenty of time to destroy the jammer. I looked down the stairs, however, and saw how quickly the spawn were catching up. Some of them ran up the stairs, some crawled up the wall, and others hissed from the bottom.

I ran to the door and kicked it down. I was on the roof, yet nothing was there. No towering jamming beacon. No tables that showed its radius. Not even a single external generator.

The spawn were getting closer. Too quickly. Without hesitation, I unsheathed my sword and waited for them to approach. One jumped out of the door and I sliced it down as it got closer to me. I sliced left and right. Killing one and slicing one across the chest, leaving it gasping in pain. If I didn't leave the roof, I was going to be overrun. I ran to the edge of the building and saw at least a dozen spawn climbing up the wall. Something was telling them I was here, and that made me uneasy, since this planet looked abandoned. One spawn was unlucky enough to be in front of me before I jumped off.

"Geronimo!" I yelled.

I grabbed its scaly shoulder with my left hand, and its head was greeted by my right fist. I reeled in pain, and a sound escaped my mouth from the agony of the impact of my fist on its bristly head. I pushed it forward, and we fell together. It seemed to know that we were falling to our death.

About one hundred feet down, I released it and activated my paraglider. The spawn squealed and growled as it fell. Its body splatted against the pavement, staining the street with its blood. My paraglider glided me down to the sidewalk. I checked my fist, only to see that it was bleeding.

"Idiot, why the seven hells did you punch it?" I insulted myself. I then shifted my view to my map. It wasn't as strong as it was when I was near the school ... I think I am an idiot.

I ran to the school. The gate was locked, but, with the butt of my rifle, I soon broke the monitor on the wall next door. I entered and saw that the whole place had been mined. Lasers had been set up, and tiny drones were hovering on the walls, waiting for some poor fool to run inside to be disintegrated. I placed a grenade on the floor, calmly pressed the button that turned on the fuse, and rolled it into the middle of the hallway. Smiling, I realized how big the blast would be and raced to the entrance to avoid being hit. Mine after mine detonated in the hallway. I entered and saw that the entire place was blackened and littered with shrapnel, and there were holes covering the walls, ceiling, and floor. I hastily made my way through because every damn spawn in the area was now coming to get me. I ran down the other hallway while lockers and rooms lined up side by side.

I wasn't going to be distracted. I reached one side of the hallway and rushed up the stairs. There was no entrance to the roof via the stairs, and a swear escaped my mouth. I was on the top floor, and it occurred to me that it wasn't too far to climb up.

The window resisted the first five blows of the butt of my rifle, but it eventually came off the frame, even though I was trying to break it, but hey looks like life didn't give everyone what it wants. Damn windows. I put my rifle to the side and looked down, which made my hands sweaty and almost made me reconsider my plan as I made my way out of the window and stood on the edge while I pulled myself up to the roof with my sweaty hands. I heard voices, but I couldn't understand what they were saying, and I decided it would be best if their words were left to the imagination. In the middle of the roof were tables, generators, maps, and a chart showing the maximum effects of the jammer—a scene that should have been on the roof of the stock exchange. The jammer was an impressive display of technology. I looked at the controls and realized that I had no idea how to shut it off. Since I was out of explosives, I decided to shoot at it, hoping that the rounds would topple it. Now the question remained: which weapon would use to shoot it. I had not used the pistol Herr Doctor had given me, but I was sure of the power that the Dark Hammer had. But an assault rifle that used plasma to fire rounds was always a good bet. I could have stayed there for hours, debating what gun to use. I weighed the pros and cons of each weapon, but because the pistol Herr Doctor had given me had not been fired, it tempted me and had the advantage of being untested; therefore it won. *Good job, brain.* As I aimed my pistol at the jammer, a voice shouted from behind me.

"Hey, what the hell?" it exclaimed with fury.

I jolted up and turned around to see the first living person I had seen on this planet. He wore a red and black urban camouflage uniform, a sinister exoskeleton suit, an armored vest, and his helmet, the two red glowing eyes above his face guard, seemed to come from hell itself. PFS patches were attached to his right sleeve, and his overcoat concealed his equipment. He appeared and resembled a shadow, something that unnerved me. Before I could fire at him, he punched the gun out of my hand. It slid to the other side of the roof and was now useless to me. The man threw a left hook at me, and I dodged it, grabbing him by the shoulders and kneeing him in the stomach. It was comforting to know that he was not a shadow, which I could tell by the way he approached me from behind. He pushed me back and got into a fight position, throwing a right punch, and I moved to the side to avoid it. I returned the blow with a quick succession of blows and, shifting my weight, I grabbed his arms, pulled him over my shoulders, and threw him to the ground. He side-kicked me down, however, when he landed. We both stood up and faced each other. With one movement, I tackled the soldier against the jammer and punched him in the stomach, which was a difficult thing to do, as his vest protected him from my armored glove. A pained grunt escaped his mouth as he began to cough up blood. His eyepiece glowed a dark red, and it burned into my eyes. He seemed to grab my very soul and absorb it into his own essence. Shivers racked my body as I saw this, and a cold thought hit me: this man probably had no eyes, and that glow was a dark desire to take my eyes. I needed to save myself from him—this creature, this demon, this human.

He elbowed my back out of pain and desperation. I saw, beneath his overcoat, a grenade belt. Reaching toward it, I pulled two pins, activated the timer, and pushed him harder against the jammer. He tried to take the belt, and a squeal erupted from his mouth, but after four seconds the belt blew him and the jammer to pieces. What was a Protectorate Federation of Systems soldier doing here, anyway?

Okay, let me confess something. I might have lied when I said the whole human civilization had united in peace. See, there was this group—well, it was like almost half the population of humanity—that didn't like the government. These people got on their ships and moved to a new world, like pilgrims. The problem was that they found a world, and the United Galactic Federation had no idea where it was. Only its name was known: Ortyra. Ortyra, the first of the Protectorate Federation of Systems planetary governments, which spanned more than fifty-six supposed planets. Its population now rivaled that of Earth, my home. Its military, also fearful, but when the human race accidently stumbled upon the Goliaths, we came together, we weren't alone, and that scared us. For the first three years after the discovery, the people of both governments worked to study those monsters. When the time came to decide what we were to do with them, the Ortyrans decided to use the Goliaths for military uses.

You can imagine what happened when word of that news reached Earth. We razed that planet, imploded it, set its sun to go supernova and tried destroying all traces of them. I know, I know, oh I just goddamn know, that was not the best of decisions. To let an entire species die—that just shows what our fear of that species did to us. The PFS broke off all relations with us and attacked us. This was now the second invasion of Helena in the past forty years. The first invasion was during the Human Blood War, or the First Cosmos Civil War.

After the first civil war ended in a stalemate, the galaxy was divided into two factions again, and nothing was heard from them other than occasional firefights between naval ships along the border. They wanted a warrior-like, expansionist civilization, but they could also be an army to hire and a pain in the ass for the UGF. Maybe they were responsible for this—of course they were responsible for this; no stupid terrorist organization could have the capacity for this.

I looked down from the roof and saw that a swarm of spawn was coming for me. Before jumping down, I noticed something unreal. On one of the tables if my eyes were not fooling me, there was a red flag with a black circle and a triangle in the center. A battleship was flying in closer to the atmosphere. They had called in the cavalry.

I grabbed my pistol from the other side of the roof and shot it at the last support beam on the jammer. The towering structure fell on its side, crashing down. My map was no longer disrupted with static. I looked again at the battleship in orbit. Even from a distance I saw that it was a crimson red with black. I jumped on the jammer and walked to its edge, which dangled far from the roof. It fell, and I slid down, away from the spawn. From a distance, a deafening boom preceded the silence—a sonic boom. I looked and saw a drop ship landing on the roof. The cargo door opened, and a patrol exited the vehicle.

"Simmons? Where are you? Ah crap." The sergeant said as he found the remains of his engineer. Another found my pistol casing and showed it to the sergeant. If they saw me, my life would be at risk. My instincts told me to hide in an alleyway not too far just to hear what they were saying. One man took out a touch pad and, to my surprise, the spawn froze in place. So they must have been controlling them.

"That's UGF casings. Eyes up, men. We aren't alone."

"Damn right, you're not," I said under my breath.

I brought my rifle up and pointed it at the patrol. They were oblivious to the fact that a rifle was aimed at them.

Two of them went to the destroyed jammer and assessed the damage. The rest seemed to talk to the sergeant to see what the next move was. I decided to give them a welcome gift and loaded the prototype round into the butt of the rifle and aimed it at the drop ship. It was a distance of about forty-nine feet, and my aim was shaky. My hand shook and trembled; my vision blurred. My fingers began to go numb. Could I really kill those men, men who had no idea what could happen to them? Set fire to them, bring them to an early grave? Although they were the enemy, they had not tried to kill me. Yet my mission did allow me to take out anyone interfering from the extraction of the king and the rest of the royal family. Morals and ethics aside, my mission came first. Yet before I could even load the round, the squad sniper turned toward me and fired.

"Sniper!" he said, mistakenly, his bullet hitting an inch from my head.

I unloaded the round from the butt of the rifle and took off to the main street, which I had first used to look for the jammer. Shots kept firing at me until I was out of their line of sight, but by then the whole PFS fleet knew I was here. Looking at my wrist map, it dawned on me that it was a new model. This one mapped the planet, my position, and everybody else's position, friend and foe. I expanded it to three dimensions and saw the soldiers mounting the drop ship while possibily speaking on their wrist communicators. I should have shot it. I should have put my ethics, morals, doubts, and all that other crap aside, because in the cruel, true world, they don't let you survive. I'm no Batman, I'm the murdering Rorschach from Watchmen, and the difference is that I don't stop to complete a mission because of doubts. I think this is the reason I retired. It wasn't because of the killing, the blood, the monsters at night, or the fear of not waking up one day. No, it was the decision to be less than human, to be a tool for killing, to give up the option of saving life. If the wrong life is saved, others die. Who am I to decide that? I don't want to be a monster, yet I alone can do what most cannot.

"Stupid, stupid me. Now they'll warn everyone else that I'm here," I cursed under my breath, and I actually hated myself for destroying the communication device on the Hyperion. I needed to warn the fleet that there was a battleship here. I had no idea how I was going to do that. Maybe the castle had a communication device? Help isn't coming ... so why bother?

Now I needed the help of the special operations unit in the bunker. I corrected my path to the embassy and took off running, every so often looking up at the sky, hoping that a ship was not following me, stalking me.

Playing paranoid cat and mouse made me imagine thousands of soldiers on the rooftops, waiting, watching, and seeing me. I imagined them aiming their rifles, and I could feel the bullet already hit my back and me going down to the floor. The loop was playing in my head slower and slower each time. How would it feel for the blood to pool around me, for me to be coughing out of my lungs onto the street. For the PFS to probe my body and laugh at it: the first UGF soldier to be killed. What would they do to my body? Hang it by the foot in the center of the city and display it to all of Ortyra? The feelings racked my nerves and even made the exoskeleton jittery. I needed to take my thoughts out of the darkness of my imagination. Concentration on my present surroundings would block out my wandering thoughts.

The streets were littered with leaves and personal belongings. Why was this scene the same in all the cities I had fought in? The wind breezed down the silent street and seemed to be trying to slow me down. I kept going and passed skyscraper after skyscraper, vehicle after vehicle. There were also spawn and a few police corpses. It then dawned on me that, a block before the embassy, I had passed the very detailed statue of a minotaur at least four stories tall and with eyes that reflected flames. It stood out in my mind, as if I had read of some monster that guarded something in an old poem or story. What layer of hell was I entering?

The windows of the embassy were smashed and cracked and resembled drops of water on the metallic asphalt. It was a mess in here, as all the UGF flags were on the floor—stepped on, spat on, half-burned, or just trashed. I bent over to pick one up and just stared at it. The wind rustled in the dark lobby. Anything the wind could carry was being dragged deeper into this pit. I stood up and set my visor to night vision, since I couldn't see in this damn place. The word "hell" rang in my head for the second time The word brought me no fear, the place brought me no fear, the inhabitants did not frighten me. Not in a theological sense, anyway. But have you ever wondered what the worst monsters in the universe are? Humans. We create the monsters, we bring them to life, we breed them, show them to our young, brand their image on everything. We voice them, we train them, we teach them. Whether it's the monsters in our minds or the monsters we are, I can't think of a worse hell than the type we build in this universe.

The stairs went deep inside the massive building. The living quarters were seven stories down, and so was the bunker. My descent was guided by Virgil, which I aimed in front of me. It seemed to me that I probably wasn't the first one to try to reach them, since there were bloodstains down there, as well as PFS boot markings and shells. I jumped the last ten stairs and the exoskeleton absorbed the impact. I then aimed at the one open door.

The air seemed cold, hostile, and bloody. Even Dante did not face this in his journey. The echo of my footsteps in this area void of life sounded louder than a million of cries of agony in one's head. My hands began to sweat through my gloves, and the sound and frequency of my breaths weighed unjustly against me. The bunks on both sides of the special forces living quarters resembled those of a teenager's room that had been searched; they were a mess.

When I did find the bunker door, It was open—blown open to be precise, but open nonetheless. That told me everything. It was all wrong. I opened my mouth, but only silence escaped. Two steps inside, I fell on my knees. I dropped my pistol, I dropped my hands, and I dropped my faith and hope in humanity even more than I already had. What I saw furthered the proof that humans are the worst monsters. Those men had not needed to suffer so. Twenty men, hanged from the ceiling. Twenty men, tortured, cut, and beaten. Twenty violent men, who had not needed to die like this, went out like animals. I took off my helmet, and ran my fingers through my hair. Everything in me shook. I stood there seeing what no one should go through. I saw ... oh, what I saw.

A rage grew inside me, a rage that made its way forth from my very spirit. It caused me to roar. It caused me to grab my fist and slam the wall. It cause me to spit, kick, yell, and whoop like a savage, throwing anything that was not secured in place. In my frenzy, I grabbed a table in the middle of the bunk and, with all my adrenaline, hurled the damn thing to the other side of the room. I grabbed my rifle and beat the thing until I couldn't lift my arms anymore. With this anger, my NOVA grenade was hurled onto the table, and it burned with my hate and disgust. I stared at that fire and bit my left finger until it bled to stop myself from yelling.

I cut the men down when I snapped out of my madness. I needed to leave. I couldn't believe what I had just done; I couldn't believe what had happened to these poor men. It was hell, and I needed to get the hell away from there. I forced myself to forget about those atrocities. With that decided, I grabbed my helmet, put it on my head, and went outside into the still and occupied night. On my way up the stairs, I took an olive-green three-day pack and filled it with explosives, water, light strobes, a new uranium battery for my electro-rod, blankets, a new engine for my glider, a more powerful exhaust and thruster, a tool kit, an exterior coat for my use, and two knives for my exoskeleton and one for my left boot. The armory was missing a few more magazines, cartridges, a one-hundred-round drum magazine, and a compensator for extra plasma for my Hornet before I left.

I set my way toward the castle. I was breathing heavily—so heavily that I felt as though I were being weighed down. The map told me the castle wasn't that far from my current position; two and a half miles stood between me and my destination. Maybe I would catch a lucky break and not run into any soldiers; I hoped so, for my little fit of rage had left me drunk with fatigue. Going down the main street, I saw that the spawn were still frozen. Without leaving things to chance, I took my sword out and sliced down spawn left and right, creating a path for me and conserving ammo. An alarm beeped, causing me to turn around, and I saw the spawn I had missed slowly start moving. Their movements reminded me that I was surrounded by them.

"Crap." I turned around and pushed the rest that were in my way while running down the street before they achieve full mobility. I turned and found myself on a main street with lines of abandoned cars on it. This had become a regular sight. I ran opposite the way the cars were facing.

For a while, the same quiet rustle of wind and phantom voices that I had heard before the appearance of the PFS overran the streets. Very few spawn were running loose and alive, but the majority I saw were the bodies of these creatures which were facedown with blood pooling beneath them. Ships began to fly overhead, and my map began beeping as it indicated their stops and landing zones. An alert that enemy troops were landing around me appeared. The map then began to show the troops a few blocks in front of me. Monitoring the enemy as closely as Big Brother did, the soldiers began to search the buildings and surroundings. Easy pickings. They didn't know that they were being watched. However, after a few minutes of me sneaking past them behind cars, between alleys, and into and out of buildings, they all stopped to listen to a broadcast in their helmets. When they finished listening to it, they pressed a button on their wrist controls and all turned their heads to my position.

Watching them look around for me hopelessly was amusing, yet seeing the way they quickly looked in my direction stopped me cold and made my breaths speed up. They stared at my position, and the feeling of paranoia hit me. They then began to run toward me. Their movements were like shadows in the darkness. They disappeared from the map, and then I was revealed.

*Run.* The word sounded distant in my head, and it invited me to follow it. My footsteps rumbled in the streets and echoed inside me. The Hornet kept hitting the chest plate that I had to protect me. The map beeped once more, and the PFS troops appeared again; they had stopped. I paused to observe them, yet they looked at their devices again. I ran, and they looked around some more and carefully moved into a defensive position. I entered a building and scrambled up to the second floor to observe them. They huddled in a circle and looked around. Running got us off of the map; it protected us so long as we had it active. They didn't seem to know where I was, and a few of them ran off to find me.

A building with an open window stood in front of me; the squad was over fifty meters behind me on the street. I was about to jump out of the building I was in when a soldier stopped in the alleyway under me. He had stopped to glance at his map, and I looked down on him and slowly opened the window to jump into the next building.

"Sir, he's behind me. It's on the map, but he isn't there. I don't understand," he said into his wrist communicator.

I couldn't let him keep talking; I needed to take him out. With my pistol in one hand and my knife in the other, I pushed open the window and stepped out.

"I don't know where you are, but come out so I can blow your head off," he whispered.

"Sure thing." A light chuckle escaped me.

I landed noisily behind him, but he kept his rifle aimed to his front. *Why didn't he hear me?* I wondered. He began shivering and sniffling as he lowered his rifle. He did not move much, but he kept shaking. For once in a blue moon, I was wrong. He had heard me, and he knew I had caught him.

"Well done. Well done," he said to me as I kept Dark Hammer aimed at his helmeted head.

His sobs began softly and didn't amount to much noise. Shaking from his shoulders, he dropped his rifle and quickly turned around. Before raising his hands, he took off his faceguard and goggles. I stared into his eyes deeply, and it surprised me that he had one gray eye and one blue eye. Why was he crying? With tears on his face, he licked his lips as he shook his head.

"Shoot me. You have to. You'll die if you don't. I'll tell them where you are if you don't." He whimpered and sobbed harder.

I hesitated. This was different from the time the PFS were on the roof. That was fair game; this was different. Every fiber in me was arguing about whether to shoot him or spare him. Even if he was the enemy, it just wasn't right, since he had surrendered. If he hadn't heard me and had kept on walking, then I could have shot him with some honor.

"Do it. Come on. Do it! Shoot me! Kill me!" He had snot on his nose and swollen eyes.

Shaking and looking deep into his eyes, I squeezed the trigger once, with a yell from my rage. I kept firing and yelling as he was on the floor. I yelled in agony, in anger, in regret. I stared again into his eyes, but I could not see the gleam that had been in them but a few seconds before.

The echo of the body dropping attracted unwanted attention. I could only imagine what the PFS thought upon seeing me standing over their comrade with a pistol in hand. Their screams of rage brought me back to reality. I don't think I'll ever forget that expression.

"You son of a bitch!" One yelled as he fired at me.

Instinct took over as I returned fire and retreated back to the shadows and to the castle. Had he really needed to die? Do we really need to die? These questions always come up when sleep can't find me, or if I don't push my thoughts to the back of my head.

I left the past on the street. My hands were in my pockets as soon as they finished wiping away the blood on my goggles. I set my path back to the palace.

The communication from the Protectorate was quick, but the processing of what happened was slow for the troops. As I ran toward a squad of listening soldiers, they dropped their equipment and made way for their rifles. The sight of seven barrels aimed at me proved that fear still lived in me. There is one teaching that no one I can recognize taught me—something that wasn't said in the academy, by Director Kayre, or by any officer I was under. Fear is a good sign; it means we can overcome the cause and prevent those that cannot overcome it from facing it. No one is fearless, for how can people be brave without fear?

As I ran at the troops, my thruster and exoskeleton linked up and increased my speed. It was a powerful feeling to be human and move like a machine. The Protectorate fighters bunched up, and the seven uniformed and armored soldiers fell back as I advanced. I took my knife from my left scabbard and was soon firing my pistol over their heads, forcing them all down to the ground.

Fear is something that can be overcome, but it is also blinding. The PFS believed that I was going to kill them. I didn't enjoy killing people, but sometimes to complete the mission and stay alive, it's either them or me. It was funny hearing their cries as they threw their rifles and hit the ground with their rears or backs. I had learned to use fear as a tool and weapon in the training academy. I had also learned, from a fictional character from an animated show, that hope was of greater use than fear.

A sign appeared overhead that read "Palace," and under it were the words "police access only." I speed-walked a little, but when I took a left onto a highway, a line of cars stopped me from advancing. *Damn hovercars. Maybe they'll stop my pursuers.*

I walked alongside the cars and looked at my map. Another drop ship was landing near the place where I had engaged in the firefight with the PFS. I knew it was probably just reinforcements, but I wanted to leave nothing to chance. My feet picked up the pace in the dark night as never before in my life. I could run ten miles in about half an hour, and the exoskeleton could double that distance, yet that night it seemed that I was trying to outrun the death itself. Even though we were old acquaintances, as I brought people to death and death took people from me, I did not want to see death yet, not now.

When the drop ship circled the school, it seemed entirely different from a normal drop ship. The cabin was slimmer, the design was longer, it had wings, and the cockpit was smaller. It was an attack ship. With its thermal imaging scopes, rail cannons, and missiles, it was perfect for searching for runaways, stragglers, and those trying to hide. I decided to shoot this one down.

I climbed on top of the roof of one of the cars and emptied a magazine from my rifle into the air. The ship's sensor must have picked me up. It spent an entire minute just hovering around like a bee over a flower. After another minute, I grabbed a light strobe—a circular plasma entity that, when disturbed, emits a bright light that can act as a flare or can hover in place and keep emitting light. With it on the barrel of the rifle, my finger squeezed the trigger. The strobe flew at amazing speeds into the air before exploding in a spectacular flash of light. The enemy ship gained altitude and headed in my direction. I loaded the prototype round that was meant for the other ship and now readied it for this one. I aimed at the ship as it got closer. My sight zoomed in on the ship and automatically employed night vision. When the ship was about

350 meters out, I pulled the trigger thrice. The round penetrated the hull of the ship and detonated, leaving a massive hole in its side. It lit the sky up in a magnificent display of explosions that made the light strobe look like a firefly.

As I perused my map, the ship fell onto a building, exploding even more when it crashed. Smoke rose from that building as I began to run away from it. There was no smile on my face; there was no glint of satisfaction at that deed.

The overpass ended, and a barrier that separated the right and left lanes stood there; it was soon behind me after a simple vault. A giant wall protecting the palace towered in front of the main plaza of the city. There was a balcony not that high on the wall and another at least ten feet above the first one. Two balconies—for what purpose? This was weird. Why would the monarchs put themselves almost at crowd level? Humble people maybe, or probably fools.

As I neared the castle walls, I noticed the sentry towers. For some reason they didn't seem right. I aimed my sight at them, and the sight switched from a normal sight, to a night-vision sight, to a thermal sight. All the visible sentry towers were occupied by at least three crouching figures. They all seemed ready to jump up and fire at my position, and that caused me to back up. It was a death trap, a perfect death trap—one that almost caught me.

"Who the hell—"

Something attached itself to my right leg. Before I was able to take the simple action of looking at my leg, something dropped me on the floor. Whatever had attached to my foot then pulled me back by an unseen force. A rock hit my back and poked me. The grass was moist and slippery. I had to make the simple decision of whether or not to scream at this unseen force. However, before I could even decide that, something turned my body until I was facing a large rock opposite the palace. A silver object was attached to my leg, and it began pulling me to the rock. Gunfire riddled the area where I had just been; the object had just saved my life—or probably doomed me to something worse. Whatever was pulling me was not gentle, and rocks and other objects were in the way. The object pulled me closer to the grand decorative boulder in a fashion that reminded me of the way a gravity handle lowered me. When I was just five feet away, the rock moved to reveal a thick blast door that was opening as I approached.

"What the hell is going on?" I shouted as I readied my rifle, aiming toward the opening and into the void.

# CHAPTER SIXTEEN

## CAPTURED

The sliver of light attached to my foot turned out to be a rope that had pulled me deep into the dark room hidden behind the rock. An unseen force closed the blast door, and the whole place turned pitch black. I turned on the flashlight on the rifle and activated the green night-vision visor on my helmet, but I still couldn't focus on anything; this made my head feel light and woozy. I tried to stand up, but a man in a Helenac Police uniform kicked me down again. I took a knife from my back and stabbed him in the leg. I didn't care if I was here to help him; he had attacked me, and that made me mad. He shouted in pain as I shone my flashlight around the room, revealing it to be a bunker. I was tackled from the back by at least two people. I turned and kicked one off of me; the exo-skeleton suit worked like a charm as I planted my foot in his face. The other one grabbed me and started to punch me in the side of the head. He hit hard; the punch hurt. I head-butted him, and a fourth man appeared over me and kicked me in the face. That's when I blacked out.

I woke up handcuffed to a swivel chair with a nasty

gash on my face. It hurt, and it made me wonder what the hell those cops had on their boots. As standard procedure, I was stripped of my weapons, equipment, food, helmet, goggles, and face cloth. I spun on the chair left, then right. I was very pleased to find out my chair had wheels. I spun and moved around the room gracefully. I spent about an hour picking locks on the cuffs with a tiny piece of metal I took from the chair. It was a tight fit, and the handcuffs cut my wrist in the process.

After I took the handcuffs off, the wait began. Some time passed before the lights turned on; when they did, they were uncomfortably bright. The door opened, and before me I saw a reflective window on the wall. Before the doors opened, I moved the chair into a position where my interrogators would not see that the handcuffs were no longer on me. Hidden from the door and the window, I waited.

The doors opened, and ten police officers in SWAT gear, like the ones from the downed cruiser, entered the room and aimed their pistols at me. Another one with a flashy uniform entered and sat down on a chair one of his goons brought.

"Ah, sweet. I'm gonna be interrogated." I smiled. "Although I'll admit, this is first time I'm on the wrong side of the table."

"Shut it, pretty boy" the flashy cop said with breath that reeked of coffee. "Do you know which planet you and the PFS tried to annex? The UGF will rain a hell storm on your asses when they get here."

This man was an idiot! A full-blown idiot! I even showed him my face of disgust. Before judging him, I checked to see that my patches said "Grey, type B positive, American, Earth, Ghost, 356th Battalion." I was hoping that maybe they had taken them off so and he had mistaken me for a PFS grunt. Unfortunately, this man was either an ignorant idiot or he was illiterate. And to say the least, I liked that last possibility.

"You, sir, are without doubt the most, if not the only, idiotic person here. If you saw my dog tags and my patches on my arm, chest, neck, back, and vest, you would clearly see that they say 'UGF.'"

He gulped. "They could be fake."

I heard shouting from the reflective window and saw the door being opened. A guard entered with someone and stood at attention.

What happened next, I did not expect. The hologram entered the room. Only she wasn't a hologram this time. She was flesh and blood. My jaw dropped at the sight of her beauty—her true, realistic beauty—a beauty that many would admire but few would truly love. She wore a knee-length white dress with a black line that traveled around its edge. Her eyes were a dark brown color. Her skin was a dark tan, and her lips were covered with a red lipstick. She had a perfect amount of eyeliner, and her hair flowed from her shoulders and moved to the left of her face. She had a beauty mark on her left cheek. She turned her eyes and smiled at me.

"What is your name, pretty boy?" I heard the officer's voice from what seemed to be miles away. My gaze was aimed at her, and my attention was only hers. The police officer repeated the question two more times before hitting me in the face, and that made me lose eye contact with the woman.

"Are you even listening to me? Eyes up her—" He froze. "Princess!" he exclaimed after looking at the woman I was staring at. The rest of the police officers turned and bowed at her.

She smiled at me as if we both knew a secret. Her smile was rich, reassuring, and strong, and it made her more beautiful to me. Feelings for her grew inside of me. They were similar to what I felt for Evelyn, yet different and stronger. Like how I felt about the hologram only real now.

"His name is Gerald M. Grey. Captain in UGF military and an agent in the UGF Defense Force. They sent him here to knock out the jammer and be my knight in shining armor, isn't that right?" Her voice was so perfect it just made me want to cry. Maybe that was the reason I had said yes to the hologram's marriage proposal. Yet this was the first time I had ever had feelings for a real female other than Evelyn.

"Thank you for knocking out the jammer. I linked up to my digital persona, and I am pleased to meet you. I can't believe you are here," she exclaimed, smiling her warm smile.

I still couldn't speak. Was I to build a wall and not let her in, as I had done for many others? I didn't think I could with her. It was the equivalent of lifting the entire ocean and moving all of Earth's sand to Mars. But I felt that if it needed to do so for her, I would find a way. She got closer to the flashy cop and looked at him in a provocative manner.

"I uh …" he said, looking at his boots while scratching his scalp. For a second I thought she was going to hit him on the back of his head.

"Commissioner, please uncuff Mr. Grey. Pretty please." She fluttered her eyes at him. He looked solemn as he walked to me.

I stood up and handed him my handcuffs. "Sorry you took too long. I decided to have a go at it."

The other police officers holstered their pistols and walked out of the interrogation room. The commissioner also walked out, but not before turning around and looking at both of us. I rubbed my wrist and returned the stare.

"Do you need anything, princess?" He asked.

"May I have a moment alone with Mr. Grey?" she replied.

"Understood, ma'am. I will be outside if you need me," he said, straightening his uniform. He turned around and left the room, making sure the door remained open. I turned to look at the princess as she walked closer to me.

She surprised me by hugging me while lowering her head to my chest. Her hands then began to clean the bloodstains on my ears and nose. For some reason, I let her do this. I did not let anyone other than me attend to my wounds anymore, and yet I think I fell in love in her when I saw her try to clean up the blood. She started to cry.

What the hell was I supposed to do now? The only person I'd comforted and hugged was my sister, but those were occasions when I knew what had happened and what she was thinking. It pained me to see the princess cry, and it made me want to help her. Not wanting to feel worthless, I put my arms around her, and we stayed like that, her quietly sobbing and us holding each other. Now I was helping her when she was weak, as she had done for me.

"Hey, don't cry. It's all right," I said to her while caressing her face with my hand. I looked around and tried to think of something to help her. I remembered when, back in my mind with the hologram, she sang me a song. I knew it was pathetic, but it was a really nice song, and I remembered it. I called her my sunshine.

She stopped crying and held me tighter.

"I don't know you that well. We barely met in person, but I need your help," she said softly. "Those creatures have killed many people and are destroying the city. The PFS are also invading and declaring it theirs. They have shot down every ship that has tried to leave or enter."

"The Goliaths are being controlled by the PFS," I said. "And what's worse is that there is a PFS battleship in orbit waiting for the evacuation cruiser heading this way. It won't stand a chance, and the evacuation and reinforcement of this world will take weeks if not months."

She looked at me and wiped her tears with my sleeves. She giggled, and I laughed a bit. We looked at each other, and even though her eyes were still red and puffy, she smiled at me.

The princess held me tighter, and I realized I was hugging a princess. The same princess that I had married on that rooftop in a memory,I needed therapy.

"We don't have any communication devices capable of communicating with the UGF here, but in the castle we have a room with equipment that can."

"Well I need to reach it—after I talk to the king, of course," I said while keeping eye contact with her. For the first time in a long while, I smiled truly.

She led me out of the interrogation room with her hands holding mine, trying not to let go of me. Wounded police officers lined the hallway. Some had gunshot wounds, and others had been wounded by the sharp claws of the spawn. I noticed that no one had a weapon more powerful than a pistol.

Near the entrance of the interrogation room sat a police officer with a wound on his thigh that appeared to be from a knife.

"Sorry about that," I muttered.

He looked up at me and shook his head. It was hopeful of me to think that he would forgive me.

A man with a balaclava covering his face was arguing with the police commissioner farther away in the corridor. He must have been on good terms with the king, because he was telling the commissioner no. There was a locker at the end of the hallway, and I was willing to bet my stuff was in there. I assumed the man was probably arguing about wanting something back from the locker, as he kept gesturing at it.

"You know the law, no assault rifles," the commissioner said in his whiny voice.

"Well, the hell with those laws!" The man with the balaclava screamed. This made everyone look up. "People are dead because of them! We are underequipped. A pistol cannot kill these damn things. We can't penetrate the body armor of the PFS with pistol rounds. We're dying because of your stupidity." In frustration, he slammed his arm on the wall. "God damn you and your rules. You don't know how many friends died in front of me because of your damned proposal to the damn council about no assault weapons. Even the king agreed it was stupid, but he was outvoted. Because of you, this is happening." He poked the commissioner in the chest with his index finger. The commissioner had a very apathetic look on his face.

"Who is he?" I whispered to the princess while admiring this man.

"Captain Eric Sherwood," she answered, "the gun enthusiast and the one who was leading the retreat to the bunkers"

"What law is he talking about?" I asked, interested. He was something I used to be. Angry, alone, quick to blame, and vengeful.

"The ban on assault rifles. The one the commissioner pushed forward in the council. However, my father was outvoted and the ban passed, and now no one, not even police, have them."

I looked at him. I needed his help, because he seemed to be the only capable one here.

"I need my equipment back ... and his rifle," I said to the princess, taking her hand. She looked at her hand and at me, smiling and nodding. She walked to the commissioner and waited for Captain Sherwood to finish talking.

"Oh, my bad, Princess," Eric said, stopping his rant for her.

"It's all right, Eric," she replied. "I just have a request for him."

"What is it ma'am?" The commissioner replied blankly.

"My man over there—yes, the handsome one—needs his equipment back," she said to him sweetly, glancing at me and smiling. The commissioner didn't even bother going to unlock the locker himself; he just handed the princess an electronic chip. She smiled and thanked him. Behind her back, she motioned for the captain to follow her. Noticing this, the captain looked at the commissioner angrily and punched him square in the jaw.

The princess opened the locker. My vest was in there with two rifles and an assortment of other interesting things that had been confiscated. One was the experimental rifle Herr Doctor gave me, and the other was a standard-issue UGF military rifle. I took both rifles and handed them to the patient captain, who was beginning to understand my scheme. I took my vest and saw that a blue vest was hiding behind it, and it held more ammunition than mine. Common sense dictated that this belonged to the captain. I found both of my knives and, surprisingly, my sword. I took the dark blades and sheathed them. I took all my equipment and closed the locker behind me. I returned the chip to the princess, and she went looking for the commissioner, who was still trying to stop the nosebleed Eric had given him. Before she left, however, she gave me a little earpiece. As I took the earpiece, I realized that the vest still had the exoskeleton spine piece, which, when reattached to me, felt like white-hot needles.

"It's a communication device. Put on the earpiece, and we can talk like that," she said before giving me a little kiss on the cheek. "You are the one I have been waiting for all my life."

She left smiling, and I touched my cheek. The captain grabbed my arm and pulled me deeper into the bunker. Yet he was only grabbing a lovestruck man that was putting on his face cloth, goggles, and helmet.

# CHAPTER SEVENTEEN

## SHADOW DEMON

I didn't know where to go, so I just followed him while holstering my pistols, sheathing my sharp, pointy blades, and attaching my rifle to its sling. We walked own a corridor and over a catwalk, and we then entered a room. Captain Sherwood motioned for me to follow him to a man looking over a holographic map in a dark room.

"Sir, it's a UGF agent," he said to the man. The man stood up straight and looked at me with kind eyes and a smile that made it seem as though we shared a secret.

"Son, come closer," he said, extending his arm toward me. I walked toward him, and he shook my hand.

"I knew the UGF would not abandon us. I knew they were good people," he said to me.

"We would never do that; we always keep our promises, sir. But I have a mission. The first part was to knock out the jamming device and to find the king and the rest of the royal family, and to secure a place for an extraction. And I'm thinking you are the king. Am I right?"

"Outstanding job. But I cannot leave my people here and head to safety; I need to be here with them," he said.

"There's a UGF cruiser on its way to evacuate car-
pet bomb this city with bombs that will kill any and all
life. But it won't destroy the city. Don't worry, sir; the
UGF has planned for things like this." I wore a look of
doubt as I said this, because I needed to make a request
of him, and the part that not all of the citizens would be
saved was best left out. "However, before your rude police commissioner took me prisoner, I saw that there was
a PFS battleship in orbit. It will destroy the cruiser when
it arrives, and it'll kill everyone on board. I need a way
to communicate to UGF command to postpone the rescue
attempts and to send battle cruisers to destroy the PFS
ship and help retake this planet."

He exhaled and looked around. He then picked up
a book and looked for something. After finding what he
needed, he threw it at me. I quickly caught it and looked
at it. It was a key.

"Are you familiar with a quantum drive?" he asked.

I shook my head.

"Well, if you haven't, don't worry; I myself am not
too familiar with the technology either. However, my top
scientists have been working with a hydrogen engine that
is faster and can fly at higher altitudes than a hovercar.
One is in this bunker; Captain Sherwood knows where,
and he will take you to the castle to find a way into the
communication room."

"This will postpone the evacuation. It'll probably take
another day for them to get here. Are you ready to have
that on your conscience?" I asked, questioning his morals,
thoughts, and mind.

The king looked at the floor. His white beard rivaled

that of Herr Doctor, and his brown eyes reminded me of a wise man. Very appropriate for his profession. He looked up at me and nodded.

I turned around and headed for the door. Captain Sherwood exited and started back along the way we had come to this room. I stood at the door as the captain walked on.

"My daughter," said the king, "she mentioned you a few hours ago. She told me you were the one. I don't want you to save us and then leave us—or rather leave her; it would devastate her. Please, I know I can't ask you, but I wish, and I know it's pathetic, but I wish, I wish you would see something in her and not treat this as another mission to be brushed off."

I stared deep into his eyes, and then at his wall. There was a glass ornament and an oil painting of a group of miners being led by a very young yet heroically posed man. The painting was very romantic and heroic. However, there wasn't much color other than black, gray, and the occasional red and dark olive green. I made eye contact once more with him, closed my eyes tight, and left the room.

Captain Sherwood saw me and kept moving to a different hallway. The king's words haunted me, but I wouldn't let myself be distracted by that. We kept on moving and passed by dozens of rooms. We turned a few times until we came to a door being guarded by two security personnel. They were dressed similarly to the captain; however, their faces were not covered.

"Crap, these guys only listen to Commissioner Thickhead," the captain said. "We need to knock them out. I'll get the one on the left; you get the one on the right. Hurry before they call him"

I slung my rifle across my chest and cracked my knuckles. Eric walked calmly and hit the guard on the left with the butt of his rifle, while I unslung mine. I then hit my target with the butt of my rifle, which broke his nose. He hit the ground but was not knocked out. Seeing no choice, I hit him once more as he tried to crawl away. He continued to move slowly away from me. I grabbed his shoulder, moved him onto his back, and hit him one last time, knocking the poor man out.

"Damn, that was fierce," Eric commented. "But hey, you know what they say—third time's the charm."

He turned to the keypad on the side of the door and proceeded to try to unlock the door while I laughed. I put my hands in my pockets and felt something. It was the communication device. I put the earpiece in and turned on the receiver. Eric opened the door and revealed what appeared to be an underground hangar or warehouse. We walked to the only vehicle in the place and mounted it. He turned on the machine, and it moved. Four flaps opened, and four engines came out of them and arched out of the vehicle. When they extended completely, the engines turned on and the vehicle hovered above the floor. We buckled up, and the captain pressed a few buttons to opening a door in the hangar. He accelerated, and my head was pushed back. We left the hanger at top speed—faster than a PFS attack ship could ever travel.

"How are we going to get into the castle?" I asked Eric.

"Easy, we get an attack ship to blow the front door and the sentry towers," he responded.

"Are we going to hijack one or make it follow us all the way back here?" I asked, loading a fresh magazine into my rifle.

"Whichever comes first" he replied.

After a few minutes, we encountered a line of abandoned hovercars on the road. It was the same road I had taken when I shot the attack ship down.

"So you've been to war? You've seen war?" he asked with a hungry tone.

After hesitating and sighing, I cleared my throat. "Yeah, I have."

"How long?"

"Pretty long. A man's got to eat."

"Have you seen a space battle? Tell me, have you seen one?"

"A few small ones, one big one."

"Tell me about them." He accelerated the vehicle and raised his tone.

"They're explosive. The big one I saw had cruisers, carriers, and battleships on both sides, not just a few attack ships defending a planet. That was on Clo. Biggest space battle since the First Human Blood War. Thousands of ships dogfighting and exploding, and people dying. After we destroyed the armada defending the planet, we dropped down and got pushed back."

"When you get sent off, how is it?"

"It's hard to believe you're a captain. It was dreary. The first time I walked onto a carrier, it was raining. The wind blew on us all, and it caused the flag to wave back and forth. It's funny; I remember it two ways. The first is when I was there, the second is when I look back at it." A smile was spread on my face; I saw it on his goggles—but it wasn't exactly a happy one.

"Tell me, what are the two ways that you remember it? I'm sorry if I'm pestering you, but I've never left this planet. I don't know of what's outside this atmosphere, this system. I want to know everything." His eyes gleamed.

"I know how you feel. I think most people feel that way in life. One way was happy, with the rain sounding like a marching tune. The cheers of the people as we boarded sounded like cheers to ascending to the stars. The other way, the way I now look back at it more frequently ..." I paused as we passed a patrol of startled PFS. "The rain, it sounded like cries. The people—I felt that those who did understand what we were going to go through stayed quiet and wept for us. It wasn't the first time they sent soldiers, but it always bothers people."

"We've never had need for soldiers here—just cops. I climbed up the ranks only to hope for something interesting in life. Did you ever know that old saying, 'Boredom can kill more people than bullets'?"

"Have you even killed anyone?" *What a sudden question*, I thought.

"One. A few years back. Hostage situation in a bank." He stared at the road.

"And how did that feel?" *How dare he glorify war.*

That stopped him.

The thought of the soldier with one blue eye and one gray eye came to mind. I soon remembered what his condition was called: heterochromia iridum. I didn't just kill him; I executed him. His stare will be with me for as long as I can see; for it is burned into my thoughts.

"I don't want to talk about it," he said.

"Of course you don't want to talk about it. Do you want to know why? Because talking about it will bring your barbaric side to mind. It'll bring out the side you try to convince yourself doesn't exist. It'll bring out the side all of us humans have. In the end, that's the side that causes the fires, the pools of blood, the broken bodies, the crushed souls, the destroyed cities."

"We're not all like that." His expression defended the goodness of humanity.

"Look it up on the Internet. Search "war." What do you see? You see soldiers from every era, from every nation, from every planet. Fighting, dying, killing. From the Babylonians, to the Chinese, to the Germans, to the destroyed kingdoms of the East moon and star, to the Earthen armies, to the separatists, and now to here, with the PFS. We can be horrible beings."

He thought about my savage point, and he told me something that brought me to a different perspective.

"Then why do you do it? Why do you keep fighting?

"I like this job as much as I hate it, but there is something that kills my humanity. Something that probably makes me inhuman."

"And what might that be?" he asked while turning a corner.

"My kill count. I have exactly twelve thousand seven hundred eighty-eight confirmed kills. Two of those kills were confirmed here on this planet today. Do you have that much blood on your hands? No, you don't." Even through his balaclava, his mouth was wide open.

I wondered how much blood Herr Doctor had on his hands—blood that only he and military records could measure.

"How?" His widened eyes feared and respected me.

"Years of service, many missions. The men I used as weapons also add to my kill count. Airstrikes take up the bulk. I reek of death. Can't you smell it, my friend?"

For a few minutes we rode in silence around the streets, until we hit a main street that was filled with abandoned vehicles.

"Watch this," the captain said, pulling a lever that looked like ones they use to increase altitude on Hyperions. The vehicle jumped over a car and stayed at that constant altitude.

"What is this thing called?" I asked Eric.

"R&D calls it a Creeper; I call them idiots." He laughed as he accelerated the vehicle.

A dark shape appeared in the sky; it had the PFS logo on the hull. Three PFS scout ships came out of a transport circling overhead. Since the transport was too slow, their command had decided to send the scouts, which were sufficient to reach the same altitude as us. However, since the ships were arrow shaped and carried three heavy machine guns, they were not able to reach our speed—shame.

They began to fire when they reached our altitude. Bullets penetrated the light-blue metal panels on our craft.

"So, here's the thing," Eric said. "We don't have any weapons mounted on the Creeper."

"You idiot! If you want to get their attention, then we

need to shoot those stupid scout ships down, and how are we going to do that?"

"Don't blame me; blame R&D," he replied.

"The seats rotate, right? There's a circular design on the bottom," I stated to him.

"That's where I was going with this. Here, you drive. It's just like riding a bike. Do you even have those on Earth still?" He pressed a button on the touchscreen control panel on top of the steering unit.

The steering unit and panel moved toward my side, but I couldn't even understand the controls. Eric hit a switch, and the seat rotated 180 degrees and now faced the scout ships. On the monitor, their red lights flickered and burned brighter as they drew closer. Eric's seat elevated a bit, and the metal panels of the Creeper moved to give him a better angle to shoot from. I took the side stick and held it in place. Adrenaline was pumping in our hearts at that moment, and time seemed to speed up yet slow down at the same time. Eric, from what I could hear, was removing the safety. In about one seconds, he went trigger happy and was an earlier, more undisciplined version of myself. I heard a crash and looked at the rearview mirror. We were missing a scout ship, and the captain was loading his fifth magazine. I decided to get off the highway, since we were traveling in circles and still getting shot at. Taking a right, I rotated the hovercar to face the scout cars, much to Eric's surprise.

"What the hell?! Tell me when you are going to do that, bastard! Scared the living hell out of me. Why are we changing route? Turn back!" he exclaimed.

"Shoot down the rest of the … oh, never mind. Switch; I got 'em."

"You don't seem to have much ammo, mate. I got this, luv." He smiled at me through his balaclava.

I then took one hand off the control stick and hit the switch Eric had used to turn his seat around.

"I hate you," he said to me as he slung his rifle over his shoulder.

"Well, I want to shoot, too, and I don't think you're qualified to keep shooting." I responded.

Looking at the control panel, I selected the option that gave control of the vehicle to Eric. As I poked my rifle out of the doorless Creeper, a memory occurred to me.

I was back in a city whose namesake was the Latin word for peace—Pacem. Most of the landscape was littered with debris from the buildings that had once stood there. I was wearing the old uniform, walking around to see the dead of the UGF—the enemy and the civilians. There were rumors that the rebel force contained a PFS element, but they remained rumors. As I walked through a destroyed building, my hands grabbed my holographic dog tags. On the back was the UGF oath. Upon inspecting the building, I found four civilians lying down with empty expressions. There were signs that they had been gunned down. I stared at each one, and the youth in my spirit vanished with these lives.

Gunfire outside made me run to stop it. I saw a man shot down by a rebel soldier, with a woman standing behind him, watching as he fell. The separatist walked away from his act, passing the woman while the light emitted from his eye goggles burned with the same red light the scout cars emitted. The woman, with a stern face and look of despair, stared at me. She walked to the man who had taken the bullets for her, and she knelt next to him. She kept staring at me, watching me, as I had arrived too late to save that man. She said everything without saying one word.

Taking my helmet off and removing my goggles, I yelled for the enemy to turn around to face me, for him to look at me. When he did, he was greeted by my rifle aimed at his chest, which spat fire and metal to bring justice to him. When I made eye contact with the woman again, we both had the same morbid expression, yet now she could see that my face was dirty from the constant fighting and held a deep sympathy for the dead man's sacrifice. She saw that my expression was not one of pity, but rather one of regret for being too slow to save the man on the floor. I turned around to face the ruins of the razed city, and my squad members ran out of the building to assist the woman. Secret was crying at the feet of the dead man; Proctor could comfort only the woman and his brother. The remaining members of my squad picked up a surviving, yet wounded, soldier from the debris. It was in that moment that we all had a question within us: "How much more are we willing to sacrifice for peace?"

Eric began to turn the Creeper around and accelerated while the remaining scout ships began to catch up. On the panel between me and Eric, I hit the switch to rotate myself. My seat elevated and turned me while the metal panels of the blue craft started shifting to give me cover.

I aimed my rifle at the front of one of the PFS scout ships. With a well-timed four-round burst of fire to the exhaust vents, the ship became engulfed in blue hellfire.

At my feet, a circular base for what appeared to be a machine gun mount was sitting uselessly. I later remembered the ban of assault weapons and thought that perhaps even R&D was not allowed to use heavy weapons or even mount them. I assumed the bases were probably placed when the Creeper was sent to a UGF military factory for inspection and armament. The last remaining scout ship began to make its debut for our showdown. It cranked its engine and rushed our way. Flashes from its three ports told me it was firing at us.

"Shoot it!" Eric yelled. "Those guns will rip us to shreds, you idiot! Why did you stop the damn car?"

"Shut up and move!"

I couldn't really tell him why I had stopped. It was a mad desire for more action, for that sweet rush of adrenaline. I was its slave, and it was my master. I could call it a drug, since action killed my friends, since it had the ability to ruin my life. It was something to take my mind off the boring ways of my life. I say this because, in reality, all humans have undesired, boring lives, whether they admit it or not. There are moments in life when we need to get danger once in a while to eliminate the boring daily routine of life. Of course, if I had told Eric that, he would have shot me for endangering him—something that did make me feel awful, since I needed him.

"Hold her steady," I said to him.

I shifted my weight a little for a better shot, and I heard a little yelp. It wasn't my voice or Eric's. A round whizzed by my head, and I looked back at the ship. The red light of the ship flickered brightly, and it zoomed quickly toward me. One of the machine guns fell off. The pilot was jettisoning equipment to lighten the craft in order to match our speed. This was an ace scout. He was likely their squad leader or smartest pilot.

Eric kept accelerating down the road and took a turn through the maze of towering buildings. Our stalking predator released another machine gun and inched closer toward us. His beams were on all high, and his machine gun fired another spray of death.

"I hate you, I hate you, I hate you, I hate you so much," Eric said while looking at the monitor, which showed the shooting speeder. He kept the car steady even while forcing the Creeper over abandoned cars. I emptied a magazine in about two minutes, since I was taking my time with this one. It would be an honor to take him out; he did not deserve a petty death like the rest of his squad. I really was insane; maybe that is why Evelyn got me to be an agent.

He let go of his final machine gun, and it clattered on top of a car. It fired some rounds into the walls and other vehicles the second it hit the street. He soon released a computer and three boxes of extra ammunition. The enemy ship shot forward and started to catch up to us. The man took out his pistol as the craft moved closer to my side of the Creeper.

"Please tell me you did not almost get us killed so you could have a standoff with him," said Eric.

"Will it make you feel better if I lied?" I said as I saw the PFS soldier's pistol.

"Look at the size of his pistol; of course not!" His pistol put both of mine to shame.

"Well, does he look like he can suck a golf ball through a garden hose like the rest of his squad?" I asked Eric. "He deserves this."

The scout ship and its rider rode to my left and stared at me as I moved back to my forward position. His helmet covered his entire head except for his eyes. The helmet and face guard were molded into the shape of a skull with spiked teeth. The unnatural part of him showed up in his eyes. His irises burned a dark crimson red, the same as the eyes of the first PFS I killed; his sclera were made of gray manner; just the sight of them seemed to hurt. Something about that creeped me out; made me feel as though I were fighting shadows and devils instead of humans. Some unknown factor was at work; something made him look demonic, especially with the skull-shaped head protection.

Eric stole a glance at him, causing him to accelerate the Creeper. I grabbed my rifle, having decided to cut our duel short. Of the many people I have regretted shooting, he is not one of them; I knew I would not lose sleep at night after putting him down or after watching him stop moving as the bullets hit his chest and jaw.

"Stop!" I ordered Eric.

He hit the brake, and we slowed down. I got out of the car and sprinted to the ship. I had to know why his eyes burned like blood. My steps echoed loudly in the dark street, and Eric ran at a distance behind me. He tackled me as soon as we were fifteen meters from the craft.

"What the hell is wrong with you?" I said. The knife

on my exoskeleton extended to his neck as soon as we were down.

"There are soldiers in the building in front of you," he explained while holding my arm away from his neck.

He took point as we moved toward the downed PFS scout ship, which had come to rest on top of some worthless cars. I held my breath, hoping that the PFS would not notice right away that one of their scout ships was down. Our careful steps to the ship and the body were soon halted, as a rocket flew into a car next to Eric. He flew a foot to his right and then quickly stood up. He tried to reload, but the magazine he had in his hand landed next to me. While firing at the flashes on the building, I swooped down and snatched the helical magazine for him. I threw it at him, and his catch was impressive. He was something special—very disciplined, very accurate, and very proper. Firing at the window as well, he took out more of the soldiers than I could.

We stopped to reload behind the scout ship. Our rapid breathing kept reminding us that we were under a lot of stress and fire.

"Enemy shock trooper and police officer behind cover!" one of the enemy yelled.

"Is it the same one that killed Dillinger?" another asked.

"Yeah, I'll keep them suppressed," a third said before spraying bullets with a light machine gun, which made my vision blurred as thundery lightning flew toward me.

"They're going to flank us," I said. "I'll return fire, and you take out the rest. Understood, Proctor?"

"What?" When he looked at me, I realized my mistake. "Did you just call me—"

He was cut off by a bullet hitting his shoulder and a yelp of agony.

Another one of my friends had been shot right in front of me. I had to blame myself; I needed to, because it was my fault that he was on the floor grasping his shoulder.

"One down; get the other one," a voice yelled.

A PFS troop jumped from the building to the speeder. He had his rifle at the ready and walked toward me with the cover of the gunner suppressing me. Eric was on the ground, and I couldn't reach him. The soldier came closer and jumped over the speeder. If I wanted to reach Eric, I needed to take the others out.

While listening to the sound of the bullets and calculating when the PFS trooper would land, my rifle was next to my chest. Eric groaned, and it made me want the PFS to hurry up, made me want them to stop taking their time.

When the PFS did fall behind me, his eyes were covered by the same goggles every black uniform regular had, the same eye protection that emitted the red light. While he had his back against the speeder, a burst of bullets stopped the soldier. I strained to turn around and threw a light strobe at the PFS. The impact shattered the clear plasma membrane of the light source, which released a flash that burned brighter than a star. The light blinded the soldiers, which stopped them from firing and gave me time to return fire. I heard four voices before I brought down the soldier that tried to flank me, yet I saw only two other soldiers holding their heads and covering their eyes. Without mercy, I pointed the rifle at them and did what I was trained to do.

With that done, my attention turned to Eric. As I

ran toward him, he turned around and pointed his rifle at me. I had saved this man's life, and now he had me in his sights. I stood there like an idiot with my mouth open. It didn't occur to me that he might not have been targeting me.

"Get down!" he ordered, and I obeyed immediately.

His rifle shot the same rounds as mine did—6.59 mm caseless ammunition, which hit the fourth PFS soldier behind me. Breathing a sigh of relief, I faced the man who had saved my life.

"For a second I thought you were going to shoot at me." I chuckled while helping him lie on the speeder.

"Why would I do that? I need your help as much as you need mine," he said to me while I was pulling my medical kit from one of my packs.

"You cocky bastard. I'm going to make this hurt."

I pulled out a transitillator, a device that would numb the wound and melt the bullet into a thin metal needle, which would allow me to remove it from his body with ease, and then it would evaporate in the air. I held the handle of the transitillator as the metal needle injected itself in him from the bottom barrel, and the condensed pulse beam began to contain and melt the bullet inside him. His stifled scream made me chuckle, but it also almost made me hit him to get him to be quiet. When the beam stopped, the copper-and-silver-colored round was sticking out, and I held it in my hand. I showed it to him, and he was about to touch it when the needle evaporated.

"You're a real good medic" he responded as I injected a foam that cleaned the wound and mended the bone.

"Nah, I never took medic classes. I took piloting

lessons and counter sniper classes," I confessed while pulling out a skin graft made of cloned stem cells that sealed his wound.

"Then how do you know this?"

"I've gotten shot more than a few times. I just learned to patch myself up. Sure made my medic happy." We both chuckled.

We made our way back to the speeder. The ship stayed in a menacing position. I moved to the body of the soldier who had made it to the speeder and saw that he had three vials in one of his chest pockets. They were clear tubes with a black honeycomb design on the label; the PFS logo was in the middle. The liquid was blue and had a yellow hue at the edge of the container. The heart sensors on the body of the PFS soldier emitted a red light, and as I watched, they faded to black. I didn't understand that, as he should have been dead since I shot him, over five minutes before.

Eric opened the vial and sniffed the contents. He raised his balaclava enough to show his mouth. He savored the blue liquid with his tongue and spat what he had out. It was probably a drug, and the tiny amount he took made him shook and drop to the floor. I took out a canteen and waited for him to vomit. I still didn't know what to expect, but when he stood up and drank the water, his iris had a red hue on the outer sides.

The enemies' steering controls consisted of a black control panel and content that was little more than large touch screens than what the UGF had aboard their scout ships. However, one of his touch screens caught my attention, since the picture of a beautiful woman was displayed on it.

"Ah, crap. He had a wife, I think," I said to Eric while removing the tablet from the vehicle.

Eric came out of the Creeper to look at the picture. There was something about the way he stared at her that made me suspicious. "One might be. The other person we know."

His balaclava made reading the expression on his face difficult. His eyes, however, showed me two things: fear and sorrow. The tablet changed photos from the woman sitting under a tree with a basket next to her, to a picture of the princess and the words "find her" typed next to her circled image.

"Well, he shot at us," he muttered under his breath while searching the soldier for his dog tags. After finding what he was looking for, Eric pulled the tags off the dead soldier's neck and read them before placing them on the man's back.

We ignored what we saw on the monitor, and Eric's reactions began to make me uncomfortable. He was acting erratically, twitching uncontrollably; his rifle seemed to shake along with his hand.

"Vulture 2-3, this is Vulture Nest. Has target been apprehended? Over," the radio roared.

Eric and I looked at each other and backed away from the ship.

"Vulture 2-3, this is Vulture Nest. Do you have the target?" The radio asked again.

"Vulture 2-3?"

"We'd better get moving before they send reinforcements to check on this ship," Eric said.

"Then hide the Creeper. Didn't we plan on hijacking an attack ship? This is the perfect chance," I said.

"That's risky," he replied, staring at the building the PFS had attacked us from.

"But it's worth it. Come on, you know it's riskier if we try to sneak into the castle," I said to him, looking at the PFS scout ship.

"Vulture 2-3, we are sending a Typhoon. Stand by," the PFS commander said over the radio.

Sherwood ran to the Creeper and got in. He rammed into a building, breaking the wall, and parked inside. Two ships flew overhead, but they were headed to a different location. I ran toward the building and waited for the Typhoon. Eric joined me and waited for the same thing.

"I think the princess likes you," Eric said, but he did so in a tone I did not recognize or like.

"I think so too. But why? I'm not a very lovable person," I answered.

"Do you know anything about her?" he snarled with furrowed eyebrows.

"N-no," I stuttered.

"Well, she read your entire bio. Your health reports and even your evaluations. Do you even know her name?"

I looked at him. That hurt me. I looked at the night sky and waited for him to hurt me more. "Do you ever wonder why we are put on this world? Why we are who we are? I think that for some reason, maybe by chance of luck or by fate, we need to do something with our lives. But that luck or fate lets us decide what we are gonna do. I think what I'm trying to say is that we can't let our lives be governed by the faults of our actions, but by the movements of our dreams. That is what I think when I look at the stars and through the celestial heavens of our galaxy." As I spoke, I looked at the stars and two moons of this planet. My goodness, they were beautiful.

"And what are you trying to say with that?" he asked, reloading his rifle.

"Maybe, just maybe, I am supposed to be with her. Or maybe you're the hero of this struggle and you get the spoils," I said, looking at the floor.

"Her name is Olivia of Helena. Her middle name is Diana," he said with an expression in his eyes that made me wonder.

I heard the sound of an engine and turbines.

# CHAPTER EIGHTEEN

## TRAP

I waited for the engines to be overhead, for the ship to hover down, and for the troops to exit. It was essential that it land for the troops to get off so Eric and I could get on. The ship crawled into a descent to the street, but its slow rate ensured that I would go insane before it reached the ground. I took my rifle at the doors of the ship. Eric did the same thing, but I took my hands off my weapon and pressed the barrel of his toward the ground. He looked at me, and I pointed at my silencer. He nodded.

The black attack ship landed with the cargo doors facing the hole that Eric had made when he crashed the Creeper in. We took cover behind some debris and waited for the doors to part.

The doors soon opened, and a soldier ran out to secure the area. Without hesitation, I squeezed the trigger and shot him down. The rest of the squad exited the vehicle, only to be handed their fate by me. I jumped over the debris and started changing magazines. Eric jumped over as well and ran to the back of the ship.

Running right behind him, I almost tripped on a PFS

soldier who had few breaths left in him. He moved and took his pistol out while turning to look at me.

"Don't. Put it down and you might live longer." He moved his pistol barrel closer to me.

I took the pistol that had been given to me by Herr Doctor and aimed it at the soldier's head. He looked young, maybe eighteen or nineteen. I looked into his eyes; he had one tear in them, and a bottle similar to the one we found on the speeder's corpse, on his lips.

"Don't! Goddammit, kid! You have a chance to keep living; don't do it!"

"For what? You killed many of my friends; you brought on this war now. We were only here for a quick mission." His own blood began to drown him as he gurgled and spat it out. "I don't have much of a choice. If you were me and I were you, would you do the same? I wouldn't show you mercy; you would do the same." His eyes began to turn red.

"Kid, I'm telling you to stop, please. You don't have to end it."

"I have to!" He quickly raised his pistol, and I shot him.

"Get out now!" I heard Eric yell.

Two pilots were pushed out by Eric; they put their hands on their heads while kneeling.

"What the hell happened, Gerald? Why was there a gunshot, and why does that poor kid having a bullet in his head and his brains on the street?"

"Tried to kill me," I replied darkly, looking at the pilots, who were trying not to make eye contact with me.

However, it occurred to me that I did not know what

I would have done if I had been in his position. *Where do my loyalties stand? For these people, or for my life?*

The pilots wore helmets that covered them all the way to their eyes with a vizor. The glass gave them the ability to see through the ship's cameras and motion sensors, and it provided a heads-up display. With the click of a button, a mask covered their face and gave them air to breathe. How much power we gave to buttons.

"What should we do with them?" I asked.

We couldn't kill them, as that was in direct violation with the rules of war; yet we couldn't leave them there, since they would give us away. This was ironic, since I had just shot the kid, who was in reality just as unlikely of hurting me as the pilots were.

Eric grabbed his rifle and hit one of them on the head; he then did the same to the other.

"You like doing that, don't you?" I asked.

"Yeah, I do," he said. He grabbed one of the pilots' helmets and threw it to me.

I caught it and took off my own helmet and strapped it to my back. We both got inside the ship and put the pilots' helmets on.

"Did I lock the Creeper?" Eric asked.

We both stopped and looked back. I shrugged at him and he scratched his covered head.

"Oh, no one will see it. Let's go," he said.

The differences between the UGF ship and the PFS ship were astonishing. The red light hit me, and the seats and equipment seemed to too close together. The cockpit door was open and gleamed with different-colored lights. It seemed that the architects and ship builders weren't fans of only red. Eric sat in the main pilot's chair. He lasted less than ten seconds before he stood up and moved to the copilot's chair. "Yeah, I can't pilot this," he said, putting the seat belt on.

I rolled my eyes at him and sat in the pilot's chair. The controls were very different from those of Hyperions and any other UGF ship. It reminded me of the time I tried to learn calculus or when I took advanced linguistics. Finally I found the elevation switch. It was then something of a hassle to find the speed and weapons controls. I was getting an idea of how to do this. I moved the elevation switch forward and picked up altitude. I grabbed the control stick and started to pilot the ship to the castle, more or less. I hoped I could reach it before being discovered.

"You are slow at this, but I won't judge you, since this isn't any design we are used to," Eric said.

"Shark 3-6, this is command. Did you find what happened to Vulture 2-3? Over," the radio squawked.

"Damn, doesn't that kill stealth," Eric said.

"Shark 3-6, sensors indicate that weight differences have decreased dramatically. Please respond."

I pressed forward with the ship. It was unbelievable that we had been able to hijack it in the first place. Eric studied the controls and found the gunner pad. The screen turned on and showed the secondary automatic cannon aiming system.

I checked my wrist map and saw that we were about a kilometer away from the castle. I sped up as the radio barked orders for a reply. Eric touched the control pad with his fingerless gloves, moving the gun around. He was ready. We reduced our altitude and made our way through the empty streets, snaking in between the buildings.

"Eric, do you think they have antiair weapons? I hate getting shot down."

"No, there wouldn't be any place to put them." I found his optimism inspiring.

"What about shoulder fired?" I asked.

"Well, if there are any, I'll worry about those."

The great gates of the castle soon appeared before us. The sentry towers were manned by PFS soldiers, and their confused expressions brought a smile to my face. None seemed to understand why an attack ship was in front of them. One officer was on a communication device, relaying information to his superior. He shouted something to his men, and that caused them to fire at us.

"Returning fire," Eric said, and he began firing from the attack ship's secondary cannon. He then flipped three switches and pressed the trigger on the control stick, firing missiles and plasma-arc cannon rounds. Tower upon tower was destroyed, along with weaponry, and soldiers were either blown off the buildings or exploded into a bloody mess. It was quick and efficient.

We destroyed the sentry towers and flew into the main yard. Soldiers and engineers began to run inside the castle, abandoning their work on who knows what. A fountain in the middle let me know that there was not enough room to land. And aside from that, I wasn't sure how to land.

I looked at the controls and red lights of the ship. As I decided to pull a crash landing, I tinkered with the idea of telling Eric.

"Eric."

"What?" he said through his balaclava.

"I think I should tell you ... I don't know how to land."

He looked at me with seriousness in his eyes. No matter how many safety features any ship has, a crash landing is fatal no matter what. This is because the fusion engine requires liquid radioactive elements that served in a somewhat similar capacity as gasoline in an internal-combustion engine. Heh, gas. I wonder why people didn't call it "liquid explosive dinosaur"—a more appropriate name.

"Open the cargo door. Get close to the ground and then I'll jump off," he said. "You'd better follow me."

I pressed two buttons, and the cargo doors opened while our altitude decreased, but the engines maintained enough thrust that the ship did not crash just yet. Eric took his seat belt and helmet off. He put his on his standard helmet while waiting for the right moment to jump. I began to follow suit.

The ship started to shake and tilt. The nose tipped forward while the altitude decreased. I stumbled a bit. I took my helmet off its strap on my back and put it on my head. The strap buckled itself, and the faceguard covered my face. The green visor shielded my goggled eyes as I jumped off the ship.

"Geronimo!" I yelled.

The ship moved toward the smoking ruins of the outside wall. The impact sent shockwaves and smoke all around as the whole ship and a great piece of the wall mixed as one. I landed feet first, and my exoskeleton absorbed the impact.

Eric ran up to me. I grasped his arm, and we surveyed the chaos we had just created.

"Talk about stirring up a hornets' nest." he said, turning around to the front entrance.

We ran toward the giant wooden door and opened it with a great simultaneous tackle. Sandbags and tank barricades stood on the front plaza. The PFS had been preparing for a fight; the kid might have been lying about them staying here only for a quick mission. Crates of antimech missiles and gun rounds were stockpiled behind the sandbags and other barricades. Antiaircraft lasers and guns were in various states of assembly, as well as missile launchers and plasma mortars. And Eric had said there wasn't room for any equipment.

I knew that the soldiers must have taken cover in the castle when we entered, since there wasn't a living soul in the whole damn place. For this reason I walked silently while checking my corners twice and listening for any noise. However, the only sounds I noticed were the screams of the spawn and the Goliath. With our rifles aimed in front of us, we entered the palace, I in my olive drab soldier's uniform, and Eric in his police blues.

"Where is the communication room?" I asked.

"There's an elevator hidden beneath the grand stairs."

Eric moved toward a pillar and made sure the area was safe. The chandelier dangled above our heads as we moved toward the staircase in the center of the room that led to the second, third, and fourth stories. However, we moved to its side, and I served as lookout for any trouble.

Eric placed his hands on the wall, his fingers searching for something. He removed a piece of the wall to reveal an elevator door. Since the power was out in the entire structure, the doors would not open. Eric strained and pulled, gasped and groaned, but still he could not open the metal doors.

"Need a hand?" My offer sounded so innocent that his eyes gave me a look that could kill.

I used my exoskeleton at full power, and the doors strained and moved to the side. Eric entered, and before I closed the doors, he placed the wall piece back into place. He opened a panel inside the clear elevator and began entering the number sequence to take us down.

"Damn, no power," he said, looking around for something to power the elevator.

It was taking too long, and he was working too slowly. I moved him out of the way. The panel had a port that seemed it would accept an electro rod. Mine fit, and it activated the elevator, I activated it and the elevator drained it's power. A blue light began to flicker above us.

Eric swore before closing the panel. "They changed the damn codes. Only one person could do that without telling anyone, and that's the damn commissioner." He cursed and spit on the elevator after mentioning the commissioner.

"Wow, wasn't that predictable. Seriously, anyone could have seen that coming," I pointed out.

"I'll override it," a sweet, delicate voice said in my ear.

Eric couldn't see my expression because of the visor on my helmet, but if he had seen me, I would have worried him. Voices and yells sounded outside the elevator. Orders were soon given out to return to building the defenses and to return to the castle to find us. A fire warning was extended regarding the downed Vulture.

"It's okay. Remember, it's me, Olivia. The code is zero nine one zero nine six," she whispered in my ear. "Now, I have been bad and hacking the network system, so I'll guide you through this castle and help you avoid the enemy. But you need to let me take control of your helmet's camera. I know you will anyway, sweetie."

I walked to the panel and entered the code as Eric knelt next to it. The elevator started stirred to life. Eric gave me a look of disbelief. This was getting predictable; I was probably going to get stabbed in the stomach when it was all over.

"How?" he asked calmly.

"Princess told me," I responded, and his look appeared shocked and discontented.

In the corner of my visor, Olivia appeared from an office down in the bunkers. She smiled at me, and her beauty kept me from saying anything. How was it possible for her to access my equipment from her position? How was it that she kept me in her thoughts and mind and she stayed in mine?

"Don't worry; just follow my lead," she said to me.

The elevator stopped after a while, and the doors opened to a somewhat dark hallway. It was agonizing and cold. Eric turned on the flashlight on his rifle, and my visor lit up to reveal all that was in my way. The sight of the Hornet changed to thermal imagining and linked up with my visor automatically. The hallway was only twenty feet, but the darkness made it look longer.

"I get Wi-Fi down here." My map soon connected to it and asked me if I would like to download any applications. This is what I love about UGF equipment, no matter what generation it is, no matter what company makes it, it is always upgradeable and compatible with any technology around.

"Of all the things you could worry about, why is that on the top of your list?"

"It's almost midnight on Earth, and servers always use Earth time instead of Meridath time."

"Meridath time? Servers? What are you talking about?"

"There's a satellite a few hundred thousand light years from this planet that directs specific signals to Earth, and then there are a few that send military communications to all channels that the military has access to."

"Sense—you're not making any of it."

'You'll see in a bit," I said as I finished downloading an application and filling in my account information.

When we reached the end of the hallway, we found that the door was locked with a hatch. I lowered my rifle, put my hands on the hatch, and turned it clockwise before slowly pushing the door.

Monitors reflected my bloodstained clothes and Eric's blackened uniform. The room was filled with computers and communication devices. Screens lined the walls, all for them bearing the logo of the Helenac Kingdom—an olive wreath outlining an ascending dove. I connected my map to a computer via cable, and the two pieces of technology connected and synced to one another.

"Now that I'm connected, I get my daily bonus!" I cheered as my virtual city received extra diamonds.

A silence told me that Eric did not approve of my use of time, but my concern for his approval was not on my mind.

While sitting down at a computer and waiting for it to boot up, I explained universal time, Meridath, and the game I was playing. When the computer started, the codes were typed in from the UGF communication platform in Earth headquarters.

"Eric, tell me why is it that all other electronic devices in this city are not working, yet here all these bloody computers are?"

He was looking out the door, making sure no one came in.

"This communication center used to be a UGF forward operation base during the First Galactic War, long before we were born. When the PFS tried to take over the planet, the king was able to repel them. This room is just a working relic of that past. This room is hundreds of feet underground and protected by layers of lead and concrete. That's why the EMP wasn't able to shut these off. Or the power in the underground bunkers."

"Why are there all those bunkers?" I asked, very curious now.

"The mines house a very unstable and rare mineral. If it accidently falls, it triggers an enormous explosion. You might think of it like a tsunami; it won't destroy the point where it starts, but the explosion gets larger and larger, and when it hits the city, it kills people that are not protected. That is why the windows here are so damn hard to break, have you noticed that?"

The connection linked up, and I tried to make contact from a dead world to the other side.

"Harvester, this is Reaper, over." Static.

"Harvester, this is Reaper, calling from the Helenac Kingdom. *Over.*" No reply. I knew this had to be karma from the attack ship. But that wouldn't have made sense. I put my head down in desperation. As I put down the microphone, the urge to curl into a ball grew from deep within me.

"Reaper, this is Harvester. How is it from the other side, son?" Director Kayre answered.

I had to smile. He had to be dramatic; he just had to be dramatic.

"Dead and hiding, sir," I answered him.

"Funny. Now what happened to your communication device?" he asked.

"It got chewed off in a fight with a Goliath spawn. Oh, did I tell you they were here?" I said, covering up my lie with some truth.

Eric chuckled at that and waved at the image of the director as soon as he appeared on the monitors. The director merely saluted Eric.

"How is the royal family? And no, you didn't," he said seriously.

"Fine, sir. Now to the more pressing matters. We have company here, worse than the Libertas. The Protectorate Federation of Systems is here. They have a battleship in orbit and many soldiers. They're digging in. I don't doubt more ships are coming, and more soldiers also."

"Whoa, say again. The PFS are there?" he asked, looking for confirmation.

He was part of the generation that had fought the PFS in the earlier war. He had proven that he was worth his weight in service to Earth; his position had truly been earned. He and all those that died in ditches, were killed off by the cold, or simply died unknown deaths, but he merely survived to be given the title. To remind him of those days was to earn a lecture of why we needed to stop the enemy, but what he really wanted to give out was a heartbreaking scream.

"PFS are here, and damn are they loaded. Call off the carrier and bring more troops, at least a fleet of battleships, and did I already say bring an army?" I said.

"You know it'll take a full ten hours to mobilize that much," he said, sounding overwhelmed by such a request.

But how could he not? Our enemy was back within our gates, and they were keeping us from peace—an action that was as stupid as the oath I took to preserve it.

"Gerald, how are you, son?"

It was strange for him to call me "son." It was even stranger for him to wonder how I was. Director Kayre had always been there for me, from when he got me my job with the UGF, to my first and last combat mission, to my fall into darkness, after which he gave me a job at the Defense Force. I could always remember him saying, "You just get back up there, Gerald; you've got to make me and your sister proud." He knew how I was; his looks always scanned me and told him how I was. In fact, he was the closest thing I had to a father figure, since he was there for me during all my greatest accomplishments and worst downfalls.

"I'm fine, sir."

"In all my time of knowing you, something has always been on your mind. So tell me, what is going on?"

Olivia's image was in my heads-up display and in my mind. However, I couldn't tell him about her or what we have talked about.

"Fine," he said, "be stubborn. You have a job to do, and I have mine. But I need time."

"I know you can do it; you've done it before," I said to him. "By the way, General Chris Rommel is here."

A fire grew in his eyes, and his expression burned into a snarl. My friend had a hateful streak, and it was easy for me to tap into it.

"Is that self-absorbed, self-naming, damned traitorous general really there!" he yelled from his side of the microphone.

I looked at Eric and took off my faceguard and cloth. We made eye contact while I winked at him. He got the drift that I had lied to motivate Director Kayre, and he started laughing quietly.

"Give me ten more hours and I'll wipe that eternal stain on my academy from the face of this universe."

"Give 'em hell, sir."

"Captain Gerald, I see your partner there, yet he is Helenac. Where are the embassy's security forces?"

It hit me in the gut when I remembered those men hanging like bats in the bunker before I cut them down. I grabbed the back of the chair; I wanted to throw it.

"They're—"

The director cut me off. "Don't. I know what you're going to say, and I don't want to hear it. We've already lost over two hundred fifty-seven men. We're going to lose more now." His eyes dropped to the floor. He hated losing people, even if he didn't know them. It was his job to save lives, not lose them. "Yet there is something that is bothering me. Only a few people on that planet knew they were there. And I mean only the embassy personnel and the high members of the planet authority knew about them."

The elevator closed its doors and went up. This stopped me and Eric. The director heard something but kept talking to me.

"Sir, the PFS know that Captain Eric Sherwood and I are here. I've got to go. Get those troops here, and damn it, hurry." I threw the microphone and chair to the side.

"Gerald, you get the hell out of there, and take care. We're counting on you."

He had never before said he was counting on me, even though he always was.

I grabbed my rifle and ran out through the door; Eric had already taken up his position and was aiming at the elevator. He was crouched and ready with a fresh magazine. I went into a prone position on the floor and pulled out three experimental rounds. I placed them, ready to arm them. Silence.

"Who was that?" Eric asked.

"Who was whom?" I responded.

"Who was who" Eric corrected.

Not many people had the privilege of correcting me. I just stared at him in annoyance.

"That one general your superior hates," he said, his rifle still aimed at the elevator. "Rommel, I think."

"A long time ago, back during the 1940s, there was a world war—the second one, not the third one from 2142. One general from the bad side—he wasn't bad, he was just on the bad side, the German side, the Nazi side—was named Erwin Rommel." I shifted myself on the floor to find a better firing position. When I did, I deployed the rifle's bipod. "Now this guy Erwin Rommel—brilliant guy, great with tanks and troops, both sides respected him—killed himself when a plot to kill his leader was discovered and he was found to be involved in it."

"So why is that general named after him?" Eric asked me.

"He isn't. His real name is Charles Miller. After they named my director the director of the UGF Defense Force and not him, he went insane, became an alcoholic, and defected to the PFS, the bastard."

The elevator descended again, and we shifted our attention to it.

For a moment, my heart stopped. For a moment, Eric stopped breathing and swallowed. The stillness played a quiet tune, and the sound of the descending elevator called unto us. The green hue of the visor made the shadows appear like a hooded figure that was ever shifting and closing on us.

There was a ding and the doors opened. The elevator was empty. I glanced at Eric, who stole a glance at me. He stood up and walked slowly to the elevator. I picked up my experimental rounds, stood, and slowly walked toward him. The moment seemed to slow down as a beeping noise registered in my ears and soon stopped. Eric stood not even eight feet in front of me as an explosion blasted against the wall to his left.

The fire and debris covered Eric as it pushed him to the floor. From the hole that emerged as a result of the explosion came a squad of PFS soldiers. They wore helmets that covered their faces and armor that drenched them in fearsomeness. When I saw who they were, my instincts took over. I slid to the floor, closed the face guard on my helmet, and aimed my rifle level with them, and the forty bullets that were in my magazine had soon been emptied into the red-eyed soldiers. It wasn't enough, though; only seven of them lay on the floor with puddles of blood growing from each of them. My breathing shook me. I pulled out both of my pistols and emptied them before my rifle fell to the floor. Two had survived this quick shoot-out. They aimed their rifles at me, and they would have shot me if I hadn't thrown both pistols at them. I jumped to my feet, and my hands made their way to the last long sword from the last surviving member of the old Ghost Battalion. One PFS soldier shouted as I sliced at him, yet he was quick enough to jump back and avoid being cut. However, he tripped on Eric's motionless body.

Eric! He was still on the ground, and he needed to get up to help save this world while I was on the sidelines.

The other PFS member took out his knife and raised it. As I walked toward him, I passed the soldier that had tripped and ran my sword through him. His subsequent cough brought up blood, and a pool began to form around him as well.

My hands went to my back and retrieved my knives

from their scabbards. I showed them to my opponent, and he swiveled his knife in the air. My lips were dry, and the darkness made my knees feel like jelly. We held our position, and I waited for him to come toward me. When he did, he came sprinting, yelling at the top of his lungs. The man swung the knife downward. I crossed my knives above my head and held his knife in the air. He grunted and head-butted me. His helmet smashed into mine but broke upon impact, making him scream in pain as the blood rushed down.

"Yeah, that wasn't the smartest decision," I said as I kneed him in the stomach.

The high-powered exoskeleton gave me a sick sense of power as he coughed up blood. After punching him in the face and throwing him to the ground, I grabbed my knife and stabbed him in the neck. His red eyes stared deep into mine, looking the way all eyes look when the life drains from them.

I cleaned the crimson blades on his shirt and put both of them back in my scabbards. I grabbed my sword, cleaned it on my victim as well, and put it in its sheath. I went to Eric and saw he was barely moving.

"Goddamit Sherwood you took that explosion like a champ," I cheered at him, slamming my hand on his shoulder.

He was lying on his side, hiding something. Darkness grew under him.

"Sherwood, what is that," I said upon noticing it. "Eric," I said in a more worried voice. "Eric." My hands rested on his shoulder as a groan escaped his lips. "Get up, buddy. We can rest later." I received no response from him. A great tingle crawled up my spine and into my heart. "Eric, don't. Please get up."

I turned him face up and saw that a metal rod had impaled him right through his stomach. Blood started to pool around him at a quickened pace, as his hands no longer were able to apply pressure to the wound.

"No!" I yelled, searching for his first-aid pack.

It was in his back pouch and was very different from mine. When I pulled it off of him, more blood began to pool around us. I opened it, took the cap off the metal needle of the anesthetic syringe, and injected the contents. It worked quickly, and he started to slow his wheezing. His condition started to worsen as he entered a state of shock. Looking back at his first-aid pack I began to search for medicine to stabilize his breathing. I threw out worthless medical equipment while searching for it. Eric put his hand on my shoulder, and I looked to the pool of blood around him. "Come on, man, you're going to make it. You're going to save the damn kingdom, and you're getting a damn medal. You're getting the guy or girl you want after this as well."

"She won't want it." His whisper sounded cold as he shook his head.

"The princess will hook you up; just stay with me." It then occurred to me what those expressions had been— the looks and sad eyes. I knew who he wanted, but she would not look at him; she looked at me.

"Eric, don't die."

Who was I kidding? I was no doctor, I was no medic. I wasn't going to save anyone. Eric was going to die of blood loss or shock. What a horrible way to die.

"Bastard," he told me weakly, or at least I was hoping he was telling me that.

He gurgled blood through his balaclava. I tried to take it off, but he weakly slapped my hand away.

"Only one bastard," he said.

I had no idea how to save him. I knew that the only capable cop in this damn city, maybe even this whole world, was dying next to me. It was sad that I was letting him die because of my ignorance in not having taken first-aid courses. I held on to him, hoping to ease his passing. He had a tear in his eyes, while mine had many.

"Knows of that hidden entrance," he said in an even weaker voice, his eyes closing.

I knew he was doing his best to stay alive. His blood touched my knee guards and was soaked up by my pants. His grip was loosening on my vest.

"Commissioner," I said blankly.

I looked at one of the PFS soldiers I had gunned down. He was crawling away from the scene. I must have missed his vitals, but at this point, the whole damn PFS could go rot in hell as far as I was concerned. Eric also noticed the dying man, and he reached for his pistol. He took it out and tried aiming it at the soldier with a shaky wrist. I helped him aim, but before he could even squeeze the trigger, he left me in a dark room with his blood on my hands.

Captain Eric Sherwood should have died fighting the PFS or the Goliaths. Instead he died ambushed in an underground bunker in my arms. He should have told me to keep the princess safe since he couldn't, or to get the PFS out of his world, or for his death not to go unavenged.

Or he should have said something defiant. Instead he said something about how we had been sold out to the PFS. What a terrible friend I was to let him die. It almost made me want to join him.

Before I let him go, there was something inside me that was fighting to be let out. It had been growing since Clo. From the deepest emotions of my heart, I let out a scream that shattered my very mind and soul.

# CHAPTER NINETEEN

## REVENGE

I was kneeling over my friend, looking at him. My only friend in this world. His blood was on my hands—literally, not figuratively, but at this point, it just didn't matter. I slipped his visor over his eyes. He was gone, and his eyes, empty and unseeing, did not need to view this world anymore.

It was a while before an idea hit me. I stood up and collected my weapons, which were still all over the place. Eric's blood was all over me, staining my green uniform even more. I placed my pistols in their holsters and strapped my rifle on my back.

In furious anger, I began punching the wall in a desperate and futile hope that I could bring him back. I kept doing that until there was a hole in the wall and a gash on my left fist. I heard laughter at that point—slow, quiet laughter. It was from the PFS soldier that Eric had tried to shoot. I grabbed the surviving soldier by the collar and stood him up.

"Where is he?" I asked him.

He spit on my visor. I balled my fist and shattered his

nose. Breaking this man was simple; he was giving me enough fuel to release all my rage.

"Where is he?" I asked him as calmly as humanly possible.

"Who?" he asked.

*To hell with the rules of war, to hell with these people.* A rage grew in me that tends to grow in people who don't vent their anger on something.

"The commissioner, the one who sold his planet to your government," I answered.

"You're going to kill me after I tell you, so die in a hole," he said to me, flashing an upside-down pinkie, a universally understood insult to my sister and mother. My response to that was to grab his pinkie and break it, right before slicing it with the exoskeleton's hidden blade.

"Damn right I am, and I might do it painlessly if you tell me quickly." I lifted him higher, and then I saw the bullet wound on his shoulder.

I put him down and crouched next to him, and I then pulled out my electro-rod and inserted it in his wound. He screamed at that action I switched to the interrogation option on the rod, and an electrical charge ran through his body; it was just enough to keep him awake and make him consider answering my question. His cries of agony were deafening in the corridor. I moved the electro-rod inside of him and pushed it in deeper so the bullet dug deeper into his bone.

"All right! All right! I'll tell you. He's due to move to the battleship in about an hour. He's on the embassy of the city, waiting for a drop ship to pick him up." At this point he started laughing and crying. What a vile man.

The blood flowing from his mouth enraged me more, as he could still bleed but Eric could not. To make sure he was not lying to me, I increased to the voltage to an almost lethal amount. His screams and cries of pain made my stomach jump and my heart pulse faster. I felt a sick pleasure at his agony; I almost wanted to continue.

"What's your plan, Captain? A drop ship and an attack ship are gonna be there, and your plan is to face them and kill him?" He laughed at my insanity while spitting his blood on my face.

"Yeah, that is exactly it," I said, getting up with Eric's pistol behind my back. "Where is he again?

"Crazy man, they'll kill you before you can touch him. He is on his way to the UGF embassy." He laughed and touched his shoulder in pain.

"Good." I took Eric's pistol from behind my back and shot him in the head.

I turned around and entered the elevator. I pressed the button before looking at the carnage in the hallway, and putting the electro-rod back into its holster. I didn't know which button I had pressed; I had just selected one at random to get me away from there. The elevator began to ascend as my eyes stared at my hands, which were bloody and trembling.

Static rang in my helmet as a beautiful voice spoke. "Okay, you're back. The signal broke up when you went lower. Wait, where is Captain Eric?"

My jaw quivered with that question, and she began to shake.

"He's dead," I answered. She covered her mouth, and her eyes started to water.

"I need a vehicle. I can't say why right now; I just need something fast," I replied.

"There's an experimental hovercycle in the hanger. It works, don't worry; I know."

She took it as my sister would take a death—sad but yet curious to see if it could have been avoided. Most times even I could not determine that.

On the control panel, I pressed the button for the hangar, and the elevator moved up. I took out my rifle and reloaded it, eventually doing the same with my pistols— just preparing for my suicide mission.

When the elevator stopped, the doors didn't open. I then remembered the power was out. I placed my fingers in the gap between the elevator doors and pulled, and I was able to open them enough to exit. This was a hangar and a storage place, something for kings. Old cars, new hovercars, experimental vehicles, and whatnot stood in rows. I searched until I found what I was looking for—a hovercycle.

Now, don't get me wrong, it would have been smarter to go back for the Creeper, or to have not left it behind. But I didn't have time to go back and get it. I needed to hurry and reach the embassy.

In the insanity of my mind, I found this funny. Just the previous day I was on Earth, bored out of my mind, not caring about anyone other than me and my sister. I was battling boredom. Now I found myself fighting for something again.

# CHAPTER TWENTY

## INSANITY

It took me a full minute to understand what I was going to do. I checked my wrist map and picked a route to take. I didn't look for an extraction, for I didn't care and had no thought of surviving this plan. I sat on the hovercycle and turned it on. Olivia was right about it still working. I would probably encounter spawn and squads of PFS soldiers. I began to hover with the craft and motioned it forward near the hangar doors. When I hit the accelerator, the craft shot faster and broke through the door. I was thinking of telling the princess when she called to me with her beautiful voice.

"You're going to help rebuild that, dear," she said.

"Yes, I will," I said in monotone.

"What happened?" she asked in my helmet.

I sped down a street and turned a corner. The events of what happened beforehand kept playing again and again in my head. Dawn was breaking overhead, and the monstrous Goliath roared somewhere in the distance. I took a deep breath and readied myself to tell her what happened. The faceguard automatically retracted into the helmet .

"We sent the message to UGF command. However, we got ambushed, and an explosion sent a metal pole into Eric's stomach. I couldn't save him. He died of shock and injury."

The day grew from its nightly companion.

"The commissioner betrayed this kingdom. You'll find he isn't with you anymore," I said to her.

She looked through the camera and into my eyes. She couldn't believe all these events were happening to her kingdom. I accelerated and hit a spawn that was crossing the road with others of its kind. Three screeched at me for my atrocity. On this ride, I began to think of my life.

In truth, I'm a harsh man. I pay little attention to my once great morals, and I have a nearly nonexistent conscience when I want to. But I am like that because I have allowed myself to be like that. A monster. Maybe this mission wasn't just a mission; maybe my luck or fate sent me there to change me. I needed to see a better version of myself. If I could not, then I had no reason to be alive.

As I passed streets infested with PFS soldiers and spawn, I said, "Tell me about yourself."

"Well, my birthday is February eleventh. I was born here on this planet. I like all types of rock and classical music. I don't know what else to tell you. Your turn."

"Well, I'm a terrible person. I've never been good with women. I have a sister, and we've never met our parents."

"You're a good person; you just don't always see it."

"Thank you. I'm glad I met you."

"I'm glad you said something first. I'm glad you came here. I've been so alone here."

It was during that moment that an epiphany was soon uncovered. The princess was a lonely spirit hoping for a companion. But that doesn't mean she was weak and fragile. No, she had a fire in her.

"So." She paused and smiled in my heads-up display. "We're married."

"We are." I hadn't even dated her; I married her straight away. What an idiot, I could hear the Ryan already yelling at me.

The first girl that I had an attraction to, she asked for marriage. Her smile was true and told me of her happiness. I couldn't bring it upon myself to kill her happiness. Would you have been able to do that to someone who cared about you, and whom you secretly cared about?

The more I thought of it, the more I realized that the Goliath was nowhere to be seen. I didn't think too much of it since I could hear it in the distance.

I knew what I wanted, yet I also knew it would keep me from my duty. Damn me.

After getting shot at by what seemed to be hundreds of squads of PFS soldiers, I made it to the UGF embassy. The towering building was actually tiny compared to the surrounding buildings. I still had about twenty-five minutes to reach the top of the embassy before the commissioner arrived.

I thought about it and decided to ascend a neighboring building. I remembered what had happened inside those walls. Those screams still sounded in my mind, but they were getting louder. We humans are monsters at times.

The building was an insurance company and was probably where all the city's money had gone to make sure no building or person was harmed during an accidental explosion from the mines. I entered the main lobby riding my hovercycle. No electronic devices were on; all screens were black, and all lights were dead. I rode to the stairs and went up with the hovercraft. It was a tight fit, but I was able to ascend past the UGF embassy high rise and saw the sun rising. Playing it safe, I went up three more stories and waited. That was all I could do.

"What are you doing?" Olivia asked me.

"Waiting for the commissioner. I'm gonna take him out when he gets on board the ship," I said to her.

"Gerald, don't do it. You'll get killed," she said.

I liked how she sounded worried about me; it made me feel a little better.

"I have to, or more secrets will get spilled," I said to her, smiling at the camera. It was a real smile.

She held her hands in front of her mouth. "Please … don't do this. I don't want to lose you." She began to sob.

I don't like seeing women cry, especially for me. It might not seem likely, because of my personality, but there have been women that have cried over me. And you might guess that I just didn't give a damn, but I just didn't know how to react to it. However, it bothered me seeing her cry; I didn't want to see her cry. I would stay alive for her. The thing I told my sister about me dying was that if all those thoughts about me dying were able to be erased, then damn me, I would take it.

"I won't; I promise," I said, and I meant that promise.

I meant that damn promise with every fiber of my body. I wasn't going to die, for her.

"Please come back to me," she said quietly.

"I will." My eyes closed when I made my promise.

She began to sing one of her songs—the one with the humming—and asked for me to return.

I took off my paraglider. The exhaust and thruster were blackened and not as big as those I had taken from the embassy. I removed the upgraded thruster from my pack and began switching it. My fingers were blackened and burned while removing the plasma converter. Then I switched out the engines and fuel tanks. The old thruster was a temporary jetpack and glider. With the task done, the old thruster was soon on the ground and the para-glider was over my pack. The intake began to charge itself, and a higher power concentration showed in my heads-up display.

From my vantage point, I saw the door from the roof opening. The commissioner came out, escorted by two soldiers that appeared to be from PFS special forces. This was going to be even more difficult than I had anticipated, and probably more enjoyable.

The soldiers dropped a beacon on the roof, and in about three minutes a drop ship and an attack ship de-scended from the orbiting battleship. The attack ship provided cover as the commissioner, wearing his black overcoat and combat boots, boarded the other ship.

The PFS special operations units entered next, which caused the drop ship to slowly ascend with the side door still open. My time to shine. I hit the hovercycle's accel-erator and held onto the brake while taking out the pistol

Herr Doctor gave me and shooting at the window, which made it crack. The attack ship moved closer to the building to investigate. The ship stood three meters from the cracked window and decreased its altitude in an attempt to provide the pilots a clear view. I released the brake and shot forward. The hovercycle broke the glass, and before leaving the building, I hit the ascending gear, making me ascend to the hovercycle's limit of five meters. I felt insane and extremely nervous, as I had no idea what might go wrong and disrupt my plan. Realistically, my plan should not have been working, but it was. I began shooting as I drew closer to the attack ship, and I abandoned the hovercycle when it rammed into the cockpit. I used the explosion of the hovercycle to push my paraglider into the drop ship. My pants caught fire as I rolled inside the drop ship's open doors.

The commissioner's eyes widened as I landed inside the ship. The special operations soldiers were taking off their rifles, and they looked quickly at me. There was one close to the doors; I punched him, and he screamed as he fell to his death. I grabbed the other one and hit him against the wall of the ship. He put his hands around my neck and tried to strangle me. His hands squeezed with an iron grip. He began to appear fuzzy and out of focus, which was likely an effect of the lack of oxygen in my bloodstream. My head began to hurt, and my grip on him loosened. I dragged him to the other side of the ship and hit his back against the ship. I then took out my knife and stabbed him in the stomach repeatedly.

While he spat out blood, I greedily breathed in the air from the planet. As I panted, I removed the knife and cleaned it on his uniform and took a vial of the drug from his chest pocket before pushing him calmly off the ship. He fell faceup, looking at me. His crimson eyes, glazed over, kept staring at me as they grew smaller. What a sight.

Apparently the pilots hadn't noticed anything, since they kept moving toward the battleship. I closed the ship's side door behind me and turned to face the traitorous commissioner.

"Now think this through," he said, trying to reason with me as he retreated to the other side of the ship. "A soldier from the United Galactic Federation is going to kill a commissioner from the Helenac Kingdom. You'll get court-martialed."

"Let me stop you there," I said, putting my left hand up, motioning him to stop.

"You stopped being commissioner when you betrayed your world, and you sure as hell became more of an enemy to me when you got Eric killed," I said, staring into his porcine eyes. "And another thing, my actions will not get me court-martialed; I have no jurisdiction over me from the UGF." As I spoke, I put out the remaining fire on my pants—not because I thought they might burn off, but because the pain was growing like a parasite.

From the glass, I noticed that we were nearing the outer limit of the atmosphere. I took my other pistol, the .454, and aimed it at the pilot through the metal wall. I fired, and the ship started to lose control and descend. I heard screams from the copilot and took him out as well. I placed my pistol back into my holster and lunged at the commissioner. He was stunned at such an action, and the coward climbed onto a tall chair, where he thought he was untouchable. I grabbed him by the neck and pushed him toward the side of the ship. Punching him in the face, causing his nose to bleed, I unleashed my full rage on him. I threw him across the ship and onto the floor, which was now uneven, since we were slowly falling. He slid toward me, and I picked him up and threw him to the ceiling. He fell onto all fours and then grabbed his gut and groaned in pain. I picked him up for the last time and pushed him toward the side door. We broke through the side doors of the ship. I was able to do that mainly because commissioner's protective armor and my exoskeleton were strong enough to do so.

"Ignem Farem!" My words were justice.

We began to fall, and this fall was very different from the first one I had. We were soon falling at terminal velocity. We were both screaming at this point. The commissioner, through his bloody nose, was screaming his head off in fear. I was yelling in anger, holding on to this pig. I grabbed a knife and stabbed him in the stomach. An eye for an eye.

It then occurred to me that I was falling also. I laughed in my head at my own stupidity. Was I doing this to show off to the princess? Hell, I might have been. Luckily the altimeter on my still strapped-on paraglider rang. I laughed aloud as I pushed the nearly passed out commissioner off me; he could die by himself. There was someone waiting for me. I flipped the switch, and the paraglider extended along with the thrusters. I ascended a bit but continued to descend overall. I looked down as the commissioner's body plummeted farther and farther, and faster as well.

It then occurred to me that my uniform had blood-stains all over it. Some were Eric's; the rest were from PFS soldiers. How horrible it looked—a green uniform stained with crimson. I came closer to the tallest building as the sun began to rise from the west, warming me from the cold embraces of the night. The green visor retreated into its compartment and was replaced by a light gold one. My mouth shield also retracted, and I let the sun hit my face.

I was about fifteen stories up when I saw where my unlucky self was landing: behind two PFS tanks and an entire company of snipers, riflemen, machine-gunners, and flying drones.

"I know where you are; stay there," Olivia said through my helmet.

"Don't! You'll risk yourself!" I shouted, but it fell on deaf ears.

I saw her stand up from her chair on my heads-up display, and she ran out of view of the camera. The timer showed about forty seconds before I landed, and I knew the paraglider would make noise as it retracted and re-fueled. As I neared the ground, I saw that the tanks and company were moving forward. Those tanks were dread-ful equipment. I took my rifle out and loaded an exper-imental round. I could now see that they were heading toward the body of the commissioner. It was a nasty sight, but he had deserved it.

I landed about fifty feet behind them—luckily far away. Yet, as predicted, my paraglider loudly retracted, and all but the tanks turned to look. I smiled, showing my teeth, while quickly running behind a building and into an alleyway. The PFS soldiers started to fire at me with their assault weapons and rifles. I heard the turrets of the tanks turning toward my position. Shouting and steps filled the air. A combat drone flew toward me, aiming its gun at me. I raised my rifle and quickly shot it down.

I saw that the way out of the alley I had landed in exited to a street lined with restaurants and stores with more floors above them. Drones quickly swarmed as I tried to shoot them down. The footsteps of about two hundred soldiers were catching up to me. I was shooting while retreating down the street.

There was a pizza store toward the middle of the street that had its windows opened. I sprinted to it, and the bullets seemed to race me there. After I jumped inside, the PFS units began to surround the exterior of the shop.

I was pinned down. There was soon a storm of lead as cracking electric rifles were used against me. When I poked my head up to see how many were outside, a round grazed my helmet and forced me behind stronger cover. Debris and dust covered me. A wall of bullets barricaded me deeper. An open door to my left provided access to stairs. As I crouched behind the register, my movements were stopped by a faint shout:

"Throw grenades in. Smoke him out!"A circular rock flew over me, making my blood curdle. It emitted a humming noise and it might have well spoken to me saying, "I'm not a rock." A shout escaped my mouth as I sprinted to the door while attempting to avoid the bullets.

As I checked my map, the drones and tanks began to close in. I took cover on the second floor and pulled two light strobes and an explosive from my pack. When I hit both strobes against my helmet, their membranes became permeable and they joined as one. Moving toward a window, I shot at the PFS at random to draw their fire. Having achieved this, the wall soon became a bullet magnet. After forcing the explosive device into the light strobe, I moved on to a different window to find a better angle from which to throw it.

I hesitated, took out a magazine, and emptied all forty cartridges into my hand. I carefully arranged them with the bullets pointing outward. The lightstrobe reminded me of a porcupine with bullets aiming out of it. I threw it over the firing crowd, and the PFS found it amusing that a floating ball of light was hovering at chest level. The electrical impulses began to heat the bullets and explosive device. I wondered if it would it be a difficult thing to watch.

Near the balcony on the other side of the building, a loud and horrible blast broke the windows where the PFS were. I was pushed down by the shockwave and shoved into a paying station.

A yell from a commander emerged. "Sound off! Vector Company, sound off!"

Very few voices called out. The tanks must have been fine, since they moved again, I didn't know how many I had killed in the blast, but I hoped it was enough to discourage them from pursuing me. I jumped off the balcony other side of the building to the ground floor, and my exoskeleton made a sickening pop as soon as I landed. A shot of pain ran through me.

"He's over here!" A soldier said from behind me when I landed.

"Don't kill him! He is to be captured alive. Alive, goddammit!"

In all truth, that made me feel a little more encouraged not to get caught. I sprang into the air, and my thruster activated and allowed me to jump toward the building on my right. My feet kicked off of it. Gliding in the air, the PFS attack troopers dropped from higher buildings and followed me in their jetboots. On my way around the buildings and along the streets, I dropped explosives for later use. The PFS took no notice, and I soon armed my detonator. The weakest of the followers couldn't reach my speed, and the fastest of the pursuers were either shot down or pushed down. When I reached street level, my glider had nothing in the reservoirs and needed to refuel. I ran into a different alley—a mistake that I hope I never repeat. The alleyway did not connect to the other street; a solid steel-and-brick wall stood at the midpoint, leaving me with no other place to go.

I had already used three magazines and had my back against the wall. So this was how I was gonna go. I loaded my fourth magazine and chambered my round. I aimed at the drones and incoming soldiers. I pressed the trigger three times, firing the experimental round that was still loaded. However, the drones and soldiers must have counted on that, because they moved out of the way. The round hit the building opposite me; the explosion ripped a hole in the front lobby and scattered debris on the street. Although it did more damage than the improvised explosive, it caused no fatalities.

"Well son of a bitch," I said, looking at the destruction I had caused.

The drones and soldiers also looked at it, then back to me. A few laughed and ran to the cover of trash compactors. The tanks covered the alleyway and aimed their guns at me. I took my sword out and slung my rifle on my back. If I was going out, I was going out fighting. Just then, a hand touched my shoulder. I looked back and saw that it was Olivia, in the flesh. She moved in front of me, as if she were trying to shield me. I tried to get her to move behind me, but she didn't budge.

What she did instead was take out a metallic controller. She pressed and held a green button on it, and soon there was a loud humming noise and a very sharp smell in the air.

"Lay down your weapons or we will fire," a PFS soldier on the tank turret announced.

"Olivia, get behind me," I said.

She instead lifted her hand to chest level, aimed the controller at the enemy soldiers, and looked at them. "Stop!" she yelled while releasing the button.

Her voice echoed into the alleyway and popped my ears.

Whatever that controller was, it released an enormous, powerful energy blast that caused the drones and the soldiers to be pushed flat on their backs or against walls.

She pressed and held the button again; this time she charged it longer. The soldiers began to stand up slowly, and the drones started to hover again. To be honest, I had also been pushed back, but only a little.

"Stop!" she yelled again as another sphere of energy expanded, pushing everybody back. This time the echo was louder and lasted longer. Call me crazy, but it seemed that the energy was coming from her.

She pressed the button again, and I held on to my pack. The air became still and the wind stopped. As princess of this planet, she became princess and master of the elements with the control in her hand. When everyone rose again—me, the PFS, and the drones—she put her hand in the air and released the button once more.

"Stop!" she yelled at the top of her voice.

A blue energy sphere surrounded us and expanded at an increasing speed. This blast was the most powerful yet. It disabled drones and pushed the PFS all the way out of the alley and onto the debris. Even the tank was pushed back to the building. This echo rang in my ears and might last a long while. The walls cracked, and PFS electrical equipment was disabled. The soldiers tried to pull the sizzling equipment from their bodies. However, that last surge of power must have drained Olivia of her strength, because she fell to the ground.

She had saved me, and now she was on the ground, in need of my assistance. I quickly picked her up and carried her in my arms. I found it strange that she had appeared behind me, since the wall in the alley cut off access to anywhere else. We were a strange sight—an olive-green dressed soldier holding a princess in his arms.

I turned around to see an open bunker door in the steel wall—and I was shocked, as I hadn't noticed anything there before—and I limped toward it. I was wondering what was causing me to limp. I thought that maybe one of the impacts had disturbed the calibration of the exoskeleton, or perhaps it had been jammed in the fall. Either way, I held her close to me. *I don't want to let her go*, I thought while placing my lips on her forehead.

# CHAPTER TWENTY-ONE

## SAFETY

**B**efore closing the bunker door, I saw the sun rise a bit more in the sky and heard the groans of the downed Ortyrans.

I descended into darkness like a space traveler exiting his craft in the starry cosmos. When I was little, back in the orphanage, I wished to be one every time I looked up into the night sky; but orphans are better soldiers, spies, and government agents than adventurers or explorers. No one misses orphans; that's why society would rather have someone famous lost in space than someone who is just another breath lost from the world. That's why everyone needs to push his or her way to the top. We must be who *we* want to be, not what the world wants us to be.

I walked down the stairs holding her close, occasionally looking at the steps or at her face. Eventually, as I reached the bottom of the stairs and walked into the dark corridor, the green visor replaced the gold one. I saw every design on the walls and floor. *Hexagons. Very nice; I like that design.* I felt fearful and cold because of something I can't explain other than by saying that it was a bad presence. I kept walking until I reached a motion-activated door. *Odd thing to find,*

I held Olivia close to me as the hatch opened automatically. Light shined on us, nearly causing me to drop the princess. The door led to the civilian bunker area. It must have been twenty miles across and fifty long, yet it was thriving with civilians. It wasn't jam-packed with them, so there must have been more rooms like these, all filled with signs and lights warning the citizens of the dangers above.

The people were walking around; couples were holding hands, people were whispering, children were being followed by their mothers, and police officers were pacing around and talking with worried mothers, fathers, and children. The whole place was fifty meters under me, and a catwalk extended from the door I was at to another door across the bunker. I began to walk on the catwalk, and it sprang to life and quickly carried me across the room. I looked at my wrist and saw that my map was showing me where I was and what was above me. It might have seemed strange to the people below to see a soldier dressed in olive green, covered in blood, carrying someone they all knew. When I reached the other side, I quickly opened the door to get in. There was a drone hovering in front of me, right in my face. It was a bit smaller than the PFS and UGF combat drones. Maybe half a foot, give or take a few inches. The drone was colored ash gray and sapphire, and it emitted green and red lights from its port. The little thing appeared to be depressed, if a drone can even appear to be so.

"You're right in my face," I said to the drone.

"My apologies, Captain Grey," the drone said in a very formal manner as it hovered backward.

"Where can I get a doctor? She passed out using some energy weapon," I said.

"Ah yes, it was the shock sphere. Very powerful, but it is quite draining on humans, apparently. We began mass production last week. Would you like one?" The drone asked.

"Yes ... no. Yes please, but just get me to a place to set her down."

"Well, Princess Olivia has many in her living quarters; you can set her down there," the drone replied, turning around to guide me to her room. "This way, if you please, Master Grey." The drone's butler-like manner annoyed me.

I followed that gray-and-blue drone as it led me to a corridor that had many rooms on both sides. All said "laboratory," but I doubted all of them were. It was strange to imagine what scientists do in their chemical laboratories, since all the good chemical findings Argon. Get it? You know because-oh forget it. If nothing else, science was one of the greatest gifts to humanity. If not for technology, I might have been in a church on Earth listening to how much of a sinner I was. I hate being called a sinner. And one other thing that would make me want to hate life more is that some of my friends would have been persecuted for choosing their own sexuality instead of being part of what was perceived to be the norm. It has never been clear to me why we don't like what other people choose for themselves. Is it so hard for people to accept others as being different?

The drone took me to the end of the hallway, and it must have activated a switch, because the door there opened by itself. In the room on the other side was a clean, organized mess. *I'm more organized than her.* I thought. Shirts, pants, dresses, blueprints, posters, electric screwdrivers, other articles of clothing, and mechanical apparatuses for anything from spaceship parts to hovercars were lying on the bed and the floor. What a mess! She had thrown these things on her bed, chairs, desk, and computers. I could tell by all this that she was a brilliant mind, but even if she weren't, I would still care about her. The walls were a dark blue, and the ceiling was black. I stared at the drone, hoping for it to tell me where to set her down.

"If you're looking at me for a place to put her, you should make room," it said.

That smart-alec drone was annoying.

"Gerald," She said weakly, struggling to open her eyes.

"She's all right; she just needs some rest," said the drone. "On account of security, however, I will not be leaving until the princess wakes up completely and orders me away."

"Fine by me, drone." I said, moving whatever gizmo she had on her bed so she could lie down.

I set Olivia down on the bed, pulled up a chair, and sat down. I stared at her while she slept. Even though I had slept for eighteen hours on the way over here, my whole night was tiring from the constant threat of dying or capture. The UGF would arrive by nightfall or the next morning. Even the strongest need help, and I know how to ask for help.

Recollecting my events made me realize what I had lost and what had been regained. Hope for me had been regained, but I had lost a friend. I had still not totally regained my humanity, but with the help of Olivia, anything was possible. I removed my helmet and placed the still-calibrating piece of armor on the nearby tabletop. I then removed my goggles, leaving my face cloth on as the only thing still covering my face. It was late on Earth, but seeing as how I had nothing to do for a long time, I assumed it was probably a good time to talk to my sister and see what she could tell me about my little change.

I scooted my chair toward one of the computers, turned it on, and opened a secure channel with my sister. Before the call went through, something caught my eye.

An unclosed tab showed a diary entry and video analysis from the surface. I clicked on the video, and it hit me in the gut to see footage of me fighting the PFS. There were more videos of me on Clo, in the Russian colony of Kyrgyz, and in the Chinese colony following the outbreak of a dangerous weaponized virus. I remembered Brain praying and hoping that the virus was a zombie virus. Even now I can hear his plea: "Please let it be zombies, please let it be zombies, I've been a good boy." The captain kicked his ass after the evacuation.

After looking at the videos of me, the temptation to read the diary entry was in my mind. Was it possible to betray the honor of being an honest man and take a peek at her diary?

It was, I realized while looking at the entry.

> He is the perfection I have always wanted.
> Disciplined, careful, and caring. How can I
> be wrong about him? I admire his courage,
> his strength, and his fearlessness. Looking
> at the way he fights, I know he will defend
> me with all he has and succeed. I know
> I promised never to have a boyfriend. I
> know what love does to people; it hurt
> me the first time. I'm glad I never gave
> him anything of mine. Neither a kiss nor
> myself was ever given to anyone will-
> ingly, but I want it to be for him, for sweet
> Gerald. Not myself, for love now has been
> too sexualized. Can it not be for feelings
> and care? I'm a very broken heart, and I
> have the scars to prove it, but he can heal
> me. The child ... the things they did to
> me ... It's been so long. I don't know how
> to tell him. Will he still see me the same?
> I'm not what I seem. I hope he kills the one
> that did that to me, since my father didn't.
> I hope he can heal me and keep me safe.
> Please, God, I don't even think you're real
> anymore. You gave up on me, but please, I
> hope he is here to help me.

There was another update on that entry, and it prompted me to save everything and download it on my wrist tablet. In that moment, something died inside me.

The feeling of mercy was no longer in me. The drone did not see it, and I would not admit this to anyone, but I felt something move down my cheeks. The salty fluid did nothing to rid me of my pain and anger. They had done something to her when I was not even aware that she existed. They had made her go through something, and I could not stop it. I hate people. I hate monsters that are humans. I hate them; I can't stand them. We ruin ourselves. We shouldn't be allowed to live. Maybe I could go back in time and save her. The space-time continuum could kiss my ass if it meant I could save her. Do you understand what she went through? Do you know what she feels? You would criticize her, call her a freak, if she were not a princess. You have my hate because you did not save her but instead criticized her and laughed at her. I hate you all. You called her names and did not even ask about her story. I would never abandon her or let anyone harm her anymore. I swore this on my life.

Before returning to call my sister, I set the tabs on the computer back to the way they had appeared before I watched the videos. The drone's fierce stare burned into my back; the thing seemed to be monitoring what I was doing, and those little eyes couldn't blink, which made it more nerve racking. Wiping the expression off my face and letting the visor hide my eyes, I waited for my sister's answer. There was a click and four rings, and finally she answered. My goodness was she tired looking. Her green eyes had bags under them, and her glasses and uncombed pink hair was not helping either. I might have had blood on me, cuts on my face and arm, but at least I was sharper looking than she was.

"Hello, sister, why is it that I could contact you but not UGF command?" I asked with a smile on my face. I just love annoying her sometimes. This made it seem as though I were the younger sibling. I did not let her see my eyes, even though she was the closest person to me.

"I hate you, but I still love you," she replied.

"Oh, I love you too, sis. Listen, you're home right?"

"I just got home. Why do you keep everything so organized? It hurts my eyes to come home from that neat office and find you have everything neat also," she complained.

"Well, you don't clean. You barely cook. I have to do almost everything, just like when we were kids," I reminded her.

"Why are you wearing your helmet?"

Her question stung.

"Because I can," I said.

"Oh my god, you're in Helena, aren't you? Gerald, do you know how bad it is right now?"

"I think I know how bad it is; I'm here seeing everything firsthand."

"Is the Protectorate really there? Gerald, have they shot at you?"

"Yes to both, but I'm fine."

"You don't look fine; you look awful."

"Some things have changed."

"I can tell; you're giving off a different aura—a familiar one, though."

A smile crept across my face. I could always count on her.

"The news is bad here. Millions of soldiers have been

mobilized and are making their way to you. Thousands of tanks, Mechanized Heavenly Devils, and ships were being moved from bases here on Earth and all over. Director Kayre is getting approval for more carriers and battleships. You should have seen the protests."

"I can only imagine. Tell me about them."

"About a billion people in India and China combined have been protesting about the mobilization," she said while trying to fix her hair. "Brazil has millions walking on the street, hoping they will be brought back. Internet polls think that this is another rogue colony being taken over by rebels. But that was five hours ago."

"What do you mean five hours ago? Do you mean something's changed?"

"Yeah, big time. The president gave a speech with Director Kayre. They showed your recording with the cute cop about the PFS. Director Kayre had us tight-lipped about your mission at first, since it was a covert one to retrieve the king and his family, but now the whole UGF knows the PFS is back!"

Two things bothered me, the first being that she had not even seen Eric's face, and the second one was just how big this conflict was now.

Running my fingers through my hair with unease, I was reminded of when I was in school learning history. It must have felt this way for children in England hearing about the German troops invading Poland, or children in Mexico hearing about the US invading Panama. This feeling was the feeling everyone got when they heard that the old Russian Federation invaded Crimea and set fire to Kiev and the rest of the Ukraine in their time. A calm before the storm of war is the worst calm.

"Who's that?" She asked, looking up and seeing Olivia.

"Princess Olivia, heir to the Helenac throne, daughter of our king," the drone said.

"Yeah, yeah, yeah, that's who," I said to the drone. "She saved me. Listen, I have a lot of time to kill. UGF will be here late, maybe at night, maybe in the morning. I'm not sure."

"Is that blood?" Evelyn asked as she stood up to look at me.

"It's not mine. It's not mine. None of it is mine," I replied, looking at my gloved hands.

"What happened? What have you done?" she asked, all worried now.

I sighed and looked at the still passed-out Olivia. I turned back and prepared my story. It was about an hour later when I finished telling her.

"Sad. I'm sorry about your friend, Gerry. You have so much blood on you," she said with tears in her eyes and her hand over her mouth.

"There's gonna be more casualties. Ryan had better send as much as he can. We can't let the PFS win," I said solemnly.

I heard a voice behind me. It was Olivia. "More soldiers?"

"I'm sorry; it's the one sure way we can get them out of the city," I answered her.

"You're Olivia. I'm Gerald's little sister, Evelyn."

"Olivia," she said, introducing herself with a beautiful smile.

"So my brother tells me you saved him," my sister teased.

"I might have," Olivia said humbly.

"Oh, I like her, Gerald. Honey, I love you like my sister now."

"You're so adorable, just like Gerald," Olivia replied, hugging my neck.

"Well, please keep him safe. I need to get ready to go back to the ..." Evelyn said before passing out.

It was night on Earth, and she needed to sleep. She had the habit of passing out like that, even if she was talking to someone. She was always desperate to sleep.

"She's fried," I said, closing the communication widow. I should explain that it was a civilian model. Civilian models could only talk to other civilian models. Same for military ones. The good thing was that after an incident with a spy agency, communications manufactures had made their products strictly two-way devices with no way for communications made on them to be monitored or intercepted.

"How many soldiers are coming?" Olivia asked.

"I don't know. Hopefully over a few million. Maybe a few battleships and a couple carriers. I don't know, but we need more than enough to destroy the PFS."

She placed her hands on my neck and noticed the tabs she had left open. At the speed of light, she closed them, not noticing that I had downloaded them.

"Mr. Cat," she said, "You are free to go now."

"As you wish, madam." The drone hovered out through a port on the door.

"Mr. Cat? I don't think it likes me."

"She doesn't like you."

"It's a she?"

Her laugh brought me joy and happiness. As I held her hand in that bunker, I wanted to stay like that with her forever.

"Excuse me, but why aren't there any PFS soldiers, or even drones, here in these bunkers?" I asked.

"The bunkers are our best-kept secret. Did you know about it? No. The UGF doesn't know. Not even the PFS knows."

"But wouldn't the commissioner have told the PFS?" I asked, worried.

She didn't answer, but she looked surprised, with her mouth open. I stood up and grabbed her hand. We left the room and almost ran into Mr. Cat.

"Where are we going?" Olivia asked.

"We have to get you and your father out," I said to her. Drone, where is the king and all important personnel?"

"Sir," said Mr. Cat, "the majority of Helenac council is off world right now. Location classified. The king, however, is with the chief of staff and some of the other planetary chiefs in the control room."

"Where are they, and don't waste any time; we need to hurry, hurry, hurry," I said, clapping Olivia's hand against mine to emphasize my words.

"Gerald. Wait, please tell me what are you doing?" she said.

I could tell I was scaring her. I held her arm and pulled

her close to me, hugging her. "I need to get you out of here. You and anyone else the PFS would execute if they were to capture you. Now come on."

But she didn't leave. No, she just stayed there with me hugging her. My brain went haywire, but I stood there with her hugging me. Where were her scars? Where would I put her back together?

She pushed me away, took my hand, and guided me to her father. We ran through corridors; Mr. Cat had trouble keeping up.

We had no idea how much time we had before the PFS came for the high-ranking officials. Or for the civilians. We passed through the corridor where I was first interrogated by the police officers; however, some now lay in body bags, others were in worse states while still alive. The ones who were not injured were tending the wounded or moving around to the places they should be.

We ran through the corridor, and I jumped over boxes of pistol rounds and dwindling medical supplies. I passed a hallway in which many doctors were either giving blood transfusions or taking blood from the uninjured. Many officers looked at us and tried to get out of our way. A thought occurred to me.

"Those SWAT guys that came in the room when they interrogated me ..." I stopped and looked at Olivia.

"Carl!" she yelled.

A cop ran up to her and bowed his head, trying to catch his breath. He stared upward and saluted her. Although he wore a very heavy vest under his uniform, he appeared to be too young to easily deal with the horrors of the outside.

"My lady. What can I help you with," Carl said.

"Captain Gerald needs the special officers. And you too," Olivia said.

He ran back, grabbed his pistol, and spoke into his transmitter. Nine officers came out of the crowd of police officers; a few were rolling their sleeves down and taking off bandages from the blood donations. I motioned for them to follow us, and Olivia took my hand to lead me to her father.

"Have you detected any breaks into the bunker or lost communications with any entry point?" Their confused faces showed me what I had feared.

"Have there been any intrusions to the bunkers? Have the sensors picked up anyone trying to force their way into the bunkers? Come on, this is important."

"We've lost communication with the king. And there was an opening to the hatches in sector four-alpha-lima-two," one of them said.

"That's the hatch we used to enter," Olivia said.

"Yes, but the PFS are still around that area, and we have visual of teams trying to survey the wall."

"Wait, when did you lose communication with the king?"

"About the same time we lost visual with a squad of PFS. Oh ..." They soon realized the gravity of my failed responsibility.

"My mission here was to extract and protect the king and his family after I knocked out the jammer. And now you're telling me that you have lost contact with the king right after a PFS squad disappeared?" According to my standards, these men were incompetent.

"Gerald." Olivia's hand was on my shoulder. Her voice soothed my anger. "It's not their fault. Don't get mad at them."

"Get your weapons ready; we might have a hostage situation," I said, turning around to face them.

They all took their pistols out and chambered rounds. Many twists and turns later, we came to a heavily reinforced door. Keeping Olivia at a distance, the police officers soon took positions. I twisted the hatch and pushed it, yet it didn't open. The officers looked worried and tried to hear what was behind the door. A crowd of other police officers in their dark sapphire-blue uniforms and doctors stood where Olivia was watching. Many voices began to murmur, and all eyes peered at me. Social pressure is a great motivator for me; it implores me to find a way to keep myself from drawing attention.

I took off my pack, and my hands made their way to the last explosive I had. I placed the explosive on the metal frame and entered the calculations for how severe the explosion was to be. I set it to break the locks and open the door. We all stepped back and covered our ears.

After the device detonated, the police breached the room with me behind them. The door had been knocked clean off and rested on the couch, smoking. Inside was the king, looking at a holographic map of his city and the movement of the PFS. If the explosion did not put the fear of me in him, then I have no idea what would. Various maps, holograms of the bunkers and all who were in them, and a hologram of the battleship were on display. With the dozen or so chiefs of staff looking at me and kneeling, it was apparent that they were safe.

"Well, hello, I was just here to check if your door could withstand a breaching charge. Which it didn't." Olivia chuckled from a distance.

"Captain, what in the hell is the meaning of this?" One of the chairmen yelled while dusting off his blue coat.

"Well, you see, a PFS squad disappeared near a bunker entrance right when communications with this room disappeared."

"And you believed they entered and came here?" The king asked.

"Yes, sir."

"Well, good thing you came; I need you to see this," the king said while extending his hand.

I walked closer to the holographic map monitoring the battleship. The councilor had a digital notebook and touchscreen pen and was taking notes. I was able to see its name: *Spirit of Vengeance*. This was the PFS forward expeditionary ship. An alarm sounded, and the councilor called for the king's attention.

"Sir! We have more ships entering orbit. We have two. No, three. Dammit, now five ships. Three battleships and two carriers."

"How can this be?" the king, said walking toward that map.

Everybody crowded around the hologram, and sure enough, that is what we saw.

Once in orbit, the carriers began sending drop ships to the capitol. Pods then ejected from the battleships and headed to the surface. I was certain that these pods carried Fallen Angels and drones. A ring sounded from one of the monitors, and the king moved to that one.

"Yes, yes I see it." There was a pause after the king spoke to the man on the monitor.

"Where the hell is the UGF?" the man asked, distraught.

More people joined the channel and began talking, all asking the same question.

"Did the UGF forsake us?" one asked.

"Are they running from this military?" another asked.

"We're doomed, I say, doomed," said one with his hands on his head.

Arguments over who should be taken to even more secure locations began to erupt. The sad thing about humans is that when our lives our threatened, few help the rest. These people had lost hope in my government, and in a sense, since I represented my government, they had lost hope in me. I stood behind the king and looked at every one of those police officers. The words surrounded my head; the shouting fought to enter my mind. Standing there to see who would break first wasn't my style. I took out my dog tags and looking at the oath on them. It was time to step up.

"I'm here." I said.

"Who are you?" one of the persons from the screen asked.

"Captain Gerald Grey, UGF Defense Force agent and current sole protector of Helena. Now, the UGF did not abandon you; I postponed their coming and told them to bring a bigger army. We first thought we were fighting spawn and Goliaths, not the damn PFS. And you damn well know we leave no person behind. Now shut up and wait. They'll be here by nightfall."

"How are you so sure? How do you know they aren't abandoning you also?" another person asked.

"Because I know my people, and they will never let the PFS take this world or leave me. There is an oath everyone who works in the Defense Cabinet swore. It reads as such: I vow in heart and spirit to defend those who cannot defend themselves; to strive to protect the gift of life, for it is a right for all; to fight for the majority and, if necessary, to sacrifice my blood and air that others may live; to uphold the peace; and to never know defeat or give in. I swear to defend the innocent, whatever the cost."

"We're all going to burn," I heard from one of the monitors, yet the rest began to clap.

"Now, King ..." I didn't know his name.

Olivia ran toward me. "Richard," she whispered.

"King Richard, we need to get you out of here. I forgot to mention that you had a traitor among your trustees. Don't worry; I took care of him. But I believe he did divulge information about the bunker and your location," I said, touching my stubbly chin. Damn five o'clock shadow, it was itchy and needed a shave.

"Who was the traitor?" one councilor asked.

"The police commissioner," I answered. This caused many shouts and much arguing. I listened for about a minute before taking out my pistol and firing it into the air. That got everybody quiet. These politicians were getting a little too annoying; they needed to learn to listen.

"Get what is important and meet me outside," I said. "We have little time, maybe five minutes. Now hurry."

"Where are we going?" the king asked.

"To the last place they'll expect us—the castle," I said.

"Are you insane?" a police officer asked.

"I might be. But we have to go now. I have to get you all out. Not for my sake, but for yours. I know what the PFS do to prisoners, and believe me; I do not want you to face that." I looked at Olivia specifically.

"Hurry, please," Carl said, pushing people away and turning off the projectors.

The king and every councilor and chief of staff was picking up electronic equipment. There were about twenty people in this room, all scattering to get equipment, all scattering to help one another.

I went outside and waited for them. The thought of what would happen to Olivia if she were captured by the PFS crossed my mind. They would torture her in both mind and body. The last thought made me shudder, for who knows what barbarian would do such a thing to her. I would rather have had all the suns in the universe explode than let the PFS touch Olivia—I mean the king. Oh, who am I kidding, of course I meant Olivia. She was the one that truly mattered to me. Had she said the word, I would have abandoned my post and the king to be with her. A minute later, Carl came outside. He was a young lad, maybe nineteen.

I wondered if they were recruiting kids these days.

"Are you serious? Are we going to the castle?" he asked.

"Yeah, but we need to hurry."

And hurry they did. Four minutes later, they all had packs full of supplies—all except the police officers—and they were all outside with me. What a group of misfits. I really didn't know what to call them all. I motioned for them to walk toward the left of the hallway. My wrist map had finished mapping the whole city, including the bunker. I picked a route that would lead us directly into the castle. We passed citizens, police officers, doctors, and children, all of whom looked at us. I felt their eyes move from the king toward the princess and finally to me, where they stayed. Thousands of eyes stared at me. My knees began to weaken and my stomach churned because of the unwanted attention. I went on to the computer of the map and attempted to take control of the speakers that ran along the bunkers. Failing to do so, I asked Olivia to do it.

"Don't worry, sweetie; it was just the code you needed, and I have it." Her smile added insult to injury.

An entire city watched its king flee, though he did so against his will. I couldn't imagine what people would do if the president walked out of the White House right now; I bet half of them would celebrate and the other half would scream.

To keep my mission from hitting the drain, the king needed to be moved somewhere else. I could see the horror in the eyes of the people as they watched the war coming home and took note of the pressing matters that forced me to carry my rifle across my chest. When politics and peace talks failed the one thing that kept me alive—my rifle—was the only thing that really worked. As terrible as it may sound, that is the frank truth.

I linked my headset with the P.A. system. Hope—I had to give that to the citizens. *Maybe they'll like me enough to stay with them here on this planet*, I thought.

"All citizens of the Helenac Empire, this is Captain Gerald M. Grey of the United Galactic Federation from the planet Earth," I said. "As you are all aware, your world, your city, and your kingship have been attacked. I understand this has never happened in many, many orbital rotations of your sun. But do not lose hope; my people are coming. We are coming to beat the Protectorate Federation of Systems and expunge them from your planet. Just hold on, please, as things are going to get messy. Just stay strong. They will not harm you, and I swear to this star that I will not let them harm your king, your princess, or you. This is Captain Grey. Over and out."

By the end of my speech, everyone was looking at the loudspeakers.

"Some hope for the people, Mr. Grey?" one of the chiefs of staff asked.

"Yes, sir. Some hope," I said, smiling.

"M? I don't remember a middle initial in your file, Gerald, honey," Olivia said, getting closer to me and holding my hand. "Does it stand for something?"

"Murdoc. Gerald Murdoc Grey is my full name," I said while walking down the hallway with everybody looking at me.

"And what is your sister's name?" she asked.

"Evelyn Amelia Grey." I answered. "Are you interrogating me, Olivia?" I joked.

"Maybe I am," she said, laughing.

I looked at my wrist and noted the direction we were headed. It was about half an hour later, after we had passed possibly a million people, when we reached the ladder to the hidden entrance of the castle. I grabbed my rifle and held it at the ready. The police officers approached, and from what I saw, it appeared that they pushed the roof up. Light shined into the bunker, and one by one the police officers disappeared from view. I motioned for the king and his chief of staff to go up next, and I waited until it was me and the princess left. I was in a dilemma as to who would go up first, me or her.

"Well here's the thing," I said, reasoning with her, "You're wearing a dress, and if you go up first ... well, you get the idea."

"You aren't leaving me here alone are you?" she said, hugging me and getting close to my face, which was still covered by my face cloth.

I could imagine my face was red, for never had I been like this with another girl. She put her arms around my neck and moved much closer to me while removing the face cloth.

"I've waited for you all my life. I knew it was crazy, but I knew you would come anyway," she said.

With that smile of hers showing as always, she put her forehead on mine, and we stood there with the light shining on us. My hands were still at my sides, and my mind was floating somewhere over Venus.

"Oh, you dummy, haven't you seen a love projection? You put your hands around my hips," she said.

"As you wish, madam." We both laughed.

I put my hands where she told me as my heart pounded. I stared into her brown eyes as she smiled and looked away from me. She was still smiling even as she looked away. I smiled at her and pulled her closer to me. She finally looked me in the eye again before shutting hers, moving closer to my face, and pressing her lips against mine.

# CHAPTER TWENTY-TWO

## WHO?

I climbed up the ladder with Olivia on my back, holding on to me. She giggled as I pulled us up. Every so often she would kiss my cheek, and I kept blushing more and more. It was ridiculous of me, but I liked it. Everyone should have a person—it doesn't matter who—to do that to him or her. The kissing and caring part, that is, not the carrying (but the carrying is optional). I reached the entrance, and the police officers offered their hands to Olivia and pulled her up to the castle. Carl offered me his hand, and I took it. A police officer then closed the hatch and placed a tile over it. They circled the area and secured it. I looked at my wrist map and pointed the way.

I took a step, and the loudest squeak I have ever made issued from my foot. I stopped and looked around, but the only ones looking back at me were the group I had brought with me.

"Sorry," I said, and I heard Olivia snort at that.

I placed my next step on a different tile, and this time no noise was made. We walked from the ballroom toward a hallway in a single-file line. I was in the front, and the police officers were at the rear. As we passed four patrols and drones that were moving equipment to the outside plaza, we could see that they did not expect us here. We walked until we reached the correct door. The hallway was about fifteen feet high, and we were able to easily walk five abreast. I looked outside the window and saw that it was already past midday.

The view was beautiful. Even with the enemy ships in the sky and the smoke, fire, semi-destroyed buildings, spawn here and there, enemy soldiers and vehicles, occasional transport or attack ship, and minor discomforts, the city was still breathtaking. I wonder how the city was able to stay so beautiful. Maybe because the king and the government cared so much for its citizens that they must have spent a great deal on the city. Helena had fountains, monuments, plazas, parks, recreational centers, government-built skyscrapers, and the most advanced transportation center in the universe. It must have been a true joy and pleasure to live there. Hell, they even had a great social security system and health care system. On Earth, the UGF debt ran in the decillions as a result of constant spending on defense. A single carrier cost forty-nine hundred trillion credential dollars. A Heavenly Demon mechanized infantry suit cost fifty billion. A single soldier ran into the millions. The point of the matter is that more money was spent on killing people than on maintaining their standard of living, and I can prove that because I still don't have an automated drone in my own house that cleans up for me and Evelyn. Not every planet that was part of the Federation was as luxurious as Earth, and even that was because of the centuries of life on that planet.

"Captain Gerald? Are you all right, son?" a chief of staff asked.

I stopped my daydreaming and turned back. I had no idea who had asked me that. Hell, I had no idea what any of their names were.

"Sorry. Yes, I'm all right. This way."

I opened the door to the security room. Inside were monitors and hologram monitoring devices similar to those in the underground bunker. Everyone except the police officers got behind pieces of equipment and turned them on. Carl approached me; it still amazed me how young he was.

"Captain, what about the PFS?" he asked me, his hand on his holstered pistol.

"Well, as I said, they aren't expecting us to be in the castle," I answered, sitting down on a bench and inspecting my Hornet by taking it apart.

"How are you so sure? I mean look at this. Look!" he said to me.

I took my eyes off my rifle and glanced at the twenty other people on the monitors and holograms.

"Don't you see, these are the most important people to this planet, and you put them in the lion's den. You can't actually believe they are safe. With thousands of soldiers preparing for a fight and perhaps a million already having been dropped from the ships, we aren't safe here."

I calmly took my kit out of my back pouch and started to clean my rifle. I couldn't look up at him, because I thought he might have a point. Cleaning the rifle brought the thought of Eric's dead body to my mind. I looked at my black gloves and my trousers, both smeared with blood. It made me stop cleaning and gave me trouble breathing.

*No, the people are safe here*, I thought. My mind had deceived itself.

"Do you believe in second chances, Carl?" I asked him.

"Yes, I do. But why are you asking me that?"

"The day before I arrived here, I should have been killed by a scorcher. A fully grown one, too. The city it was in ..." I paused there. "The whole city was destroyed—everyone killed. It was hell there. Yet I was able to save two nurses and four babies. But I saw that when I fought the scorcher, I should have been among the bodies. But I wasn't. I can't let this city face that same fate."

"Thank you. But you are not answering the question about the PFS," Carl said. Wow, he was stubborn.

"Well, since you asked, I'll take it to mean you volunteered. We are going to take the fight to the PFS and take your king out of here to a safer location."

That made his blood leave his face; he was paler than a scorcher. He trembled at the thought of such a new objective. I was glad that worked.

"You ... can't be serious," he said, stuttering.

I finished cleaning my rifle and began putting everything in my kit. I removed the remaining ammunition from my pouches and the hundred-round drum magazine from my belt, and the pistol magazines from the pouches on my leg and back. There was one plasma grenade in the backpack. The plasma compensator was also in there, and when I assembled the rifle, I made sure that it wasn't left out, since it was extremely useful. If I ran out of ammunition, the compensator could temporarily shoot superheated plasma shots like combat drone rifles.

"Who is your fastest shooter?" I asked Carl.

"Church is. Yo, Church, Captain needs you!" Carl yelled across the room.

A police officer ran toward us. He apparently didn't know what to do, as he offered his hand for a handshake but quickly retracted it to salute me.

"Put your arm down before I shoot it down," I said. "Now, I need you to help me."

"With what, sir?" he asked, appearing to be a little shocked.

"Below this castle lies another bunker. I need backup to get there." I scratched my chin.

"Just that?" he asked.

"Well, if we don't run into trouble, yeah, that'll be it."

He sighed in relief. I hoped that it would be just a simple in-and-out operation. I stood up and felt incredibly sleepy. All this running around had me at the verge of exhaustion. I decided to take a nap and go to the bathroom if I made it back. And maybe eat something. But I would definitely go to the bathroom..

"Come on, you two," I said, moving toward the door.

A shock raced through my body, and I was paralyzed. The exoskeleton was locked; it emitted sparks while sending electrical impulses to my nerves.

"Where are you going?" Olivia's voice said in my helmet.

I was able to turn my head and look at her on a monitor. She pulled the screen's holographic projection with her fingers and placed it on a tablet.

"I need to get some things and communicate with UGF command about stuff," I said.

Carl and Church at this point were trying to push my legs forward and remove the armor plates. "Save your strength," I said. "This exoskeleton is stronger than both of you. Just wait for me outside the door."

"You can't leave me, Gerald," Olivia said, lowering her gaze.

"I need to do this. I promise I'll be back," I pleaded. *How the hell did she hack my exoskeleton?* I wondered. The scientists back home were not going to be happy about that. She got off her monitor and stretched her arms. She then grabbed her bag and took out a pair of white gloves with blue sensors and lights on them. She put them on and looked at me.

"Look what I can do now, honey," she said, turning the sensors on.

"Remember how my program told you about our link? When I was a little girl, I had an accident. I had to get a chip implanted in my head. Now, after many years, I can control or hack into equipment. Including yours."

"What are you gonna do?" I asked her.

She switched the gloves on. I heard my exoskeleton beep, and no longer was I able to will it to move. Olivia, from her position, reached to her back and grabbed something. I, in turn, had my arm moved by force. The exoskeleton was under her control, and I did not like this.

"Promise me that if you come back alive, you and I will go and talk," she pleaded.

"Just that? That's a small request, but I'll do it. Just let me go, please, I need to send more intel to the UGF."

"Remember, you promised," she said, taking off the gloves and showing me her beautiful smile.

The exoskeleton powered down and recalibrated. I was again able to move and walk. She looked at me and came running. I opened my arms to her, and she embraced me. We stood there for a minute, and then I walked back, leaving her where she was standing. I turned around and put my face guard on. I couldn't think straight, something distracted me, and even I didn't know what..

I opened the door and walked out to find Carl and Church waiting for me. I walked in front of them and sat down on a bench that was near a window. I was feeling depressed. I had made promises to people I might never see again. The sun was setting, and I needed to move before the fleet arrived. And also try not to get killed— no forgetting that. But I think I preferred it that way. I walked back to the grand hall and made my way to the stairs and elevator.

"Captain—"

"Keep quiet. And hurry," I ordered, cutting Carl off.

I didn't want to talk; I just wanted silence and time to think. To be honest, I might have been walking aimlessly, thinking of what I had done with Olivia.

Who was I? I was, in reality, a nobody. I was an orphan who had kissed the princess. I was not the perfect person for her. And in the back of my mind, I had the feeling that the princess might not really like me. Unfortunately, I really liked her.

I pressed the button for the elevator to open, and I stared at the glass doors of the palace. I could see the PFS preparing their defenses.

I entered the elevator and inputted the same code Olivia had told me.

"Zero nine one zero nine six," I said blankly as I pressed the numbers on the touchpad.

"Hey Captain, you know where we're going, right?" Church asked. There was fear in his voice.

"Yeah, there's an unconnected bunker here, and I need to reach it," I said, thinking of my last visit. I then remembered what else had happened.

"Hey, none of you happen to have a body bag do you?" I asked.

Carl and Church looked at each other with their eyes wide open. Their faces were as pale as Nosferatu.

"Not for you, you idiots," I snapped at them.

"Ye ... yes," Carl said. He handed it to me from his back pouch.

"You know, if you have one of these with you, it worries me," I said to him.

The elevator reached the bunker and I exited. Eric's body was still there. I handed Church the bag, and he nodded. I approached my friend's body and saw that his eyes were open.

"Sorry, Eric, I couldn't save you. I'm sorry I couldn't do anything about the rod." I knelt beside him. "You didn't deserve this, man. I'm sorry. I avenged you. I killed him. Did the stupidest thing and destroyed two ships, but I got the commissioner. He's dead. If only I could undo what has been done, then you would still be alive. I'm sorry. I'm going to take your ammunition. I need it to do what you should be doing but can't." It was strange to talk to his dead body like this. He wasn't gonna reply; why bother?

"Sir, ready?" Church asked, having set up the bag for us to place Eric in it.

I grabbed his magazines and placed them in my pouches. There was a lot of ammo, but I took what I could. I grabbed Eric by the arms as Church grabbed him by the feet. We set him down on the bag, and Church closed it up and started writing on the tag his cause of death, rank, and name. I went to the squad of PFS soldiers, where I picked up two rifles and whistled at Carl. He turned around, and I threw him a bullpup rifle. He caught it and inspected it. I handed one to Church, and he looked at me strangely.

"Grab ammo; you are both weakly armed," I said to them.

They went scurrying for ammo as I walked to the communications room.

I sat down on the same chair I had sat in last time and opened a communications window with the UGF Defense Network. This was an open channel heard only by the UGF.

"UGF Network, This is Captain Grey in the Helenac Kingdom, over."

"Captain Grey what is your status?" a woman with an Indian accent answered.

"I need a direct line with Director Ryan Kayre."

"Hold on." There was a pause. "Logs indicate he has departed from the Havoc station. He is on the carrier UGN *Schatten*. I can try to connect you; please hold."

*The UGN* Schatten, *I thought. That is the newest carrier in service.*

"Schatten? What language is that?" Carl said upon entering the room.

I stood up and jumped to the door.

"It's German. Means "shadow," I think. Anybody answers, tell me." With that, I left the room.

I went to the nearest PFS body. I ransacked his packs and found explosives. On his belt were a thermal grenade, an impact grenade, two detonators, and a food pack. There was more equipment in his packs, but Carl called me from the room.

"Captain, there's someone on the channel!" he screamed.

"On my way," I said.

I had found some interesting stuff on the soldier, so I grabbed two other PFS soldiers and dragged them to the room.

"Well, um ... hello, Director. You look sharp in that uniform," I said of his new, well-starched naval commander uniform, trying to break the ice. It was a dark olive-green uniform with the UGF eagle and sword surrounded by the Earth on the cap.

"And you look like crap. The hell happened to your uniform?" he asked.

"Well, some of it is these guys' blood, and maybe their friends'. Some of it is from my friend. Doesn't matter. You got the fleet, didn't you?"

"You're damn right I did. People do not owe me debts anymore. I got you two carriers—"

"There are six ships here. Four battleships and two

carriers. A Leviathan-class carrier and a Torment-class carrier. Four battleships of the Terror class. These guys have the worst names for their stuff."

"Says the guy codenamed Reaper," he countered.

"Hey, I was assigned that name; I didn't pick it," I said.

His melodramatic sigh broke my fiction and implanted itself in my conscience, sorry neo-Freudians, he was right. The more psychologist tried to disprove Freud and push his theories to the outskirts of our thoughts, it ironically proved his theories right. Well, a few of them anyway.

"Don't you remember? You did choose it. You took on the name of the man who trained you and who you saw die in front of you."

"I did it to preserve his name, his legacy. He had no kids, no brothers, no way to pass his name."

"We all miss the cap terribly."

"Some more than others," I commented to him as he took out his dog tags.

"What the hell are you doing with those two bodies," he asked disgustedly.

"I'm robbing them to buy drugs. No, you idiot, I'm just taking their explosives and maybe some ammo. Transmitter works, so I'm taking that also."

"Whatever. Now, do you know the names of the battleships and carriers the PFS brought?"

"PRN *Spirit of Vengeance*, PRN *Dreadnought*, *Mikesa*, *Siren*, carriers PRN *Leviathan* and *Space Storm*. Why do they call it Protectorate Royal Navy? It sounds so goddamn idiotic."

"I don't know. They are war idiots, just in it for the expansion and glory."

"What ships did you bring?" I asked, noticing that the other guys were looking at me.

"Remember the Kepler-22B fleet?" he said.

"Holy crap, you brought that many ships?"

"No. I did bring two carriers, six battleships, four frigates, and a support ship—a French one!" He cracked up.

We both started to laugh.

"Did you position the French one on Earth or tell them to arrive after the battle was over?" I joked, hitting the touchpad repeatedly while laughing.

"Both." Ryan laughed; the man was already turning red.

"What are ships you're bringing?" I asked, trying to control myself.

Ryan kept laughing. Carl and Church looked at each other, not really understanding the joke. I just found it humorous that there was a French support ship here to help. I hoped it wouldn't surrender, as terribly stereotypical as it may seem.

"UGN *Schatten* and *Enterprise*." He started to calm down, letting escape only a little chuckle and giggle once in a while. "UGN *Missouri*, UGN *Parabellum*, UGN *Hunter*, UGN *Yamato*, UGN *Hood*, UGN *Red Star*. Frigates are UGN *Lightning*, *Thunder*, *Earthquake* and *Hurricane*. The support ship is the *Bastille*."

Carl jumped up in excitement.

"That's thirteen ships! Twice more than what the PFS have!" he exclaimed.

"By count, yes," Ryan said. "However, PFS ships are

bigger, with more guns and troops. Oh, and maybe more space for ships. Our ships do have more firepower and almost as many troops in them."

"So we're still screwed?" Church asked calmly.

"Don't think of it like that; we have a chance," I reassured him. "I knocked out the jammer and have the royal family and the chief of staff safe. What are my next orders?"

"I need you to get them to a safe point so we can extract them," said Ryan. "What is your current location?"

"Is it Marshall or still Director?" I asked him.

"For the time being, I'm Marshall. Your location, Gerald?"

"I'm in a bunker under the palace. But there's an infantry battalion here in the courtyard preparing defenses. Don't come near; the antiaircraft defense system is tightly knit. Too many antitank and MAID guns and missiles."

"What about their air power?" he asked. This was much-needed information.

"Not many birds in the air. I figure they're at the station or maybe still in the hangars of the ships. However, drop ships and attack ships are patrolling the skies."

"What about civilians?"

"Underground bunkers that were built in case of emergencies with the mines," Church answered.

"So they're safe. Goodness, you couldn't ask for a better thing. We arrive in about five hours. I'm sending you the coordinates to a possible extraction location and a backup one. Be there in six hours. I'm counting on you, Gerald." With that, he terminated the transmission.

Six hours was a long time. My map beeped and I checked it; it had a new objective marked and was beeping.

"Did you guys by chance find silencers on the PFS?"

"Yeah," Carl answered.

"Good. You know how to put them on?" I asked.

Church nodded. Carl shook his head.

"Look, I know you don't have that much training. I'm going to ask a lot from you; you can say no. I need you to help me when we go to the extraction point, because contrary to what you or anyone else may see, I am no super soldier. I still have the same fragilities as you two do; the same weaknesses, same blood and organs. It'll be dangerous; you could get killed. I'm asking you, will you help me for your planet?"

Carl, who was the youngest, thought long on this. He licked his lips and swallowed hard. His doubt made me reconsider asking for his help; it would be too much to have his blood on my hands if he were to fall.

"I don't want to be known to have sat on the sidelines when I could have made a difference. I'll help you," he said.

"Attaboy," Church said, slapping him on the back.

"Good. First get all the rifles and ammo from the squad. We need to make a little stop with your comrades first," I said to them.

"Yes sir," they both replied.

They turned around and started off to the hallway. I sat down on the chair and tried to rest a bit. I was exhausted after almost a whole day spent running around and shooting. I hadn't eaten since a little MRE I had in the apartment before the Goliath attack the previous day.

*Oh, goddamn it. I forgot about the Goliaths.* This is how I kept stressing myself out. I rolled around in the chair, letting my legs rest. If it hadn't been for the exoskeleton, I wouldn't have still been here.

What about the battalion? Who was the lieutenant major or the colonel? Who was the major? Who was the commander of this invasion? I scratched my neck with these questions in mind.

As if the galaxy turned around and said, "Hey, you know what would really mess up his day?" The power went out in the room.

"Captain?" Carl cried out.

"Don't move," I said, pulling out a strobe I had.

I hit the end on the chair, and the glow illuminated the room.

"And as a controversial book that people have used to justify a lot of bad actions in the past says, "Let there be light."

"I see him, come on," Church said somewhere in the darkness. They ran up to me, and I handed them each a strobe. They ignited their own and went back to scavenging ammo and supplies. I approached the two bodies that I had dragged and took their vests off. Heavy little things they were.

"Ready?" I asked.

"Yeah, I am." Carl said.

"Hold on, one more," Church replied.

"I'm on my way," I said.

I walked to the hallway and realized that the elevator was out. We must have been one hundred feet below ground, and I wasn't sure how we were going to get up.

"Captain, you have a rope, right?" Church said.

"Yeah, never leave home without one."

"Well since the power's out, we can open the doors of the elevator and use a retractor to pull us up."

"I don't know what that is, but all right."

We moved to the open doors of the elevator. I positioned myself under the panel that led to the roof of the elevator. I put my hands together and gave Church a boost. He went up the door. I then gave Carl a boost, and Church pulled him up. I jumped and grabbed Church's waiting hand, and he pulled me through the hatch. All three of us looked up.

"Okay, so who knows how far underground we are?" Carl asked.

I looked at my altimeter; it read -150 feet.

"We are one hundred fifty feet below ground. Not that deep for a bunker," I said.

Church pulled out a pistol that looked like a grappling gun. He set the distance the rope would travel and aimed at one of the sliding doors. He fired, and the projectile struck true. He pulled his rope out, tied it around him, and connected it to retracting mechanism. He then yanked on the rope and was pulled upward. I saw him open the door and jump to the floor. He threw back the mechanism.

"You know how to use it?" Carl asked.

"No, teach me."

"All right, so you grab the rope, tie it around you as if you were fast-roping down a building, and connect it to this little thing. Yank the rope, and it pulls you up."

"Seems simple enough," I said, doing exactly that.

It was weird being pulled up. I found myself hanging above the door, and I let go of the rope enough to lower myself into it.

"How you holding up, sir?" Church asked.

"Exhausted."

"Well, let's get back then," he said as Carl came out of the elevator.

"Do all UGF get a sword?" Carl asked.

"Yes, it's standard issue. And it is convenient and looks so damn awesome."

We covertly made our way back to the king and chief of staff. It was a miracle we weren't discovered, there were more enemies wandering around the castle than the first time I was here.

# CHAPTER TWENTY-THREE

## WAITING DREAM

**W**e reached the room where we had left the king and the rest of the group. I slumped down in a chair and started to rub my eyes.

"I've been up since I have gotten on this planet," I said. "I have fought who knows how many damn spawn and PFS soldiers. I need about an hour or two of sleep. Then we talk."

They all looked at me and talked among themselves. Olivia came to me and sat down on my lap. She hugged my neck and leaned her head on my shoulder.

"Stay here, please. Please help me know what is real and what is not," I whispered into her ear.

"As long as you don't leave me, I won't leave you," she whispered back.

My eyes felt heavy as my conscience started to leave me.

In my dream, I was in a space suit. It was a well-fitting one that I was able to move freely in. The sensors on the suit flashed blue, indicating that my oxygen and heartbeat were normal. I was sitting cross-legged on the hull of a spaceship. It was a mining ship or a transport ship; I really couldn't tell the difference (nor did I care). I was sitting outside the airlock, just drifting peacefully with the ship. I was in the vacuum, the holy vacuum, which no one could survive in and nothing could be heard in.

"How are you, sweetie?" Olivia said into the communications device.

"I'm fine. It's pretty peaceful here. You should join me," I answered.

"You really want me to put the suit on, don't you?"

"Yeah, you look even more beautiful in it. You might shine brighter than any of these other stars," I said.

"Oh, stop it, you."

"You know it's true."

"Yeah," she answered.

I heard beeping and muttering in my suit. Someone screamed in the radio, sending shivers down my spine. An alarm rang inside the ship.

"Gerald! The cargo is escaped! We have a scorcher escaping from the cargo bay. It is about to reach the bridge and sleeping blocks," the captain said.

"What cargo? The hell do you mean a scorcher?" I asked.

"Gerald, no time. Just get in … oh my god! Shoot at it! Fire! Kill It! Kill it!" he yelled before letting out a scream—the type of scream one hears in a horror movie before someone is killed in some nasty way. It told me that horror is real and that monsters are not in one's head anymore.

"Olivia, open the airlock," I said.

The look she gave me shot adrenaline into my

bloodstream, and my breath took in more oxygen than was usually needed. She was making her way to the airlock when a noise made her look back. She shook as she heard a pounding at the door. The door itself started to glow red. It was beginning to melt when a blade pierced the softened metal.

"Olivia!" Her name escaped my mouth as my arm smacked on the airlock.

She grabbed a pistol that was in a locker, chambered a round, and stood still.

I kept yelling her name and telling her to open the airlock. The blade melted the door more and revealed the face of its wielder. Its vertical-clawed mouth and bright orange eyes made themselves known to us.

Olivia fired six precise shots at the scorcher. The rounds melted before penetrating. I watched with horror as it slowly passed through the doors. It slashed at the room as Olivia stood looking at it. It then occurred to me that she still had one round in the chamber. To my horror, she pressed the barrel of the pistol to her left temple. Right on—God's little joke, her left temple, the thinnest part of the skull and covering a major artery. She turned around with tears in her eyes, smiled at me, and pulled the trigger.

I woke up with a start. Olivia was not with me, though her face was still etched into my closed eyelids. I checked the time on the wrist map. Only twenty minutes had passed since I first entered space, having a leisurely stroll in the cosmos. I got up and looked around. The room had many real books on the shelves. Paper books—that was something I didn't see often. I walked toward the king, who was still monitoring the holograph of the city. I saw the positions that the PFS were taking and noticed how many still patrolled the area Olivia and I had disappeared from. Many soldiers were near the explosives I had left behind and armed. I changed my map to a detonator, and my hands soon brought fire and brimstone to many unlucky soldiers.

"Did you see that? An explosion just killed an entire group!" the king shouted at everyone.

"I know; I caused that." He wasn't sure how it was possible.

Viewing the troops' movements made me feel like Big Brother. I was watching their every move, looking at their very fates. *So this is what God must feel like*. At least God doesn't choose sides. The holographic projection made me feel as though UGF command should have access as well, since the planners needed all the intel they could get.

"Sir, I think I should send this intel to UGF command. They'll need this," I said.

"Will my people's city be destroyed?" he asked.

"I can't promise you it won't," I answered, lowering my head.

"This will minimize the damage and quickly end the fighting?"

"Yes, I can tell you that."

"Upload it to your map, then send it," he said to me.

I grabbed the touchpad and connected the map with the frame. Both synced and updated. I grabbed the hologram with my fingertips, and it shrank as I shoved it toward my wrist map. I opened the options and sent it to the marshal.

` I had time before getting ready to go to the extraction point. I was extremely hungry and still sleepy.

The king looked at my stomach as it growled in hunger. He motioned for me to follow him as he moved to the door. He opened it, and we both stepped outside.

"You know," I said, "this reminds me of back when I was in training. Back then we didn't have all those food colonies. We were starving. Me and a buddy, we, uh, sneaked into one of the officers' mess halls. Damn, they had meat and cheese. That was a long time ago."

He nodded and kept motioning for me to follow.

"All those years ago, the PFS and Libertas fought the UGF for planets that would be useful for food. I remember that I sometimes gave up eating. I was determined that if my people were starving, so would I."

We walked into a kitchen. Massive white walls and cabinets covered the place. Huge refrigerators lined a wall. I opened one and grabbed whatever food I could. I took enough to feed everyone back in the room.

"Hurry, there might be PFS walking around the place," the king said. As if on cue, I heard rough voices coming closer from the hallway on the other side.

I moved along carrying the food, which were simply marked "food." It might have been easier, or quicker, if he had helped me. I kept taking my eyes off the corridors and peering out the windows. The sun was going down, but it wouldn't be dark for another few hours. I looked at the city and imagined how it would look when I first landed. I thought that this city would have already been destroyed, with millions of spawn crawling in every hole, or debris, fire, and ash covering the whole city. The latter would soon be corrected by advanced PFS and UGF firepower.

"It's so peaceful here. Why did they attack?" I asked the king.

"I don't know, son. It's not worth it. But they still did," he said, stroking one of the arches on the wall. He looked at the window and saw the occasional spawn in the distance.

We made it back to the room, and I set down the containers. One by one they were disappeared into the hands of the others.

I grabbed one myself, opened the container, and saw a sandwich, a container of water, and a bag of small ellipsoids in a cluster. I moved the bag and found another that held some odd-looking nearly spherical items.

"What the hell is this?" I asked.

Olivia came up, took one of the bags, smiled, opened it, and placed one of the items in her mouth.

"It's a grape, honey, and that is a cherry."

I grabbed the grape, popped it into my mouth, and bit down on it. How do I explain the taste? Never had I eaten a grape or cherry, only cherry- or grape-flavored drinks, candy, or medicine. Never the real thing. This flavor was just amazing; even better than the sweet synthetic version. It was juicy for such a small thing. The more I ate, the more addicting it became. Real fruit was expensive on Earth.

"Don't tell me you've never had any of these before," Olivia said.

"Actually no, I have not," I responded, finishing the bag of grapes. Then came the cherries. Delicious little things. I bit into something hard and spit it into my blood-stained glove. It appeared to be a rock.

"You spit the seeds out, dummy," Olivia said.

"A seed ... weird thing."

A distant rumble shook the building. Everybody stood up and looked worried. The PFS transmitter I had commandeered started picking up signals. The quick dash I took forward almost made me trip, I found myself listening to what had happened.

"Nova three to Nova two, there was an explosion or artillery near your position, over."

"Nova two to Nova three, yes there was an explosion from artillery fire *in* our position!" I heard coughing and groans. "Where the hell did that come from?"

"Nova two, this is Meteor six one actual. You were in the line of fire of our guns. General Beketov ordered the barrage in that position. I'm sorry; we protested, but orders are orders."

"Why the hell did he order a barrage in that area?" Nova two asked.

"Get this, the real reason we invaded this damn planet—it ain't political, it ain't economical or to threaten the UGF; it's because the son of the damn chancellor wants the princess of this world."

"Hey, hey, hey, watch that mouth; that's treason to say that about the son of the chancellor," another voice said.

"That brat can go to hell," said yet another voice. "I wasted fifteen years of my life putting down rebellions and fighting deep behind UGF lines in this service, and the only thank-you I get is an order to invade a crap world for his pleasure? Where's my pleasure? Where's my family bonus?"

"Stuff your complaining; that's probably a rumor," a more authoritative voice said.

"Meteor six one actual, please tell me that is not true," Nova Two said between coughs.

"And that barrage is to clear the area of anything and to make the son of our beloved chancellor look like a hero," the third voice said.

"Goddammit! I have dead and seriously wounded here, just so the damn kid can look like a hero?" he kept on coughing.

A new voice entered this mess of traffic. The transmitter told me this was an officer's voice as the color of the background changed to a very majestic crimson red.

"Nova two, Meteor six one actual, and all listening to this frequency, yes, it is true about the real reason of this mission."

I stopped listening and looked at the princess. Her expression was somewhere between shock and disgust. She stood up and walked to the window.

I stood up and followed her. She was shaking from the news. Nobody blamed her; they all stood and watched her.

"Hey, hey, look at me," I said to her, holding her hands. She kept looking at the window. I held her closer. "Look, I won't ever leave you behind. I'll fight to my last breath if I have to; I won't let him take you. Look, please, look at me. I put my life into your service; I swear to use my meaningless life to protect yours."

"Please don't say that; don't tell me that. I can't let you do that," she said weakly.

"I'll do anything for you, even die if I have to. Kill too, fight whole armies. But I need you to trust me; to have your hope in me."

Another explosion sounded in the distance. This time Nova three called out to Nova two.

"Nova three back to Nova two, what the hell, are you guys still out there? Over."

Silence answered that question.

"Nova three to Nova two, answer me, dammit."

Another silence passed along the emptiness of the radio wave transmission.

"Goddammit, Frank, answer me! Wilhem! Chester, Harper, Ramirez, Lee, anyone!" Nova three yelled into the radio.

"They're gone, son," Meteor six one actual responded. "We were ordered to launch another barrage into the area. I'm so sorry."

"No ... no, no, no, please no. Harper had kids, Lee had a wife. Frankie—I think he had a partner," Nova three said.

This was a shock to me. In combat school, UGF propaganda, Earth shows, films, and stories always depicted the PFS as monsters; soulless traitors to the Earth's government; sadistic, hateful people who didn't care about anyone. But this conversation proved otherwise.

"Gerald, please come over; you have to look at this," the king said.

I ran toward him and the holoprojector he and another counselor were looking at. The whole area was in ruins. The floor was a giant crater about a mile wide. The building began to collapse as the medical ship approached for the dead men. It had to return because the bodies were crushed and there was no way to get them out.

"That was an orbital bombardment. It was a miracle they survived the first barrage—a freaking miracle. Goddammit, those higher-ups ordered their subordinates to shoot their own men." I began to laugh a maniacal laugh. I put my head down, laughing all the while. All this just for her. Insane. Anything for the beautiful princess, my sweet, beautiful princess. I guess if the tables were turned, my actions would be the same. The idea of shooting my own men for her caused me to jump. My thoughts ran haywire; this was horrific to me.

# CHAPTER TWENTY-FOUR

## LANDING ZONE PRIME

I made everyone take only incredibly useful things for the trip to the landing zone: weapons, light strobes, and ammunition.

The king led us to a secret side exit of the castle. It was luxuriously, built unlike the noble outer wall. We exited to one of the main streets away from the main gate, where Eric crashed the ship—yes, it was Eric's fault.

We were leaving about three hours early to make it in time in case we got sidetracked or ran into trouble. We had a long distance to cover.

A thruster from a distant ship greeted us to the cold city. Olivia's teeth began to chatter, which bothered me.

The sky was again turning red, and the evening was transitioning to night in a slow process that did not match our fast march. It was funny seeing all of us quiet, with me looking at the map on my wrist. The king, even at his advanced age, was keeping up the pace with everyone.

The city was riddled with spawn that seemed to ignore us. However, the occasional PFS patrols, tanks, and vehicles appeared, and we had to hide in alleys. Olivia's teeth kept chattering with the consistency of a cricket at night.

"Olivia. Up front with me," I ordered when we entered an alleyway to avoid a tank.

"What is it?" she asked.

I took off my pack and dug in it until I found my jacket.

"You're cold, aren't you? Don't tell me that you're not cold. I can see that you are."

"Shut up." She smiled and greedily put on the jacket.

I put my hand on the spine of my rifle, and my sensors linked up with the jacket and began to warm Olivia up. She had probably been exposed to an electromagnetic pulse that fried the sensors on her clothes, keeping them from warming her up. Bad day to wear a dress.

At one point, we came up behind a patrol blocking the route, and the only way to keep going was to eliminate them. I took Church, Carl, Yuri, and another officer behind the patrol. Olivia, the king, and the king's men, along with the other five police officers, stayed behind a line of cars, waiting for the patrol to be taken out. When we were each behind at least one soldier, the police officers used their knives to cut the other soldiers' jugular arteries. I did not kill my target, but I used my electro-rod to merely knock him out. I left mine alive for some reason; I could have killed him, yet I didn't. I didn't know why, but it was probably the fact that Olivia's sweet eyes were staring at me from the distance. Her perspective of me mattered so much that I tried not to stain my appearance in front of her. However, as I turned to face the others, a shadow grabbed me and turned me to face him. The red glow from his visor burned from his eyes and the coldness of his warm exhaled breath beckoned me to do nothing. If death has a face, I'm sure it looks like that one: humanlike with red eyes, and stubble on the exposed parts.

The figure must have been hidden in the dark, since he emerged from it, like all the other PFS I had face, they were like shadows. He had his knife ready and was already going for my throat. I grabbed his arm and pushed it back. He struggled harder to try to stab me. I punched his face, grabbed his necklace, and yanked it off of him while forcing his arm down to his stomach and making him stab himself. How seemingly mesmerizing the process was for him to nearly seduce me with death, and for my instinct to bring me to stop it.

I grabbed his head and repeatedly bashed it against the roof of a car until Carl tried to stop me. I pushed the figure to the ground, and with my whole being, I tried to crush the dead man's head with the car.

A distant cry attempted to call to me across time and space. "Gerald, stop!"

Sensations twisted, rotted, burned, and were reborn in my very being. All the while I was senselessly shoving a man's head into the car. The five men I had brought eventually pulled my arms back and pushed me to the ground.

"Let me go! Let me go, damn it! He tried to kill me with a knife! A knife, damn it!" My hand still clenched the necklace as I tried to stand up.

Olivia grabbed my head and hugged me. Her touch calmed a sea of emotions and forced me to stop squirming and kicking with the same appearance as a fish out of water.

I read his necklace and saw it had an inscription that read, "To the best scout teacher, from your sharpshooting student, Ann." I had grabbed his dog tags too, and I threw them onto the street.

My helmet sensors scanned the sniper's weapon. The UGF database had no name for it, but it was apparent how easy it was to use. I took the weapon and carelessly slung it on my back. The ammo pouches he had been holding soon belonged to me as well.

The many eyes of the group soon peered at me. *What did I do? Oh right, I brutally killed an enemy soldier and stomped his head into a car. Not to mention that I pushed a police officer away so I might continue smashing his skull. Damn, I sure bet they still love me after that.* The sharp, piercing stares caused my nerves to boil. My hands scratched at my nose, my foot stepped abnormally. My brain began to think of larger words, and my fingers fiddled with each other.

The steps of the group sounded like drums: one two, one two, one two. A whisper sounded like my name. Enough! I opened my map, selected a location to rest, and sealed up my helmet to avoid hearing them.

We marched for one or two hours before arriving at a warehouse. We had passed too many patrols, too many spawn, and one too many brushes with death.

I found myself at one point with the police officers, telling them what I feared would appear in our way.

"What do you mean there is something worse?" One of the police officers asked. I think it was Raffael.

"In the military, you have your standard infantry soldier, then special forces, then flying drones, then combat foot drones, then tanks and armored personnel carriers, then infantry fighting vehicles, then ..." I bit my lip.

They all leaned in to hear the rest. Teaching is important, but telling people of the many ways to die always left scars on my heartstrings. I wonder if the guy who made that website about how to commit suicide felt the same, doubt it since his advice didn't work.

"Then what?" one asked.

"The um ... mechanized armored infantry division. Also nicknamed MAID. You probably know what they are—mechas, big ones. About seven to ten meters tall, usually. Have a powerful gun on them, powerful missiles, strong sword. A fusion arc reactor with turbines to give them a boost. Can sprint about one hundred seventy-five miles an hour. Very mobile, fast, agile, and can move quite smoothly, like we do."

"Okay, so we can avoid them—" Church started.

"Are you insane? No we cannot. Those MAIDs have sensors that detect motion, infrared thermal imaging cameras, and some other weird science crap. Look, that is why I am afraid of them." I looked down at the floor from the catwalk we were on. My eyes hesitated on Olivia as she brushed her hair aside with her hand. "No, I've seen what they are capable of doing. They can wipe out entire battalions, destroy an entire armored division. They'll grab you like a rag doll and throw you against something until you splat. They are always in pairs. We will not have a chance of beating them unless we have a huge amount of firepower." With that, I walked toward a bathroom across the catwalk.

I locked the door behind me and took my helmet off. I sat down on the closed toilet and rested my head on my hands. The mirror also showed bloodstains on my face. The water was still working, so I wiped the blood off my face and fingers. My hair was covered in blood too, which that struck me as odd. I poured handfuls of water over my head to wash the blood out.

I noticed that my gloves were filthy. Goodness was it cold. But it was necessary to keep me awake and to wash the blood from my face, hair, and fingers. My face was pale when I wiped the water away. I replaced my gloves, and yet my clothes were still bloodstained. A knock on the door alerted me that someone was waiting to use the bathroom. After quickly throwing some blood-soaked tissues into the powered-down incinerator, I hurried out of the bathroom to be greeted by the Princess.

She didn't say a word but put her arms around my neck. She held me there, and I had no idea what to say. We stood there for a few moments before she reached out and played with my hair. She then placed my helmet on my head and left again.

The warehouse must have held food, because it was now empty. The food had probably been eaten by the PFS. I went down the catwalk and exited the building. My gaze went up to the stars, and I saw the battleships and carriers. Pillars of metal, men, weapons, ships, and destruction moved in orbit. They looked peaceful there—so far away from me, so far away from the group, so far from hurting Olivia. At this distance they reminded me of fish floating in the deep. That thought took me back to a time when I took Evelyn fishing on Mars.

A green light began to blink on my map. Whooshing noises filled the city and made me look at the ships again. They looked peaceful, even though they were trying to find me and kill me. Had the noise been just my imagination? I kept pondering on that.

However, before I had pondered for long, the battle began. How simple a way to put it for such a large event that happened. It's not something one easily forgets; the imprints of the flashes of light always remain burned in one's memory.

In the red sky, an explosion erupted on the front of one of the battleships. Then the starboard and port sides were hit by similar explosions. The whole city must have looked up at that sky and wondered, "Are the heavens fighting?"

As if they were ghosts in space, the UGF fleet appeared to solidify on the battlefield with heavy guns blazing. The fleets were fighting and shooting at each other, and yet all I could do was watch. It was a spectacular sight. Green and blue plasma rounds were fired and bounced off of the ships. As I watched, I was protected on both sides by ramparts. Red tracers glowed, showing the trails of missiles. If only space had air, I could have heard the bombs bursting. I hoped that my fleet would survive the night and still be there in the morning.

Three UGF ships soon entered the atmosphere, and as if they were giving birth to smaller ships, fire came out from the exhaust ports of hundreds of thousands of transports and attack ships. Streaks of blue light began to fall from the dropped troop pods, which I knew might even hold powerful mechanical troops. I got a running start, and the exhaust on my back soon erupted to life and helped me jump to the side of the building parallel to the warehouse. I ran along the wall, my feet securing my body to the vertical surface. I continued this process until I was directly on the roof of the warehouse. My thrusters automatically inhaled hydrogen ions in the warehouse.

The sight above was like a happy dream. It was a movie in the sky, only the music was missing. While lying on my back, staring at the stars, I heard loud footsteps off in the distance. They sounded metallic, but not Goliath sized. I opened my map, and some movement three blocks to my east concerned me. It was no squad, and it was no Goliath spawn; it was metal, and it had a fusion core and an ion weapon. I hoped it was a combat foot drone, but the way it moved made the PFS shadows look like ants stuck in honey.

I gripped my rifle and jumped off the edge of the roof. I landed on the side of the building and ran, with the thruster keeping me afloat. Footsteps sounded in the distance; they did not sound human.

A sharp, cold pain gripped my waist, and I was pulled to ground level. A metallic face stared at me. The four lenses focused on my face and then retracted; they seemed to have a cheerful appearance. I was unable to move my face, and my legs felt like lead as I dangled seven feet in the air. On the shiny metal hull, my pale face appeared right next to the UGF flag etched on the metal.

The machine moved its short metallic fingers over imaginary lips and soon pointed to my wrist map. I followed with my eyes and saw that hundreds of soldiers were moving from the opposite direction toward us. Without saying a word, the MAID showed me with its hand that there were five other units surrounding them and attempting to ambush them.

The suit of armor and death set me down and let me go back to the warehouse. I ran back as if the devil were behind me, as gunshots soon quieted the lives of who knows how many. Three soldiers rushed past me without seeing me. They were probably tasked with outflanking the MAIDs and relieving pressure on their pinned-down comrades.

I held my rifle at eye level. The unsuspecting victims ran down the street, two of them jumping on the walls and gaining altitude. I fired a burst from my rifle. The recoil hit my shoulder, and the rounds traveled at supersonic speeds in a spinning motion before tearing cavities in the soldier still running on the ground.

"Man down!" the man said as he fell, choking on the last word.

"Sniper!" the other cried out.

Once again, an enemy had mistakenly called me something I was not. Sure, I could do what snipers did, but that wasn't my name or title. As they rushed toward their fallen comrade in a mad dash to get him off the street, I took off running, and pulled the trigger of my device, which handed judgment from a person who had no right to decide who lived and who died.

They fell the same way as their comrade did, but more comically, I could almost hear the Wilhem scream as they twisted in an awkward fall. Breathing a sigh of relief, I plopped down against a wall and took out a water container. I placed the elixir of life against my lips, and the sweet taste of the filtered spring-sourced liquid quelled my thirst. Standing up, the blood stood still in my head. I then made my way back to the others; time was lost to me at that moment.

With my rifle at the ready, I entered the warehouse and called for everyone's attention.

"They're here! They're here! I told you they'd be here!" They covered their ears against my excitement, and a missile slammed into a street not far away.

"What are you bloody ranting about?" Seth asked.

"Take a look out the windows and into the sky. It might be the only time you'll see something like that." With that said, everyone went to a window and looked at the sky. I knew they would never be the same. Some laughed; most cheered. Only the king had a solemn face.

"Now, everybody stay here; I need to make sure the area is secure before we move on."

The officers nodded. Half of them came with me to check out the area. I decided to look only at about three blocks in all directions before deeming the area all clear, as there were some firefights near our area but outside that radius. I sent everyone to different locations and ordered them to meet up with me near the shopping center in five minutes.

PFS communication was skyrocketing. From time to time, I was able to pick up phrases. One of the reports indicated that one of the battleships was too heavily damage and might be needed to scuttled. Another report stated that UGF troops had landed on the north and south edges of the city and were advancing to the center. This was good news for us. However, in my stupidity I just stood there on the sidewalk, listening to radio transmission and looking at the fighting fleets until I was tackled into one of the buildings. A PFS soldier had taken the opportunity to strike while my guard was down.

This one was smart enough to pin one of my arms down with his whole body while trying to reach for one of his knives. That would be the end of me. Using the power of the exoskeleton, I pushed my body up and knocked him off of me. We both quickly took our pistols out; strangely enough, he also had two pistols on him.

He shot at me and was either a bad shot, or still trying to figure out where to shoot. I shot back at him, and we ran through the building, parallel to each other and still shooting at each other. We ended up behind a fountain, taking cover from one another.

"You rat bastard. You tackled me into a building," I yelled at him.

"You deserve it, Earth scum!" he yelled back in his harsh, deep voice.

"Go to hell, Ortyran fascist military dog!" I shouted.

My pistols had no bullets, so with a swipe of my hands I loaded full magazines into them. He must have done the same, because when I jumped up, he did the same, and I fired rounds into his left shoulder. The shot sent him flying onto his back, but not before he was able to shoot me in the most heavily armored part of my vest, the chest. I must have hit him with the powerful and wise Virgil, because he fell back hard.

While holding our hands over the areas in which we

had been shot it, we both scurried back to cover. Pretty good place to take the damage in the armor—shoulder plate. It didn't go through all the way, but it did go in enough to get stuck in the skin. I head a pull as bullet came off. He then threw the armored plate to the ground. I exhaled as I heard the other guy cough.

"You shot me in the chest. You shot me." I cried out.

"And you shot me, but missed. And I'm still alive," he chuckled.

"Don't worry, I won't make that mistake twice," I promised.

We jumped up, but we did not shoot at each other. Rather, we tried to injure each other with our pistols in hand. When he would punch, I would block him with my pistol, and he would do the same. This went on for about a minute before I threw my pistols at him, drew my sword, and skewered him next to a glass panel in the middle of the room. With a single motion, I cleaned the sword on him and picked up my weapons. I panted and searched for any useful ammunition on him. To my amazement, he had none. That reminded me of the ammo I had gotten from Eric. I took out the magazine and saw that the ammunition was marked with a dark-grey tip. I needed to show the others.

With this deed done, I headed outside. I noticed that the building we had fought in was a science museum . I was pretty happy with myself until I went outside and saw an entire squad waiting with their weapons aimed at me.

"Drop your weapons and surrender, ya UGF

necrophiliac," a sergeant ordered with a pitiful accent that was a cross between Irish, German, and Ortyran.

"I'm sorry, did you just refer to me as a necrophiliac?"

His entire squad started laughing at that. It was a very bad joke, and it made me want to confront him for telling it. Well, at least his squad didn't make him feel bad. Motion behind them in the buildings above them caught my eye. Figures in dark navy-blue uniforms were sneaking up in the shadows. I started laughing at them when I saw Church, Carl, and the rest of the police officers appear on the building opposite me, aiming their rifles at the PFS soldiers from the windows.

"What are you laughing at, worthless UGF litter."

"I am laughing at your stupidity for not seeing the bigger picture."

"Get a load of this one. Telling us we're blind. What an idiot," one of the grunts said.

"Now, when I give the order, you too will see the bigger picture—or should I say you'll feel it. Especially you; don't ever call me a necrophiliac. I do have someone, and she is alive. Now die." With that final word, the police officers lit up their weapons on the unsuspecting squad.

I calmly walked to the now dead sergeant and proceeded to kick him in the ribs and groin. I might have also kicked his face, but I couldn't be sure, because he was covered in blood, and so were my boots.

The police officers descended from the building and took ammunition from the PFS they had just gunned down. Which reminded me of something.

"All of you, there is something that is totally cool

that I need to show you," I said, taking out the special magazine.

"What is it?" one of the police officers asked; I'm pretty sure it was the redhead.

"This is SABER ammunition."

"What?" Carl said.

At this point I was tired of them interrupting me, and to show them how annoyed I was, I grabbed an empty magazine I had on me and threw it at him.

"Oww!" he yelled as it bounced off his head, to my delight.

"Great, now anyone else want to interrupt me? See what happens. No? All right then. Now, as I was saying ... well, come on, walk and talk. To the warehouse. Now, as I was saying, this is SABER ammunition. Smart airburst explosive rounds. They detonate within a certain proximity of an object directly in front of them."

I turned away from the police officers, loaded the magazines into my pouches, and took my rifle off safety.

One of the police officers took a rocket launcher from one of the dead soldiers before returning it. "Needs fingerprint recognition; useless to me," he explained.

We neared the warehouse before noticing weird footsteps. Very weird ones. Inhuman ones, but not metallic ones. And it worried me that they were in great quantity, and approaching very quickly, almost as if the beings making them weren't even bothering to quiet them. I held my arm up, signaling for the officers to stop. They looked around, trying to see what was going on. The footsteps persisted. I took out my map to see what it was. While waiting for the map to calibrate, a scream made everyone turn around. The scream was a spawn's.

It jumped, grabbed a police officer, and began to tear at his vest. Carl quickly took his pistol out and grabbed the spawn's head. He yelled as he emptied the magazine into it. He was lucky to shoot it in its eye socket; the damn things were hard to kill with weak pistols.

"Get up, are you all right, man?" Carl asked.

"What the hell? Just what the hell was that!" the shocked officer said as his face paled.

"Oh you're fine. Get up." I ordered.

His torn vest was still hanging on him as he tried to stop his lip from shaking. I heard more footsteps and checked my map. We were almost surrounded.

"Hurry, run! Follow me!" I yelled as I sprinted.

They all followed me and didn't ask anything. However, some of the police officers shot to the sides in order to deter what I believed to be spawn. We couldn't lead them back to the warehouse; they would tear everyone to shreds. We kept running, but I didn't know where to lead them. More yells and growls told me that we had a whole horde of them behind us. And yet more were coming from the sides and in front of us.

We passed streets and vehicles with the whole horde behind us. More joined the chase, jumping out of buildings and windows. I heard a yell of pain behind me and stole a glance that way; I saw a police officer being pinned to the ground and having his arm ripped off. He looked at me with pain in his eyes as more swarmed in on him, clawing, ripping, and biting him. I stopped and quickly shot the man in the head. The spawn kept tearing at him, but with less savagery than before. Another spawn got Raffael. It shoved him to the wall and bit his throat out. It yelled with blood in its mouth and on its disgusting face. More swarmed him and threw his body parts into the air. They were drunk with bloodlust.

"Don't get left behind, goddammit!" I yelled.

I had already lost two men in this party. Two more added to the multitude of those I had already lost because of my failure to save them.

We crossed an intersection, and out of the corner of my eye, I saw figures—a lot of them—and what appeared to be a tank. We crossed the street when the firing started. Rounds shot down spawn, ripped them apart. I took cover behind the building and waited for the shooting to stop. I covered my ears with my hands and yelled. Who were they? Were they here to help me? A high-explosive round annihilated the spawn, temporarily ending their approach.

"Identify yourselves!" a voice ordered in a robotic monotone.

"Did anybody see who they were?" I asked.

"Let me peek," Church said.

"No, don't," I said, pulling him back before he peeked around the corner.

"Captain Gerald Grey. And who the hell am I speaking to?" I responded.

"*The* Captain Gerald Grey? Reaper? I don't believe it. All right, Captain, if you are UGF, answer me this. Who the hell is the high minister of the UGF council?"

"Oh, that is so easy, it's—" Carl said before receiving my fist in his face.

"Shut up! It ain't the answer," I said to him. I then shouted to the UGF soldiers, "How the hell should I know?"

"What! You idiot, you're gonna get us killed!" the other surviving officer said.

"Captain Grey acknowledged. Marshall Kayre gave us two important orders. First was to push the Protectorate Federation out of the city, and second was to radio in to him if we were to find you, so do you wanna guess what I'm doing?"

"Oh, I bet you're doing nothing. Hurry up; that's an order."

"Sheesh, calm yourself, Captain; I'm working on it. Lee, get on the channel and contact Marshall Kayre. Tell him we found Chuchie, or Reaper."

"Yes sir!" the private said.

His equipment looked very bulky on his thin body. The rest of the soldiers were reloading their rifles, and the tank ejected its spent round.

The tank commander was sitting on the gun of his tank. The medic went to treat one of police officers who had received a nasty gash on his back from the spawn. His vest must have been able to withstand only small-caliber rounds.

"Hey Captain, I did a head count, and, well, you seem to be missing some very important people. You know, the high-value personnel."

"Yeah, let's go get them. Damn spawn," I said, kicking one in the face. My boot sunk in and came back all covered in blue blood. "Made us go away from where they were, so we're about a klick away from them."

His look of need to prove himself told me he was going to come with us. Well, the good thing was that he was on my side and that the tank was not the reason I was glad they were going to come with us. However, his look also worried me. It was the look of a man willing to sacrifice his men for ribbons, medals, and honor—something I did not approve of. This was a man desperate for the sweet taste of war—an addictive compound that either hooks you, traumatizes you, or kills you and the others around you.

He gave orders to his squad, and the tank commander listlessly reentered the tank. Some of his troops rode on the sides. We walked over the bodies and body parts of the spawn. I might more accurately say we trudged through puddles of blue blood, guts, and brains.

We marched next to the tank as we made our way back to the warehouse. The fighting of this titanic city seemed to be escalating. Artillery shells, rockets, bombs, and guns were blowing buildings to bits. All the action grew louder. However evil fighting may seem, however horrid people describe it as being, the sound of it was always like an ancient piece of classical music to me. It would grow louder in one area yet quieter in another, just as one instrument bellows its sound while another dies down. The red sky looked like a mirror image of the red blood of us humans below.

We crossed the bodies of Raffael and the other police officer who was grabbed by the spawn. They were all over the place; bits of cloth, equipment, skin, boots, body parts, and blood were scattered where they had died. Nasty sight.

Lee had a weak stomach; soon he was throwing up at the sight of it. One of the soldiers began to whistle a tune. It must have been old, because no one recognized it. It had a nice rhythm to it.

Transmissions were pouring in. They were sometimes about squads successfully overrunning PFS positions. Some were about PFS wiping out entire battalions, or vice versa, or about enemy soldiers who surrendered without even firing a single shot. Very few were those of officers calling out to dead soldiers. Some were those of medics being called and drop ships being deployed to pick up wounded or dead. It must have been depressing to be a radio operator. An officer in charge of the dead. What a fitting name. I wonder how those people lived with themselves.

But people don't care about that. They care if you are immoral, rude, speak obscene language, have bad hygiene, are free spirited, do not believe in what they believe in, or are open-minded. Since centuries past—before wars, before writing—we have gotten that message across: "We don't care about your struggle; we care about the way you act in the present." Sad, sad story.

"Pens are old, but so is fighting, and we use that to get a message across a lot faster," I mumbled.

"What was that, Captain?" one soldier asked.

"Nothing, just nothing."

I then got this feeling that my gut should have felt ever since I arrived on this planet. It was a feeling of tininess. All around me, the buildings were hundreds of stories tall. The roads were able to hold up to eight hover-cars going each direction. The smallest street, maybe four.

Even with all these men around me to help me, I was bothered by my perception of the enormous world around me.

We got to the warehouse and waited for something to happen. When nothing did, I opened the huge doors only to be greeted by a pistol in my face.

"Oh, it's you. Sorry, handsome; thought you weren't you." Olivia said, lowering the pistol. Everyone came into view after that. The police officers came down from the balcony with their rifles aimed at us.

"Where are the others?" one of the police officers asked.

"They …" Carl said, "They didn't make it. They're dead."

This was an emotional struggle for them. The look of shock was new to them. They had never taken casualties like this. This world's people were new to it, to people dying in war. The tank commander jumped out of his module and counted the Helenac as they exited the building. He plopped down again and presumably sent the number to the Kayre.

An explosion high above made everyone jump. A flashing red light blinded everyone in the city. That probably wasn't good. When the light died down, I looked up at that sky and saw a star falling. Only it wasn't a star; it was a carrier.

"Oh my god, is that one of ours?" a soldier asked.

"Nah, looks like the *Leviathan*," another answered.

"The hell with you all, that looks like *Space Storm*," a third answered before taking a swig from his water pack.

"Tennant, shut the hell up. That's *Leviathan*," The sergeant said.

"Don't look like it."

"Oh, you are so Scottish," someone said to him.

An explosion in the descending ship's engines made everyone drop to the ground. Fighter ships exited the carrier and began engaging the earthen ships. Debris and parts of the ship started falling as the ship tried to crash land outside the city. A Terran carrier descended miles above the falling Ortyran ship. A green energy built up in front of the bow of the UGN carrier. It then tilted enough for the bow to point at the PFS ship. The energy must have been plasma or some godly power. However, in that concentration and amount, it could have been a weapon. And that must have been the point. There was a loud hum, and the plasma descended in a circular vortex-like motion at incredible speed. At that moment, green electricity sprang from PFS carrier. The black metal where it was hit turned white. That paused the fighting in the city, for the ground troops at least. A storm started and stopped in a single second. All ships departed from the area, both UGN and PFS, running scared. The ship imploded, then exploded, and finally imploded again. The blast wave pushed everybody back, even though it happened kilometers in the air.

In the heap of the sky, an entire ship turned into a metal coffin. Millions dead. The great distributer of judgment, the mighty trigger, had been forced. The greatest weapons used in wars are those we were never supposed to use: Greek fire, nuclear weapons, torture, poison, biological weapons, the human mind. My past self argued that these actions were necessary for peace. He might have been right. The self that had now taken on many of Olivia's ideals argued about using such a powerful weapon. He might have been right as well.

With great anger, I pushed toward the sergeant and grabbed his radio.

"What the hell are you doing, Marshall Kayre!" I roared over the radio waves.

"Testing an experimental plasma rail gun," he answered calmly.

"Do you have any idea how many people you just killed?"

"How are you shocked at that? I just blew an entire carrier, and you're mad at me. A simple thank-you is enough."

"You don't just kill entire generations!" Something grabbed my hand; it was Olivia.

"Oh we've done it before. Entire worlds sometimes. Remember? Generations who threatened our lives, our people, our worlds."

"This isn't the same. They don't want to be here; they're forced to be here."

"Why do you do that?" he asked as the destroyed carrier crashed outside the megacity's limits in with a deafening boom.

"Do what?" I asked him, sitting on the floor, hand over my eyes, still holding on to Olivia's hand.

"Make them look like us. You know, Earth people."

"Earth people? Earth people? You make them sound as if they didn't start from Earth"

"None of them were born on Earth, remember?"

"You bastard," I whispered.

"Oh, I'm the bastard?" He sighed over the radio.

"Now, I quote you directly. Begin quote: 'Damn it, how long before they kill every damn luckless bastard who gets left behind.' End quote."

Olivia looked up and pushed my hand away. She stood up and looked at me with her beautiful eyes, but her expression was one of fear.

She moved back as I moved toward her.

"Ryan, stop."

"Oh, you're giving up now? Did I touch a nerve? Good."

"What did you do?"

"Well, you hurt my feelings, I just did the same," he said, turning off his transmitter.

"Olivia, please, listen to me," I said.

"No!" she yelled, raising the pistol to my face.

That action caused everyone to raise something, rifles mostly. UGF soldiers to police officers, police officers to UGF soldiers. The king and his men raised their hands.

"Olivia, what are you doing?" the king asked.

She didn't answer. Her eyes stared deep into me with an expression that did not suit her.

"Olivia, look at me. Look at me. Please just trust me," I said, putting my hand on my chest. Words are powerful, more powerful than men in uniforms with weapons, and advanced pieces of technology, but only if you use the right ones.

"Tell me you didn't say that." She had tears in her eyes.

"Olivia ..."

"Please just tell me you do care about my people. If you care about me, you will tell me the truth."

I put my hand on the barrel of the pistol and lowered it. She looked at me with eyes of mistrust.

"Sir, permission to open fire?" one of the privates asked.

"Captain, your orders?" the sergeant asked.

"Permission denied," I answered.

"You came for a reason. What was it?" Olivia asked, still holding the lowered pistol.

"To rescue you."

"Please tell me you never meant to do what he said."

When she said this, I took the pistol away from her. She was strong, independent, a survivor. This gave me some peace of mind. If I died, she would not end up like my sister—lying on the bed, crying, wishing it hadn't been me but someone else. She was a fighter, and there was nothing wrong with that. She could take anything they could throw at her, and she could fight back if needed.

I hugged her and pulled her close to me.

"You didn't say that; you couldn't have. Promise me you didn't."

*A lie will hurt you. A lie will hurt her if she finds out*, I thought. I couldn't lie to her. That is, I could, but if I wanted to start anew, I had to stop being what I was before.

"You know me. You need to trust me." I wasn't going to lie, but I wasn't going to tell her the truth.

"All right," she answered, hugging me tighter.

"We have to go to the hospital. They'll be waiting for us there."

With that, just as quickly as it had started, the situation cooled down; everyone lowered their weapons.

The tank moved down the street and, everyone followed it. The sergeant was talking to the tank commander, and they seemed to be arguing among themselves. We passed seventeen blocks before coming to a major intersection, and there we received the bad news.

"Captain, we … uh, how do I put this … we're being ordered to move out. Marshall Kayre ordered this, but listen to this, he is assigning units from the mechanical division to come assist you. This is where we part."

"Damn. Where are you headed?"

"Pullit, where we going?"

The tank driver got out of his station and pointed to the center of the city. Right where the major fighting was.

"There," the sergeant said.

"Keep your heads together. I'll lead them straight to the hospital. Tell Kayre to tell his mechanicals to meet up with us." I hit his helmet with my palm.

"Will do, Captain," he said to me "All right men, back to the fighting."

He and his men departed from us. Some rode on the tank; the rest walked alongside it.

"Captain, who will accompany us now?" one of the counselors asked.

"Armored division. Maybe some armored personnel carriers. I could use a ride." I said.

We kept walking and passed many more buildings. I checked my wrist and saw we only had about four more miles to march. We also had about an hour left.

"Gerald, do you hear that?" Olivia asked.

"Hear what?" I replied, stopping and raising my rifle.

"That stomping."

I stopped and looked around. I shushed everybody, yet I couldn't hear anything. She had said "stomping," so I got on my knees and put my ear to the ground. That's when I heard it. It was soft and steady stomping. I couldn't determine the distance, but I had an idea of what it was, and I feared the worse.

"Get moving; hurry up. Just hope we meet up with the armored division soon. Or we're dead."

That caused everyone to start running. Running away from what was catching up to us. The thumping reminded me of the building the Goliath had brought down. The far-off footsteps were getting ever closer. They didn't sound too close, so I assumed we had a good amount of time to run and hide.

However, just moments later, the stomping vanished. For whatever reason, the thing I thought to be the Goliath stopped. Everyone noticed my pause and stopped as well. Two loud crashes disrupted my train of thought. The building in front of us caught my attention. Glass was falling down from the front and side of it. That caused me to look up, and when I did, the blood drained from my face.

Hanging upside down on the front of the building was a cross-armed MAID, accompanied by another one hanging on the side.

"G'day, ya freaking Yank," the MAID hanging upside down said with an Australian accent. And if that was not the most fearful thing, was the fact that the word misadrist was painted on the chestpiece, and the female symbol on the head.

# CHAPTER TWENTY-FIVE

## REALITY AND TRUTH

"**D**emi, be nice to your superior officer," the other MAID said, also with an Australian accent, but this time in a male voice.

"It took us a while, but Truth and Reality always catch up with your bloody arse," Demi said, falling from the building. She and the other MAID fist bumped at that. The suits both had Australian flags marked on the armored plates covering the machines' torsos. The words "Liquid Flesh" were printed on the MAID that was hanging from the side of the building; "Solid Blood" was printed under Demi's other kind word.

"Captain, m' name's Finn. First Lieutenant Oliver Finn. At your service. Now, you're probably wondering how we got here so fast, and I'll tell you. You see, we were—"

I chimed in, finishing for him. "Fighting inside a ship high in orbit before being told to disengage and assist in an extraction mission by Marshall Ryan Kayre. Therefore you jumped from orbit and landed near a point where we would pass."

"Bloody arse, I like saying that," he said, annoyed.

"Yank thinks he knows us well. I wouldn't date him, if I ever dated men."

"Oh, a feminist. Careful guys, she might yell at you for not treating her as equal and scream at you for not acting like a gentlemen," I joked.

"Who the hell told you to assume stuff about me? You hear me? Now I don't give a damn who you are; you leave me alone, you understand? Oh, look at the bloody time. Best be hurrying up to make the extraction point."

The second MAID dropped to the ground, and the two jumped around checking for enemies. Funny things those vehicles were. Strong enough to take any amount of fire and tank rounds, but light and agile enough to out-maneuver the enemy—thanks to aroeminium, a material stronger than titanium but lighter than aluminum.

When the MAIDs determined we were safe, they marched with us. Carl came up to me to ask me something.

"Sir, what's an Australian?"

"Well, you see, for thousands of years, the most dangerous and weird creatures just so happened to be in Australia, an old state that joined the UGF to avoid being wiped out. Those bastards are tough; must have evolved to survive the animals on the continent."

"And is that why they scare you?" Carl asked skeptically.

"Oh goodness no. The woman scares me only because of the word imprinted on her MAID, but quite frankly, I'm actually glad we have Australians here and her. They are tough; they are survivors. And I like to mess with people, I don't actually hate her although it seems like I do."

"Do you think we can ... oh, son of a bitch," he said.

The MAIDs stopped when we turned the corner. They raised their pulse rifles and powered all essential fighting sections while raising their metallic and energy shields. The hiss deafened my left ear.

In front of us was the thin son of the PFS leader and his advance special operations squads.

Three drop ships, a gunship, two speeder ships, five tanks, about twenty cloaked snipers, squads of infantry men clothed in crimson and black, a MAID, and infantry fighting vehicles and drones were in the way. The force amounted to over fifty troops.

This impressive array of soldiers and fighting machinery made the police officers freeze. They quickly dropped their weapons and raised their hands, while I raised my rifle at the enemy.

"Princess Olivia of Ortyra—I like the sound of that," the PFS leader's son said in his gruff Ortyran accent.

"Pick up y' freaking weapons; y' embarrassing me," Demi ordered.

"You heard her. We never give up. Even if it means the end of us," Finn added.

They bent over and retrieved their rifles.

"Orders, Captain?" Finn asked.

"Well, normally, if it was just us, I'd make us charge, take out as many as we could, and then die. But I have the cops and the princess. Damn it, what do I do." Indecision had me by the throat.

"Look at you now. Cut off from help. Cornered. No chance to survive if you choose to fight. I have here what you don't have—a way to win. What do you have?" yelled, shifting his officer's coat.

"Will and a reason to win. You think having the best toys is the way to win? What would you do to win? I'd chew my own leg off. Die if I have to. But I don't quit, I don't accept losing. Do you?" I answered, grabbing Olivia and moving her behind me.

"Willing to die to win a medal?" he asked.

"No, I'm willing to die so you don't win.

"Captain, orders?" Demi asked.

"Let me think," I said, looking around.

An orbital bombing was too dangerous, reinforcements would take about twenty minutes, and this situation was not getting any better.

"How did you even find us?" I asked, him trying to stall him.

He in turn took out a device that looked like a map. However, it pulsed, and a red mark appeared on it.

"Tracked the king's signal. Took us a while to isolate it, but we found him. Checkmate." He smirked.

This caused everyone to look at the king. The one way I should have found him was the way the enemy found him. Everyone groaned and cursed at his signal. Richard looked offended at that.

"Look, how about this. The whole city is fighting. But what are they fighting for? How about you and me fight for her?" He pointed at Olivia.

"Don't!" Everyone said to me almost simultaneously.

I looked at them and saw how much they were against it. They had the chance to tell me no, to say there was a different choice. Having someone I cared about being threatened, having my back against the wall—I could see why people in movies did stupid things now.

I scratched my neck and put my head down. I knew that a fight between the two of us might give the rest of my group a chance to run to the landing zone. I thought it was a stupid decision for me, a great one for him.

"Winner gets the girl and the other's life." His smug face annoyed me.

The wind breezed around us. The whirring of the MAIDs' joints and parts sounded in the distance. I stole a glance at the snipers on the building and noticed that one of them was a woman with black hair under her jacket's hood.

"All right," I said. "But our forces cannot intervene in our fight. Just one on one." I slung my rifle over my shoulder and made sure my pistols each had a round chambered.

"Gerald, no. Don't do this. I can't let you do this," Olivia said, holding onto my arm.

"Don't worry. Have some faith. But when they're distracted, I want you and everyone to run to the landing zone." I tried to smile, but her face stayed frozen with shock.

"No, I don't want you to make this decision for me," she said, hitting me on the helmet and chest.

"We don't really have any other choice." That was the last thing I said before turning from them.

I got closer to my opponent. I didn't want to study him, because I was going to kill him and didn't want to bother knowing what he looked like, other than that fact that he, like every other PFS soldier, had red irises. It was probably from that drug that Eric and I had found on the body on the speeder. A scar on his mouth stretched to his cheek and made him look as though he were angry. His crew cut was the complete opposite to my long hair.

The MAID and tanks cleared a square in the middle of the road by moving the hovercars. The infantry units lined the square to watch their leader fight me.

"You think your side is winning? When I get the girl, I'm going to destroy this city with an antimatter bomb. Sure, I'll lose a few million soldiers, but so will you."

Typical antagonist thinking.

"Shut up. Let's get this over with," I said. Somehow, I knew this fight was not going to end well.

I opened a container in one of my pouches. The pill inside was for emergencies only.

"The hell is that? Painkiller?" the PFS leader's son asked.

I swallowed the green tablet, and a surge flowed through my brain. The exoskeleton fired electrical impulses, which caused sparks to shoot out of me. I held the yell in my throat; the pain almost became too much before everything stopped. Then the pain went away and the colors set in.

"It is a psychological chemical that allows the user to employ the entire brain. Yes, from the normal eleven point two percent to one hundred percent."

He started moving around a lot. It was movement that reminded me of a frog jumping side to side.

"Are we going to fight or do seismic dancing?" I asked.

That made him lunge at me. I grabbed his fist that was moving toward my head, but I was slow to get the one moving toward my stomach. He was fast; I'll give him that. I threw a punch with my left fist, but he blocked it and returned my punch with one to my chest. That made the PFS cheer. I took a step forward and distracted him by faking a right punch to his chest only to knee him in the stomach.

This made him angry. He lunged at me and brought me to the ground. He then tried to choke me and pin me down. I kicked him in the back of the head and pushed him off of me, gasping for the sweet scent of the planet's air.

Hunching over and watching the entire scene, Demi and Finn were the only ones that were still paying attention.

"Fool, do you think there is a chance you can win?" he asked.

From his overcoat, he produced a great bayonet. It was about eighteen inches long and attached to a six-inch handle. Its reflective, mirrorlike metal appeared menacing as it was thrust toward me. From my back, I defended against his bayonet with my black sword.

I could never match his speed with the long sword. Unable to go on the offensive, all I could do was defend. My opponent then proceeded to take out another bayonet, which he used to slash at my chest. If not for the vest, I would have been cut. I couldn't keep this up for long; I was simply watching and waiting, hoping he would make a mistake. One stroke of his blade pushed me down to my knees; I was in a position in which his bayonet could go through my throat. That would have happened if I had not activated the paraglider and jumped back with my wings extended and the thrusters on full blast. I hovered in the air for a while before returning to the ground and lunging at him while my wings retracted. *Where is his mistake?* I wondered. Then he made one when he tried bringing both blades down onto my head. I quickly held the handle of my sword with both hands and pushed his blades out of his hands; his grip loosened, and they flew into the air.

With a single motion, I placed my sword back in its sheath and readied my fists to continue. He yelled while running up to me. I grabbed his fist and threw him over my shoulder. While down, he kicked both my legs, taking me to the ground.

"Would you just hurry up and die? If you do that, I won't even blow the city up; I will take her and leave," he blurted.

"No! I'd rather you blow up this city than take her," I wheezed.

"Listen, I don't want any more deaths on either side; just let her go. You can stop this fighting, but give her to me."

"I'm not giving her up," I said.

We both stood up, panting. Running at top speed, the son took me back down to the floor. He clenched his fist, and there was a metallic crunching sound as it came down on me. I moved my head at the last second, and his fist broke through the asphalt. If his fists could do that to hard asphalt, I sure as hell did not want to know what they could do to my head. Slower than last time, he began to punch my face. The first blow did not hurt as much as I expected; it was still painful though. Ten more punches and I began to spit out blood. I collected all my strength, and my head made contact with his. He was off me. My hand made its way over my nose. I looked down at my glove and saw the red liquid as he began laughing at me. I spat out more blood, and more flowed from his nose down to my lips.

The PFS leader's son stood up once more. His fist attempted to make contact with my head, but with great speed, my left arm blocked his punch as my right arm hit his stomach. He might have been telling the truth about stopping the fighting, but honestly, the way he spoke about leaving really greatly enraged me. I cornered him against the wall, and that's when he cheated.

While I had him in the corner, he took out his pistol, positioned it on my thigh, and fired. His bullet lodged in my right leg. Now, I consider myself stoic, but I had just been shot. My leg felt numb, and I started to feel cold. No matter what you are told, there are no words to accurately describe how being shot feels. Needles don't come close to that feeling anymore. Knives and slow torture are the closest feeling you can get.

My body hit the floor, and my blood hit the pavement. He started to close in on me. *Charles*. His name was etched on the left side of his jacket. *Rank: Lieutenant General*. Demi and Finn were nowhere to be seen. I was hopeful that they had taken the king and everybody else while I was fighting.

A needle pierced the skin on my right leg. *The exoskeleton's auto-injecting anesthetic!* I swiped the heir to the PFS succession to the ground. I pinned him down and grabbed his head, slamming it to the pavement once. Wasting no time, I held onto his head with one arm and continuously pounded his skull with my armored glove.

He couldn't take it anymore. I had won. His life was now mine. This made me laugh. It was not a happy laugh, but an insane chuckle.

Something snapped in me. It echoed into the streets and made the PFS step back a bit. I stood up and had an idea. I grabbed my defeated, broken opponent by the collar and dragged him to a stop light. His troops were puzzled as to where I was taking their bloodied commander. How dare he want Olivia.

"No, no, let me go. Stop! Don't do this!" His wheezing voice pained my ears.

"Shut up, you. Oh, come on, don't be a coward. It'll only hurt a second."

I limped closer to the stop light high above me. When I reached it, I aimed my wrist rope and let it hang on the light. I then grabbed Charles and tied one end of the rope to his neck before cutting the rope from the firing mechanism on my wrist.

The PFS MAID rushed toward me before being tackled by Demi's MAID. Finn's MAID jumped down from a building and started shooting the other troops. He got all but one sniper and some of the infantry troops by the time he landed. I quickly pulled Charles up and made sure that the rope was fastened. My insanity was echoing with laughter. This was its only cure. There was a reason the pill was only for emergencies; the side effects weren't good.

He struggled as the life was being choked out of him. I turned around and limped away with my pants continuing to grow heavy from my blood. Demi was pushed into a building as the other MAID readied its sword. Demi took hers out and kicked a car out of her way. The devilish woman screamed and laughed at the gruesome fight she was having.

Finn, in the meantime, was under heavy fire. He sent me a radio message.

"Sir! We came back when we heard the bloody gunshot. The others are running to the LZ. We'll hold them off."

"Negative. Disengage and assist in the extraction," I said. My deep breaths helped steady my aim as I used my sleek rifle to fire at the infantry.

"Sir!" Demi barked at me at me as sparks flew from her and the other MAID's clashing swords. "Ya can get me later for insubordination, but you can take yer damn orders and shove 'em up yer arse. We won't make it five minutes with these bastards on our tails. Now go!"

"Just go sir!" Finn said as a tank crushed his MAID's foot. "We'll hold them off. Besides, you have to get to Olivia; she took a liking to ya, mate. Go; we'll hold them here." He activated a missile that flew at supersonic speed, and the turret of the tank broke off. This sent the gunner running out of the vehicle, on fire, falling to the ground. Finn's back turret mercilessly gunned down the gunner. Antiaircraft missiles fired from his back launchers into the ships swooping down on him.

I turned around to where the king and the whole group used to be. I took a look at the map and saw them moving around the fighting. Limping as quickly as I could, I headed after them. Three rockets detonated near me.

I passed buildings as I heard ships overhead. Some were PFS, and a few were UGF. The fighting escalated as the light-red sky darkened. I was captivated by the beauty of the fight. I had a feeling of admiration for those who could pilot an airship better than I. A fighter pulled up and engaged another fighter. Explosions and turbine exhaust fumes came trailing behind the ships. The air battle was magnificent, orchestrated, precise, intelligent. It was fought by Hyperions, drop ships, fighter ships, bombers, attack ships; anything that could fly was caught up in the fight. Some ships broke off from the fight and assisted the ground troops. This was the modern-day miracle and beauty of seeing nature on Earth, or seeing the nature of the cosmos. I moved my eyes off the sky and back to the ground.

When I was a few blocks behind them, an attack ship swooped down. It had been fighting Finn, but it started shooting at me. A missile hit two meters to my right on the building beside me, which caused shrapnel to hit my temple and eyebrow as I flew to my side. My body must have looked like a rag doll. The feeling of not having control of my trajectory got to me. The green visor was now broken, when I landed; so were the goggles that I wore under them. My head felt light and warm; crimson liquid flowed from my wounds. My right eye could not open, my hands shook, and my knees wobbled. I took out my data compressor and used it as a mirror. I could see a metal shard sticking out of my eyelid; it appeared to be about halfway into my iris.

"Ahh. Ahhhhh. Ehh, no, no, no." A yell erupted from my lungs and shattered my heart.

I pulled out the shard. More blood gushed from my eye, and an even louder pained grunt escaped from me.

The ship came back for another gun run before a UGN attack ship challenged it. Both flew higher to dogfight. The group was hiding in an alley when I reached them. I sat down as one of the police medics ran up to me with a sickly expression and started taking off my helmet and addressing my head wound.

I tried pushing him away, but he held my down. He asked for someone to keep my arms down as he applied gauze compresses to my head. Rick, Carl, Church, and Yuri helped the medic as he cleaned the blood and wrapped my right eye and the right side of my head. He put my helmet back on and tried to look at my leg wound.

"No! We don't have time. We need to get to the landing zone, and fast. We have to go."

"Gerald, where are Demi and Finn?" The king asked, his eyes darting from side to side.

"They're buying us time."

"You're hurt!" Olivia ran up to me and hugged me.

"I'm all right. We have to get going.

"What happened to your leg? My god, your eye!" Her face paled.

"Oh damn, that's a gunshot wound!" the medic said. "We need to get you to a med-vat, Captain."

"No time. We have to go." The words left my mouth as my right leg limped behind.

The dogfights were getting more and more intense, as were the city bombardments from orbital cannons.

There was arguing among the planet's leaders, but they soon quieted.

I heard gunshots in the hospital and behind us, where the MAIDs and enemies were fighting. It was hard to see well with only one eye available. My walking was getting worse also to the point that Carl and the Medic had to put their arms around me as support. I kept getting shivers and twitches in my body.

It became harder and harder for me to move even my fingers. My strength was leaving me to rot. *How much blood did I lose? A pint? A half liter?* It was hard for me to tell, the stupid pills had left me groggy.

"Sir, stay with me," the medic said. "Stay awake, sir."

"Shut up," I wheezed slowly. "I'm not dying, just losing consciousness."

"No sir, you've lost a lot of blood. Don't fall asleep." He dragged me along while looking in my medical pouch.

He found what he was looking for in the pouch—a syringe with a green substance in it. It was an erthanstetic, a medicine that kept patients from losing consciousness and kept the heart pumping blood. It was also a painkiller and antibiotic with an effect of temporarily stopping bleeding. Very useful to medics.

He stopped Carl and motioned for everybody else to keep going forward. He pressed a button, and a needle came out. He looked at Carl and then at me while deciding where to put it. When he reached his conclusion, he stabbed my arm with the needle. Almost immediately, I felt a jolt of lightning hit me. Energy started rushing through my veins as the substance worked its way into my body. I pushed the pair away from me. I, stretching my arms, and my back cracked as I sat up. I didn't feel too bad now. This was good news. I checked my wrist as

I limped toward the group. Olivia hugged me and put her head on my chest. To her I was back from the dead, even though I hadn't died.

Oddly, the sound of gunfire was growing louder. I looked at my wrist again and saw friendly troops ambushing a squad of PFS soldiers. It made me wonder, *Why have humans always killed humans?* Was it psychological? Was it in our nature? Was it some undiscovered gene humans have? It takes many by surprise when their survival is threatened, what they become just to survive. We put up the cloak of civilization just to barricade our nature. But in the end, it appears that our care for others stops us from grabbing a rifle and running into the streets and firing at everybody passing by, or bombing a school.

But that latter thought stopped me. Even if we have people we care about, humans still kill. Many terrorists, killers, and wretched people had people they cared about at one point in their lives. It was scorcher shit to think that humans controlled themselves for the people they cared about. So why do we do it? For the same reason I hanged Lieutenant General Charles. Because deep down, humans are insane people with thoughts, doubts, emotions, and desires. We are peaceful one day and violent the next. I love humanity. Creatures that build progress, make inventions of benefit, take actions that help them live better, and make discoveries to keep their species alive, but they leave the dead and weak behind. Darwin was right; only the strong can survive.

"Sir!"

"Gerald!"

"Captain!"

"Son!"

I snapped back to reality. The faces of a number of frightened people looked at me. I must have zoned out in my thoughts. My previous thoughts had brought into question what I've done and said. They also made me realize something.

"It's the duty of the strong to protect those who cannot protect themselves from those who wish to do harm." I whispered. "What?" I shouted

Everyone looked at me strangely. Trying to look oblivious to their stares, I pressed forward toward the hospital.

My thoughts kept going back to that thought. It's a truth, and it had been a United Galactic Federation guideline for some time. I had been living it through war after war, fight after fight, death after death. Protecting those who cannot protect themselves against those who have oppressed for selfish reasons.

There was shouting and whistling among the group when we reached the hospital. It was like the rest of the city—a giant in nature. It was also in defiance to nature, as its heavy ship port hung from its side over the ledge of the hill.

Three soldiers came out of the hospital and helped carry some of our wounded.

A lieutenant approached me, probably the one in charge of the battalion.

"We've been expecting you, Captain. We've been holding the hospital for a while." His expression showed that he was oblivious of what we had been through.

"Where's the extraction ship?" I asked as my eye searched around.

"I'll call it in right now."

"Good. Now two questions. Is anyone here of a higher rank than a captain? And are you under direct orders to stay here even if I order you elsewhere?"

"No, and no."

"Good. I need you to take your battalion and assist two friendly MAIDs fighting a PFS battalion," I ordered. I had to help Finn and Demi.

"Sir, we have wounded," he said. "Can we leave them with you for extraction?"

"Yeah, just go. Hurry now! There's another MAID there, and you're still here." I pointed to where the MAIDs were.

"We cleared a path to the landing pad," he said. "Wasn't easy, but we did it." He opened up a line to his wrist radio. "All right, Ghost Battalion, we're moving to assist friendly units taking fire. Captain Grey here will take care of our wounded. Let's kick ass!"

His troops exited the hospital and began making their way to the kill zone. A medic reached me and asked him to take care of one of his wounded. The police medic, having overheard that, ran to us and asked where he was. Both medics ran into the hospital, and a few moments later, the medic ran out behind his battalion.

"All right, everyone inside," I ordered.

The police officers covered the king and his men. I held on to Olivia. She looked at me as she moved her hair to her side. I pretended to do the same with the outer part of my helmet. She put her hand on my bandaged eye, pulled me closer, and kissed it. It took a great deal of restraint to avoid crying out in pain. Clenching my teeth, I managed to smile.

"Let's get inside," I said to her, and I accompanied her as we entered.

"Gerald, what's gonna happen when this is over?"

"I'm not sure. We'll think of something."

"Gerald, there's something I need to talk to you about."

"Later. I need to see how many are wounded."

I saw about ten soldiers in the lobby. Some had gunshot wounds; some, very bad shrapnel wounds. I picked one up and helped him through the exploded doors.

# CHAPTER TWENTY-SIX

## THE SACRIFICE

**A** radio squawked. A wounded soldier called me and threw the wrist device to me. I caught it in my right hand and answered.

"This is Reaper, over."

"Have you reached the landing pad, Gerald?" Ryan sounded as though he was not going to give me a short speech.

"I'm inside the hospital, making my way there."

"Good. I'm sending a drop ship to extract you and everyone you brought."

"So after the extraction, what then?"

"Two of the Protectorate battleships and three of our battleships have taken such heavy damage that they have had to leave the fight. Their fleet is slowing down. Our ground troops already control fifty percent of the city. We will begin the assault to take the palace once we lighten up the remaining ground troops and spawn around it. By the way, there seems to be a crashed PFS ship along the walls of the castle, but no one shot it down. Any ideas about that?"

"I can't say I have any," I said, lying to him—and remembering it was Eric's fault.

"And we still have to worry about the colossal Goliath."

"Any signs of it?".

"No sign of it."

"That's bad."

"Especially if I have twenty percent of my manpower looking for it. And its babies are making an even greater mess around the battlefield. More soldiers are getting killed by them then by the damn Protectorate troops," he confessed.

"How can we lose a giant creature like that? It's taller than most of the freaking buildings."

The group moved deeper into the hospital. The darkness outside and the lack of electricity rendered the whole place darker than the insanity of man. The only source of lights came from portable light strobes Ghost Battalion had left behind.

"I can't see anything!" a frightened casualty yelled. It was the one the medic was in charge of.

"Hey, hey, calm down. You're with Helenac forces. You're being extracted off world."

"Where is my squad? Where am I?" His eyes were covered by gauze, his right arm had multiple bullet wounds, and half his clothes were bloodied.

"Right behind you, Chang," one of his squad members shouted.

"Oh damn, thank whoever the hell I thank, Serg. What the hell happened?"

"You got your ass kicked," another one of his squad teased.

"So did you," a fourth voice said.

There was a hole in one of the walls, caused by a CED5, or controlled explosive device five. We made our way through it as everybody spoke about different topics. I counted how many people were with us, and the number was thirty-two—thirty-three including me. A drop ship had enough room for everyone.

We followed the lights that showed the way to the landing pad. In the semi-dark corridor, a different light appeared at the end. There were cheers at the sight of this. This was the pleasant sight of victory. The hospital's landing pad had the capacity for three ships to land on it. It had an amazing view overlooking much of the city. In fact, the elevation was great enough that observers could see to see the other end of the city, thanks to it being built on top of the tallest cliff on the planet.

"Hey, look at the embassy!" someone shouted. We all ran to see what was happening.

The last time I remembered seeing it, the UGF flag was not on the flagpole; rather, it was the PFS flag. I peered at the building through my rifle's scope and saw a squad lowering the PFS flag. The one who tore it down threw it into the wind. Up went three flags. The top flag was the UGF flag, the second was the newest flag of unity—it was all the flags of the colonies and former Earth countries in one—and the third was the Helenac dove flag.

The squad of soldiers saluted the flags. The group cheered at the joyous scene. I, however, did not cheer yet.

When we were in a drop ship nearing the carrier, then I would cheer.

The pink sky made the city even more breathtaking. But did we really need to see things get destroyed to appreciate it?

My radio crackled to life. "Reaper, this is Eagle Star, we're approaching to extract you now."

My hand went for the device and pressed the talk option.

"Eagle Star, this is Reaper, roger that."

We made room for the ship to come down on the landing zone. I threw a homing beacon to guide the ship while landing. A flicker of light appeared in the sky. The drop ship! Wonderful things, able to carry forty troops and their equipment.

However, life had turned the *L* in my luck into an *F*. As everyone's hopes were raised, as freedom was in our minds, a spawn egg hit the side of the ship. The ship lost altitude and a little control but was able to regain it. Five more eggs hit the ship's turbines, and an alarm began to sound over the radio.

"This is Eagle Star. We're hit. Repeat, we're hit! We're going down! We're losing altitude. Something hit us!" The doomed pilot's voice was drowned out as his falling ship crashed into the hospital and exploded into a hellish fireball.

"No!" My yell demoralized the group more than it should have.

This act was destructive. I knew this feeling of dread was new to some of them. It could be seen in the few who were shouting nervous yells. It could be seen in the majority who fell silent but demonstrated the loudest emotions. The ground moved underneath us. An enormous hand placed itself upon the platform. Another hand appeared, and a Goliath's head rose to meet us.

It had been a while since the Goliath and I met eye to eye. Only this time, it was literally eye to eye. The eye I had wounded was a bloody mess. The blood had dried there; and the giant would probably never see from it again. When it recognized me, the slow creature opened its mouth and released its god-awful shriek.

Windows behind us shattered; all of us covered our ears. This was the most demonic, unnatural shriek anyone could hear.

"Oh, I knew it! I knew it! We're dead." The blindfolded grunt shook and began to sob.

The Goliath began to raise its hand when I heard loud music. Gunfire and missiles hit the back of the creature, and it lost its grip and fell.

An insane laughter filled the air, but this time it wasn't mine. A phantom ship and its ghostly crew landed on the platform.

"See! I told you he was still alive, Dimitry. You owe me fifty credits!" Emanuel jumped from the open side door, holding on so he didn't fall out.

"Bah! You should have died, sad man; now I'm fifty dollars poorer."

The Russian's whining annoyed me. "Both of you can go to hell! All right, we need extraction to the *Schatten*. Captains and women go first! I'm joking; everybody in now. Can you open the cargo door at least?"

The door descended, and everybody got on.

"How did you guys even survive in the first place? I thought you were destroyed for sure," I asked, holding on to Emanuel's head.

"Well you see, when I kicked you, I shut the doors and strapped myself to the nearest seat. Then Dimitry's quick thinking hit the light-speed drive, exploded the projectile, and made us go back to the Havoc station."

"You sly dogs." I applauded them.

I held on to Olivia's hand as she entered. I took off my helmet off and put it on her, and the confused look she gave me as the air filter activated delighted me. Everyone else complained about and gagged at the smell.

"You're coming with me, right?" she asked.

"I'm right behind you. I've come too far to leave you now." I winked at her with my good eye.

"Captain, this ship has seats for twenty-five. Thirty is the limit. We can't take everyone," Emanuel confessed to me in private.

As I processed my thoughts, a heavy feeling hit me in my stomach. I knew my mission was to extract the royal family and anybody useful to the throne, not the wounded, and not the police officers. But I also knew what my thinking was. I couldn't abandon the wounded here.

"Gerald. Leave me here," the king said softly.

Such a great man. But I couldn't even consider that.

An enraged shriek made this decision-making moment to begin to shatter.

"I made this kingdom, and if it is to die, then I would die with it."

"Sir, thank you for offer." I put my left hand on

his shoulder, displaying my kindest smile. "But I can't take it."

I was already throwing a hook with my right arm, and Emanuel flinched when the blow landed. His lightning-quick grab stopped the king from hitting the floor. I looked inside as everyone stared at me.

"Who has SABER rounds?" I asked the shocked crowd.

Three soldiers threw their magazines at me. Emanuel dragged the king inside, cursing in Spanish.

"Well, who's staying?" Emanuel's question hung in the air.

I looked down at my bloody boots. "Take the wounded and leave me."

He didn't question me, but it made him uneasy. He wanted to ask me it if I was sure. At least I hoped, with my entire mind and body, for him to want to ask me it.

I smiled at him. "What are you waiting for?"

He wiped a bead of sweat from his brow. With grief, he saluted me. I put my hand on the Dragula. The shriek from the injured Goliath grew louder. I slammed my palm against the bulky cargo door, indicating that the ship should take off. Olivia's brown eyes watched me break my promise. She ran up to me, but Emanuel grabbed her before she was able to reach me.

"No! Gerald, get in! Don't leave me." She jumped, trying to reach me from the ship, but Emanuel held her back. She reached for my back and grabbed one of my knives. She pulled on the handle and took it out of the scabbard. Emanuel brought her inside the ship as the door closed.

I turned and looked at the ascending craft. I saw her

tearstained face. Her eyes were red and wet. There was a stream under them. Her shouts burned holes into my soul. The Dragula picked up altitude and grew smaller and smaller. The image of Olivia crying made me weak inside. I could still hear her crying in my head. My hands found themselves in my pockets. Even from this distance, her cries echoed in my mind so strongly that I could swear I still heard them.

"Goodbye, farewell, and amen," I said. "I love you."

Immediately, Olivia's sobs quieted down. I didn't understand that.

"Gerald, I love you too." Her voice was in my head.

The transmitter she had given me! It was still on.

I took off my headset and took the little earpiece out. With great difficulty, I let it go. It fell to the ground, and I crushed it with my foot. I cast my gaze downward. In my imagination, it began to rain, and the only area it impacted was between my eye and the ground.

The Goliath picked itself up again. I was left to my fate, but if my time was due, I was damn sure the Goliath was coming with me.

I wiped my eye and smiled at the ugly bastard.

"I have a bullet in my leg and some metal in my head and chest, dread in my stomach, and two damn shaky wrists, so if bringing you down is to be the last thing I do, let's just hurry up." My words were going to die with me.

"You think I will die so easily? Do you hear me? I can do so much more—so much more! I could change. I have changed, and now you want me to join my squad members, the police officers your children have killed. Will you just give me a minute to enjoy myself? Will I not enjoy what I deserve? Don't I get another chance at happiness? I don't know who I'm talking to now, you or God, but you're both are so unfair. Just so unfair!"

I kicked a rock on the ground and threw my hands in the air before crossing my arms.

"But now I've gotten myself into a situation that will end me. I couldn't be an explorer, I couldn't be a man of honor, I couldn't even spend time with the girl. Just remember, killing me is going to be a pyrrhic victory." I turned on the communicator for air support.

"All available air units, this is Captain Grey. I have in front of me the Goliath. My location is the Grand Helenac Hospital. Bomb the hell out of it, regardless of me. Tell Marshall Kayre the VIPs are on their way."

"This is Ocean five, I'm near the area. Are you sure?"

"Captain Grey, this is Wolf three. Heading there now."

I received messages from at least seventeen ships nearby that were prepared to bomb the area. I wasn't listening; I was shooting the Goliath, keeping its attention on me. I shot my last remanding SABER rounds. I could tell that it hurt the damn monstrosity, as wounds began to open on its face. It punched the building above me. Debris came down behind me, and I moved to avoid it. I loaded an experimental round and shot at its arm. The round penetrated the skin and exploded, leaving a gaping hole.

The Goliath roared as it pulled itself up more. I fell back on some debris, and my back hit a big piece of concrete with metal poles sticking out of it. That is when I saw a little parachute land next to me. I took the parachute off the object it was attached to and noticed it was a box. My Hornet broke the metallic box, revealing an antitank missile delivery system and a note written in Cyrillic, I don't read Cryllic so it was useless to me. I grabbed the system, and my unwounded leg moved me into the damaged hospital. The sound of turbines from ships was getting closer.

"Captain Grey, this is Hunter-Killer six two. Twenty seconds to bomb drop. Danger close," One of the ships said. I heard that and the sound of a hand breaking through a wall. I was grabbed by the Goliath. My body was pulled out and squished at the same time. This worried me now even more; I feared being eaten alive. The ships were closing the distance.

I was face-to-face with the creature. I aimed the delivery system and waited. The Goliath roared again, causing the glass of the aiming device to shatter. A missile emitted a screech, and an explosion blasted a hole through the Goliath. More missiles struck their target.

Valkyries—slow attack ships that were used as ground support only, propelled by two twin-repulsor engines on each side—started shooting at the creature. But the injuries I gave it made it focus on only me.

Jazz hands; trigger fingers; high powered, highly explosive controlled bombs; rockets; missiles; plasma; and even bullets were used against the Goliath. It kept bleeding until it finally tried to put me in its mouth. Its last supper.

This was just what I had been waiting for. I squeezed the trigger, and a missile accelerated to twice the speed of sound. The projectile I launched hit the Goliath's mouth and made a hole inside of it. It let go of the landing platform, with me still in its hand.

The grip lessened, but physics made me fall into its mouth when I pushed myself out of its hand. Even after it was dead, the Goliath hurt me. The razor-sharp teeth of the monster grabbed my hip and cut my vest, and my skin tore as I fell deeper into darkness. I was cut from my left leg to my ribs.

When the Goliath fell, its many delicate bones broke.

"Am I dead?" The darkness answered with nothing.

Who knew if I was dead or alive? Who stilled cared if I died? Olivia. *My mind, I like the way you think. Maybe. It's like you are your own person. Are you? I think, therefore I am. I'm getting delusional.*

It was funny to me that I was in the belly of the beast, lying down in this corpse, this god-awful smelly monster, whose stomach was darker than starless space. I stood on my wounded feet. My arms were covered with gashes and had been stabbed with bones, but I was able grab my sword.

I raised my arms and poked around me. My hands hurt, so I took off my protective gloves and rubbed my sore, bloody knuckles. I put the gloves back on and stretched my fingers a bit. I walked around until I realized I had fallen down the Goliath's throat but had not reached the stomach. With my rifle on my back, I made my way to higher ground. The little light my exoskeleton's sensors emitted allowed me to climb higher to the "ceiling," which I hoped was the inside of the stomach. When I reached it, I raised my sword, ready to make an opening. Then I noticed a piece of Goliath bone in my arm.

My arm shakily lowered, and I pulled the bone out with my other hand. With that done, I made a cut in the monster, and reached one hand out. I stuck my sword out of the darkness and used it to pull myself out.

The Goliath was still twitching, and premature spawn were being shot out of its turned back, dying quickly. Now they were like humans, born only to die.

My hands went for two things: my rifle and the experimental bullets. I loaded a round and walked to its head. I took quick aim. The round left the barrel and blew another hole in the monster. That was my sixth experimental bullet. The Goliath had stopped moving now; it was finally dead.

"My sixth bullet? Ha! I, having received the seven bullets like Caspar from the wolf's den, have instead defeated you, you black huntsman, Samiel. Now you are the one who is dragged to hell. I, the Jaëger, have defeated the Titan." I cried in victory, falling on my back.

"It is only humans that can defeat monsters. I am no longer a monster. I'm sorry, Evelyn. You're right. I am now too weak to accept death instead of making a bargain with darkness to be a monster again." My hand took out the vial containing the red liquid I had obtained from the body of the PFS soldier.

I was exhausted. I was lying on my back on top of the dead Goliath. My hand went to one of my pockets, and out came my bottle of Coke that I got on the Havoc station. I sat up and drank from it. It was damn good. Or maybe it just seemed so damn good because my thirst was so damn great. Or maybe the fact that I was now dying made it taste even more damn wonderful.

"Olivia. Olivia. Olivia. Olivia," I said.

Her face came to mind as I lay back down. I couldn't

stop thinking of her. I lay on my back, Coke in hand, waiting to die, now humming "You Are My Sunshine."

"You really think we're gonna let you die alone, you moron?" My old captain said to me as if he were standing next to me.

"Well, I have a bullet in my leg and am losing blood, so why not?" My taunt would have enraged the original Reaper.

"Because you finally met someone. It's would be dreadful if you died and left her alone. You're crazy if you think I'll let you do that. If *we* let you do that."

"Oh, don't you dare call me crazy," I snapped. "I'm not crazy, though I should be after all I have seen."

"You are such a liar. You are talking to me, a figment of your imagination. We, as in I and the rest of the squad, are in your head now. I think, therefore I am. *I* can't think. We can't take physical form. We reside in your memories."

"All right, so I might be a little crazy, but we both know all people are. And that is fun."

"True, but I need you to live for her. And also there's a squad of PFS climbing up to kill you. No time to reload. Godspeed, Captain Gerald. Live for her. Accept that our deaths were nothing you can control. Be happy and free."

I stood up and saw that my mind was right. A squad was climbing up the body to kill me.

I grabbed my slightly stolen sniper rifle, which was still slung around my torso. My breaths soon steadied as the rounds traveled from my commandeered rifle to distant targets. Two behind me, three in front of me, almost twenty crawling up the body. The rifle had a heavy kick, the barrel felt wrong, and the sight weighed me down; this was something that hadn't been built from new material. After I ran out of ammunition, the damn thing was of no use to me.

I took out my sword, holding it up into the night, and stood momentarily in the light around me, almost as if it were a spotlight. Lights from the soldiers' exoskeleton suits showed me the ghost of the night.

I slammed my sword down on one of the enemy soldiers. Another was still trying to climb up behind me. While I was distracted, one punched me in the face. My retaliation was to stab him in the chest, take out Virgil, and shoot him in the head. Before he fell, I retrieved my sword.

A kick deadened my left leg. I stabbed the one who did that with my remaining knife. I stood up and, with both pistols drawn, shot at two soldiers coming toward me.

A rifle crack made me jump. One soldier was running toward me, firing his weapon with the same consistency as my wild heartbeat. A sting in my stomach pushed me to my knees. A jolt crawled up my spine, and I spit up blood. I raised my pistol, squeezed the trigger, and brought down the firing assailant. I wasn't going to die here by their hands. They needed more to bring me down. I quickly stood up. I was bulletproof. Titanium. Invincible. The toughest soldier on the block.

Death always tries to get us, and it always tries harder when we have the feeling of invincibility. Now I felt that my grave had been dug. It was a feeling that pierced my chest, from my back to the front. The bullet had shattered my dreams. The blood pushed itself out in front of me.

Three PFS soldiers grabbed me while I was on my knees with my blood flowing from my mouth.

A female Ortyran sniper drew closer; I think she was the same one from the holdup with Charles earlier, maybe the only surviving one. Her red-and-black uniform moved quite graciously with the wind, and her coat moved with it. A hood covered her head and hid her black hair. The metal plate on her chest bulged out too much; something was making it pop out. She checked the wound she had given me and played with my hair. My eyes were closing. My vision was fading as well. My thoughts had been slowing down. My panting didn't do much to help either.

"Hello darkness, my old friend. I've come to talk to you once again. I fought the war, but it won't stop for the love of God." More blood fell from my mouth as I chuckled at that stupid phrase.

Was that honestly the best line I could think of before I was to die? Couldn't I come up with an insult instead of that stupid chuckle and weak welcome?

The light sensors attached to my vest, knee pads, and most likely on my back were flashing red. That was known as the color of death, since every freaking thing that resembled death was either black or red. This was probably it. But half of me did not accept it; my dying brain was already making a plan of how to get out of this situation. A discomfort on my wrist reminded me of the device I had taken from Olivia.

"Damn, you're cute. It's a shame I have to kill you. I would have probably dated you if you weren't on the other side." She gave me a light kiss on the mouth.

"Don't worry," the sniper said, "I'll be quick and gentle."

She gave me another kiss, this time on the head, and it goddamn annoyed me that she did that.

My eyes moved down to her breast. It was unfortunate, but that was where my eyes were looking. She drew a knife. It looked familiar, as if it had a twin that had tried to kill me before.

She seemed to struggle with doing it; she hesitated. That's when I had a sudden realization. My perception of the movements and environment around me was now clearer than ever before. The breeze felt like sunshine after the rain. The sounds of birds were like rain after too many sunny days. The warmness of the sun radiated onto my shivering body.

As a blow to the stomach, the realization hit me. My mind finally accepted what that knife was going to do. It accepted what these people would do with me. My good eye stared at the dawn sky and saw the few fading stars. As I shifting my attention back to the woman in front of me, I remembered who I wanted to see before I died. Maybe my mind rejected the idea of my entire life flashing before my eyes; I might have seen my mother or father after so many years, or maybe I would not have seen Olivia.

My breaths grew more shallow and rapid, but before I ceased forever, I heard the sound of turbines. The sound of boots and footsteps also filled the air. Or was it my imagination? It didn't matter; I was going to die. If I meant anything to you, if my story touched you, if you have tears in your eyes, please forgive me. At the hour of my death, at the hour of all our deaths, death means nothing. The days we spent alive mean the entire world.

"Hands in the air!" A voice yelled before I closed my eyes and fell to my side.

"Weapons up" was the last thing heard at that moment.

The last image in my head was a figure in a white dress wearing lipstick smiling at me with a stream of tears running down her face.

# CHAPTER TWENTY-SEVEN

## REDEMPTION

Iopened my eyes again. I blinked and adjusted to the lights. My body was lying down on a bed. Bandages covered my right arm, right leg, left leg, hands, waist, chest, and stomach. A tickle in my throat made me cough, quite possibly for the first time in a while. I was in a giant room that had hundreds of beds. I looked around. On my right was a wounded PFS prisoner of war. To my left was a UGF casualty. Across from me, wounded from both sides were being treated by medical drones. Two hands were holding on to my hands.

I squeezed my left hand, and someone shifted her head on the mattress. A drone then approached me.

"Good morning, Major," the drone said.

"Major? I'm a Captain." My voice was hoarse from lack of water.

The drone produced a cup and poured water from its side compartment. It handed me the cup, and I let go of my sister's hand. The crisp water refreshed my throat and gave me strength to keep talking.

"So tell me, what happened?"

"Records indicate you have sustained wounds on your right arm, your right thigh, your stomach, your arms, your stomach, your thigh, and your chest, including a punctured lung, a severed artery and three bullets and also shrapnel in your eye. For your bravery, you were posthumously awarded the rank of major. You were rescued from a squad of an elite Protectorate Federation of System infantry battalion."

An alarm rang, and the drone excused itself and went to other injured soldiers. Olivia's hand tightened in mine. My head weakly turned to her. A set of footsteps alerted me someone else was coming.

"You took a hell of a beating." Ryan approached with bleary eyes.

"Goddammit, I'd never thought I'd be this happy to see you," I said, giving him a handshake and a manly hug.

"Gunshot wounds, Goliath teeth, punctured lung, foreign objects in you, and a busted eye? I thought we lost you for good. Well, we did lose you; you just came back to us." He smiled as he patted my shoulder. His uniform was a mess.

"You lost a lot of blood; we barely got you out of the med tube. That was like twelve hours ago. You've been dead and sleeping for a day now. Your sister—god, she is amazing. When she got here, she threatened to blow the whole ship up if I didn't tell her where you were." I then pieced together that we were in the recovery room of a carrier.

"I died?" That was the only question that seemed to matter at the moment.

Ryan hesitated at first. That's how he is when you ask

him a big question like that; he hesitates. He looked at me, saying everything while not even opening his mouth.

"Yeah, technically, you did. For about five minutes too."

I didn't know why it bothered me. It just stood there as a thorn in my conscience, knowing that I'd died. I'd wished for it for a while, but now I couldn't stand the thought of dying.

"Don't let it get to you. You're alive, and you completed the mission. Your sister would be proud of you." He hesitated again. I liked the man, as much as I hated when he did that. "Speaking of your sister, she and the princess have not left your side since you got here."

"What happened on the body of the Goliath? You know, with the PFS."

He chuckled at that. Laughter always meant good news.

"Just a random squad." It obviously didn't convince him either.

"Well, I can't feel my leg. Did we win?"

"I can't lie to you; I promised to you, when I found you and your sister the day after you both were released, that I would help you and always tell you the truth. We still haven't taken all of the city. One more carrier is left. The rest of their fleet has surrendered or were destroyed." He hesitated again. I braced for worse news. "Okay, I'm joking, we won. When we picked you up, half of their army had already surrendered. But damn did they take casualties, as you can see here." He pointed around the room.

I looked around and saw many PFS soldiers. The

occasional UGF soldier was also on a bed. Then it hit me—everyone was the same. Sure, some skin color was different, but that was it. We may have had different uniforms, but in the end, every damn soul in there was human. It is sad to think that we kill each other because of different ideologies, even though we all originated from the same planet.

"We're picking up the pieces ..."

He kept speaking. However, I just faded away. I couldn't listen because I was in my own little depression. I heard him talking, but he might as well have been galaxies away. In my mind was the teenager I killed back when I brought down the gunship. Had he really needed to die? I really couldn't answer that. No, but he did reach for his weapon. He did have an intention to kill me. But did that give me any right to kill him? Him so young, with life and hope, did he have a right to die? It was funny, so funny in the stupid ironic sense, that my eye twitched in a way that made a tear fall. It was an emptying feeling, to feel humanity in me after letting it go for so long. Maybe I should have died. The hardest two days of my life were over. The time had passed in a flash, yet it felt like a year of experience.

I let go of Olivia's hand and got up. Ryan stopped talking as he saw me leaving. I looked around me and saw the consequences of war: men with bandages, broken spirits, sunken eyes, no will, missing body parts, and dread. I checked on my leg and I found that I had an exoskeleton support for it.

It was amazing that when I left the room, injured soldiers were still being brought in for treatment. I remembered that one had blood on his face, and his eyes were focused a thousand yards away. *Dread*, I thought. I walked around the carrier and saw people trying to fit weapons back into lockers, only to fail and keep making the same mistakes. On benches, people were sitting down looking at their devices; most had pictures of comrades. That was all they could think about. "It's all right, man, I'm sorry. You couldn't do anything; he died painlessly." The words sounded familiar.

I had to get out; I had to leave. If I stayed any longer, I would break down at the sound of these voices. On the left side of the wall was a screen. Names and service numbers were displayed there. It was unmarked, but we all knew it a list of the names of those who had died. A man had his hand on the screen and was weeping.

The carrier was playing soft, slow music. It was supposed to keep morale high, but these people had been pushed far past the bounds of sanity to keep it high.

I eventually found myself looking out of one of the carrier's massive windows. I held on to the rail infront of the windows and looked at the outside. We were in orbit, and it was a sight that not many people ever had the chance to see. What choices had led me to this carrier? What decisions had led me to be a soldier? Ever since the orphanage, I wanted to be an explorer of the universe. However, I found out life is not so kind to dreams. And I am a dreamer. The profession in which I was best able to see different planets and stars was the profession I was in now.

However, every planet we reached was dead.

The stupidity of that thought made me hit my fist on

the rail. I hadn't always been like this, my sister use to tell me I was a happy kid, I would play virtual games with friends, I would always smile.

Was I really unhappy with life? Had I really started taking life for granted?

"You only take life for granted because you're not a ghost." My old captain approached me with his infamous synthetic Cuban plasma cigarette.

"And the reason you are unhappy, kid, is because you think you have it worse than anyone else. You have had a better life than you think; better than most people have had." He crossed his legs while leaning over the rail.

"I mean, look at that damn view. Damn—and I speak of you, for obvious reasons—but it is a good time to be alive to see that."

"Why is it that I am still living but you died? What the hell did I do right to deserve that? Why were so many of my people taken, and here I am wondering why they haven't taken my life?" As we orbited, that planet was a sight that could make the Grand Canyon jealous.

"*Gerald*. You know what that name means? Master of the spear. You know what? You are the person that fights for others." He hit me on the head. He might have been in my imagination, but it hurt. "Not all good people get good things, and not all bad people get bad things. Do you understand that not everyone alive gets what he or she deserve? But it's the things we appreciate that we should value more than the things we deserve.

"You need to be the one that fights to defend others. You, like everyone else in this life, want to make an impact in this universe. If you can do something in life, it is a disgrace and a cowardly thing to not do it. Did you think it would be so simple, though? Did you think you would not take any casualties? People die every day, but it is up to the living to make sure their deaths were not in vain. And it is the job of the dead to remind the living of that." He pointed his finger at me as he spoke.

"You do things, or you don't do them at all. You don't BS them. It's simple like that. You grab your goal, and you do whatever the hell you do to achieve it. And don't you ever tell me or anyone else that life doesn't let you achieve that goal, because that is a goddamn lie. Everyone makes his or her own destiny, if they choose."

I looked at him and reflected on what he said. He inhaled on his cigarette deeply. He began to smile when I made up my mind. I smiled at him and took off running back to the sick bay. I had gotten a new horizon in life, a new message.

"Good luck, Chuchie, good luck," he said as I left.

I passed all those who were mourning—those who had fallen into a deep, dark hole. We as a species always fall; we fall into darkness. But we always pull ourselves up from the rubble. If we don't rise, we stay behind and are forsaken.

When the sliding doors of the recovery room opened, I went back to my bed. I must have been gone for a while, because Olivia and Evelyn were awake. Marshall Kayre was talking to Evelyn.

"He's been different since he came back from his first combat mission," said Evelyn. "He came back, and his eyes had that blank stare."

"Who knew twenty missions later he would be the

only surviving member of his squad," Ryan added. "Speak of the devil, here he is."

I rushed past them and grabbed Olivia by the hand.

"Sorry, I need to borrow her." My words were as quick as my actions.

"Gerald, wait!" Evelyn yelled.

We ran out of the room, hand in hand. Olivia giggled at the circumstances. She had this adorable giggle that made me melt inside. We ran to an elevator shaft and called one up. A few seconds later, a doctor and a drone walked out of the elevator while we entered it.

I held her hand and pressed the button for the engine room. No one went there unless there was a problem.

We got out and hugged right there. I held on to her and put my hands around her waist. "We need to talk."

The morbid look in her eyes worried me. This was the moment I learned that that one sentence had the power to remind me of all the bad things I had done in my life.

I pressed my lips against hers and didn't let her speak. When she finally let go, our eyes met and she smiled at me, and that smile was her most beautiful signature smile. If I had been born a woman and had met her, I would still have tried to make her mine.

"Charles was my cousin," she confessed to me.

"Ew, incest, that is nasty." I began to laugh at this coincidence. "Small universe."

"He's like my third or second cousin."

"That's still nasty," I answered.

"I know it is. What did you do to him, anyway?" she asked me.

I thought of how his body must have still been hanging in the wind.

"Well, I beat him up, and then I left Demi to deal with the MAID. So not much," I answered, scaling back the truth.

"Gerald. There's something that is bothering me."

"What is it?"

"What's going to happen to us?" she asked me.

My breath slowed down, and I am willing to bet my oupils expanded.

I let her go and turned around. It was warm in there; the nuclear fusion and mixing of the dark matter and plasma irradiated the room. My own doubts about the future returned to me. I couldn't leave her, but I couldn't abandon my duties.

"Didn't we get married on that rooftop?" she asked. "Didn't we catch each other? Have we not cried on each other? Have we not saved one another? Does that mean anything? It means something to me."

"It meant something to me, too." I regretted whispering those words and not saying them loud enough.

The elevator came down to our floor. Olivia didn't say anything but went and faced the door. When it opened, Evelyn standing there, gazing at Olivia.

"When you have an answer, I'll be ... waiting for you."

"Olivia, wait."

"Please don't; I don't want to lose you."

"I don't want to lose you either."

"Then why didn't you answer?"

"Because I'm not sure how to feel about it. I don't want to be without you. But I don't know how to hold on to you. Because I'm afraid. Afraid to lose you because … I don't know. I don't want to hurt you like that."

My words hung in the air. I clasped my hands and cupped my mouth with them. Olivia's eyes pierced into mine. She didn't know how to react. Even Evelyn stared at me in amazement. The low hum of the reactor and the sounds of our breathing didn't let silence in.

"Do you forgive me for almost shooting you?" she asked.

"I'll always forgive you. I guess I can't be mad at you."

Olivia stared at Evelyn and walked toward me. I closed my eyes and waited for her to do something. She put her hand on my face and hugged me. Her fingers caressed my scar, moved my hair to the side, and then rested on my waist. I opened my eyes and stared at her. She gave her smile, and I returned it. Her white dress showed bloodstains and dirt.

From the corner of my eye, I could also see Evelyn smiling. Olivia was mine. Helena was as safe as it could be. The PFS were beaten. Yet something still bothered me.

Beeping from Olivia's wrist caused her to pop up. It was a message.

"I need to get to the deck with my father. Gerald, I love you."

Her smile made me forget my worry. "I love you too."

I meant it. It was my first love, my first attraction, and I was being unwise by telling her I loved her.

She got on the elevator and blew me a kiss. The door slid closed, and I responded by sliding down the wall into a sitting position.

"How did I do?" I asked Evelyn.

She slid down next to me and sighed. She put her head on my shoulder.

"Love isn't how you do with someone; it's how you hold on to someone that matters." She punched me on the shoulder.

"I know I've done something right when I make her smile."

"I'm proud of you." She said. "But, I'm also disappointed in you. How can you die like that, you asshole."

"Jeez, I'm sorry; like it was my fault I got shot through the chest with a nine-fifty caliber bullet."

"It wasn't, but I'm still mad at you."

"Sorry." My sarcasm came back. "Why do you make me seem and feel bad?"

"Because, I'm your sister. C'mon, we need to go see the marshal." She stood up and brushed off her uniform.

"Yay, I'm bursting with excitement to talk to him." I heaved a deep sigh.

"Why can't I date someone?"

I hugged her and kissed her forehead. "Because if someone ever hurts you, I'm gonna have to kill him. And if he hurts you by dying, I can't kill him, and you'll still be sad."

"You care so much about me." She smiled and held me tightly.

"Maybe someday you'll find someone who won't hurt you," I whispered to her.

"Let's go to Ryan," she said.

I touched the bandages on my palms and chest. My head wounds had scabbed over and were closing, but they were still there, above my eye. I wondered how I must have looked when they picked me up from the Goliath's body. Speaking of looking, I noticed my clothing when I entered the elevator. I was wearing an untarnished and clean olive-green battle-dress uniform. I wondered who had put that on.

When we reached the bridge, I wanted to go back to the lonely engine room. Officers were running back and forth, and technicians and engineers were manning stations while pilots and other airmen and women maintained the colossal vessel. This motion of men and women reminded me of a stage where everyone played his or her small part as the whole play moved along as a result of the collective motions and acts. I found the good marshal on an elevated platform with the admiral of the fleet. A blonde assistant was next to him, and she looked exhausted and overworked. In her hands were many tablets and a holographic communication device that was transmitting to the Earth's government.

I was saluted by a number of people who drifted into my way as I neared the marshal.

# CHAPTER TWENTY-EIGHT

## FUTURE

"**B**ack through time? You need to stop listening to the damn theories they talk about on those shows you watch, Marshall Kayre. It ain't good for you, and it sure as hell won't be true or legal," the admiral said to Ryan.

"It's just a theory. Hey, faster-than-light-speed travel was just a theory, and we're doing it now," Ryan answered.

"Sir," the blonde said as I walked closer to them.

She had bags under her eyes and a look that told me she was stressed out and needed a three-week vacation. And she was barely in her early twenties. *Stay in school, kids*, I thought.

"Ah, the man of the hour. Admiral, I would like to introduce to you Major Gerald Grey."

The admiral extended his hand, and I firmly shook it.

"Admiral Jesse Beckett. I've heard a lot about you. Most of it good. Now tell me, son, what happened on Helena?"

I sighed at his request. My eyes shifted to the blonde officer, who had the name "Rose" etched to her uniform. I simply smiled at her. My story began at the beginning with the jump from the Hyperion. I then went on to the destruction of the jammer, the dark findings at the embassy, my capture of the traitorous police commissioner, and the death of my friend Eric Sherwood. I told them about the hunt for the commissioner and the moving of the king and the rest of the VIPs, the rendezvous with the mechanical infantry units, and the encounter with the son of the leader of the PFS, including how he wounded me. I avoided telling how I killed him; I merely used a dry military euphemism to say I took him out.

They took an interest in my encounter with Ghost Battalion, and they seemed proud of my sacrifice with leaving myself behind to let the princess and the king be rescued. I took special care to not mention my relationship with Olivia; it would have spread throughout the entire universe. A soldier being involved with the princess— that would have made both of us targets for many insane people.

"You make us proud." The transmission startled me. It was a female voice of great importance.

"Um, thank you, sir ... madam? Who are you again?"

"Oh, very funny. It is I, the representative of the United Galactic Federation, its prime minister."

"Oh, no wonder I didn't recognize you; I didn't vote for you." I regretted nothing.

"Interesting." She had nothing to say to hurt me.

Ryan and the admiral smirked at such a response.

"Now, Gerald, it is important for you to know, that this was an act of war from the Protectorate. It is not something to be taken lightly. Hundreds of thousands of lives were lost to rid this planet of their rule. It is now our time to take the offensive. Would you like to lead the charge?" I felt honored to receive such a request from the prime minister.

My sister gasped at the mention of this. She hugged my arm and looked at me. It was an honorable position to lead an army toward war. Although I wondered if I could get a job closer to Olivia.

"What's the matter, Gerald?" said Ryan. "You don't seem too enthusiastic. If they offered me that job, I would be on the floor having a fit of pleasure."

My head felt light, which made the bridge seem to spin like the planet below. In all certainty, I knew I was going to die if I led the charge. I would be leading the proverbial six hundred into the valley of death, into the mouth of hell. I knew this last fight would be *my* last fight.

"Well, don't rush the man right now, we have two weeks until we depart. Let him rest and give us his answer later," the admiral said.

I nodded, thankful for having been saved by the admiral.

"Sir! Incoming transmission, Origin unknown!" A communications officer shrieked, offending the celebrations.

"Put it through." The admiral said in a monotone voice.

A pale face appeared on the monitor. His receding hairline and dark uniform quieted the entire bridge and demanded our attention and fear.

"Good evening. I presume this is the flagship of the United Galactic Federation fleet orbiting the Helenac system. My name is Presidential Chancellor Tyseus Hopkins, leader of the Protectorate Federation of Systems. I wish to speak to whomever is in charge." He seemed elegant, beyond educated, and charming, and his words terrified me.

The admiral and director both stared at each other before stepping forward with the handheld hologram of the prime minister.

"Two of you, eh? And a hologram of who I presume to be Prime Minister Manali Fitzgerald Clinton. No matter. As you are all aware, my son was killed fighting your troops on that awful planet Helena. I wish for you to know that, despite my infinite patience, you have done a wrong to a man you should not have wronged. The brashness of my son was not to be a declaration of war. He misled me in what would have been a quick operation in grabbing the daughter of the queen, lord rest her soul. However, it is I who am declaring war on you. A total, pure war. It isn't a cold war anymore; it is a continuation of an old war." Evil, pure evil, came from his mouth.

"Big words for a man who is hidden in a system we don't know the location of. You're army was defeated in one day. What makes you think you can win against us now?" The prime minister was as cool as the words of the chancellor.

"Quiet, woman; do you not see I am talking to the men of the military?"

I stood up straighter and stared into the tyrant's eyes. "Well, that's very rude of you, you chauvinistic, inbred swine." I could not believe I was finally the one who would be able to call someone chauvinistic, given my past actions and sayings.

"And who is this? A man of actions or a man of

words? Judging from your leg wound, maybe a man without judgment."

The admiral laughed.

"This man is the one who took out your son," said Ryan, making the chancellor's face redden in anger. This man is a hero and is more capable than any of your regulars or your advanced troops."

The chancellor bit his lip and restrained himself before opening his mouth once more.

"I shall see you burned to the ground. I shall see Earth beg for us to stop before it is razed to its core. You think I am but a coward. Oh, you have no idea what we are capable of. Call on your troops, and come if you dare, but you will find that none of those you send into the darkness will ever return."

"You shall see that we are not about to let a tyrant win," the admiral said. "We have the right to win; we believe in what we do. Can you say the same? Or is your abyss something that blinds you and your people. Transmission over." The admiral's words burned into my head, as did his expression.

Ryan dismissed me, and I walked with Evelyn down to the elevator.

"Don't worry; we'll see his threat turned against him," the firm voice that commanded millions said to us.

I passed a control terminal that monitored the prisoners of war. The female sniper came to mind when I saw this. My hand made its way toward my chest. I could still feel the bullet, the sharp metal piercing my chest, the one that killed my hope.

"Gerald, are you all right?"

Evelyn's eyes turned to the terminal and tried to make out what I was watching. She put her hand over mine and went for her sleek communicator.

"I'm fine. Where is the king?" Such a strange request that must have seemed to her.

It took me eleven minutes, three grasps at my heart, and a moment to catch my breath before I arrived at the Helenac king's assigned room. The king was staring through the polarized glass, watching his war-torn planet, his prized city.

His eyes glazed over, he reminded me of an old man staring at the beauty and might of the ocean. He looked like a man seeing his heaven, or maybe thinking of his past. Either way, he was that planet's flame and hope.

"Sir?" I said.

I brought him back to orbit with me. He turned with the caution anyone would use when hearing a ghost. Apart from the cut on his right cheek, which was my fault, his eyes still had the gentle kindness and wisdom from when I first met him.

"Gerald." He slowly smiled while hugging me.

"I'm glad to see you. I also have to admit, you have one hell of a left hook."

"Thanks. It was mostly the exoskeleton suit."

"The underground bunkers kept the civilians safe. However, much of the city was razed. Many lives lost to greed of man. Monsters were brought from a pit to this peaceful world. Tell me boy, why did this all happen?" The king's eyes grew distant again.

I thought of a reply for him—the man for whom I

had risked my life to save his kingdom, his life, and his daughter.

"I remember watching a show that modeled the lives many people would face if the UGF went to war with the PFS. It also showed the famines and destruction that could follow the war. It showed that there would be death and hopelessness if we went to war. Do you think we can win? Do you think we will stop at a standstill? It makes me question hope. I know it was just a documentary, but still, what do you think? Can hope just die?"

I breathed slowly. I took a deep breath before saying anything. These words were to inspire the king. It was these words that could be used to mend relationships or to give hope.

"I was watching this show, and it made me think. It made me ask if our sins can be forgiven, if our kindness will be paid back to us, if we will really do anything for those we love. It made me think about whether the most seemingly perfect beings really make mistakes and whether we can really be less than human and more than human. It made me ask whether what our past has done to us can really affect whether those we care about treat us differently. Can we really try harder for forgiveness and move along together, and can we still live with darkness and uncertainty yet still have hope, even though we think it's dead? I keep wanting to say no, but the answer is always yes, no matter how much we try to deny it."

He looked at me with a shocked expression. *Can words really inspire people?* I wondered. *Do they have that much power?*

"Gerald!" I heard a voice behind me.

Olivia ran up to me and jumped into my arms. I held her and saw how she was dressed. She was no longer in the white dress. She was in a simple black T-shirt and black pants with white-and-black tennis shoes. But I thought she looked cold like that, and it made me realize something I had mistaken about her. When I first met her, I thought she had a suntan, but in fact she had olive skin. She was still the most beautiful person from all corners of the galaxy. My smile brought her to smile.

I took off my green dress shirt and put it over Olivia. Now it acted as a jacket for her. I still had a black shirt underneath, and the cold didn't affect me. She put it on gracefully and shot me a smile.

"Did you hear the word?" Olivia asked.

"What word would that be, sweetheart?" the king asked.

"We can go back down to the castle. The UGF technicians will detonate a transimitanacal hypertensive pulse. I think that's how you say it."

"A pulse? I think you should see this, both of you," I said, motioning for them to follow me to the window.

A few ships were flying to the poles of the planet; they made a cube-like enclosure and waited a moment. A bluish-red energy began to emerge from the hulls of the ships. In a few minutes, it shot out like a pulse toward the planet. Olivia's hand found mine, and we stood there watching the energy fly down toward the planet. The dark side of the planet began to brighten with light. The damage from the EMP was now being reversed.

# CHAPTER TWENTY-NINE

## THE LAST LIVING SOUL'S TEARS

I stepped off the Hyperion, rifle in hand, waiting for the king and the counselors to step off. This time I wasn't getting shot at, and I wasn't alone. I had at my command a platoon, although they were more a ceremonial unit than a combat unit. I ordered them inside the castle single file, while the point man carried a UGF flag. Interestingly enough, the whole city was done picking itself up. It had no debris, no buildings in pieces. The engineers were to thank for that; they had pulled damaged buildings off their foundations and placed new ones from factory planets whose only purpose was to make buildings.

The Helenac population ascended from their underground holes. They greeted the soldiers with a respectful fear. The troops weren't that frightening, but it might have been that they feared there were PFS stragglers who had not surrendered yet. People slowly began returning to their homes and possessions.

The unfortunate need for the soldiers to turn into peacemakers proved popular, as they actually listened to both sides of arguments and were the Solomons and

Justices that they had fought so hard to protect. It was a nice thing to see at last.

I had hoped to see the glory of the city, and by God was it something. The sky had a pearly pink color; I would never get over that sky. We had suddenly walked past a group of workers from the castle. They looked at me with a fear that scared even me. In such a uniform, I was feared, even though all I ever did was help.

I didn't want to be feared. Not anymore. I just wanted acceptance from these people. What caused them to have such fear in their eyes? Was it my uniform, my expression, the fact that I had a loaded rifle and what I could do with it? I didn't want to be feared, for it hurt me to see that.

Maybe all I had to do was stay on this planet and show the inhabitants that I could offer kindness and protection; that they would never have to fear another attack. Maybe then they would have smiles on their faces and not fear in their eyes.

"Honor guard, halt!" I shouted. The innocent soldiers flinched.

The fountain had not been cleaned yet; it was still bloodstained, and there was something in the bottom. I reached in and grabbed it, and I almost threw it back. The fingers were still clutching a pistol, and the bone reminded me of bleach-white sand.

I called to two honor guard members at the end, Vampire and Werewolf

"Need a hand?" I asked them with a chuckle before sending them on their way to turn the remains in to the logistical officers and the casualty department. Each would then code and identify who the deceased was and inventory the weapon.

The king took a step toward the hastily assembled podium as I turned around and saw ships hovering in the air. Press drones also hovered near the king and recorded our ascent up the heavenly stairs of the last castle on the opposite side of the Milky Way. There was also a crowd in the gardens, listening to and watching the king. They were mostly civilians of this world, very few from the UGF.

The whole crowd seemed to breathe in the figure. We positioned ourselves behind the king and stood guard. Seventeen people, including me, protected the man who ruled this world, but would soon rule less.

"People of Helena and of the United Galactic Federation, the enemy has been overthrown from this world. It came with a price—a price too heavy to bear. But bear it we must. Know that not one sacrifice is taken for granted. We are the only people in such a giant galaxy. We have found other creatures, but they are not like us. We strive forward. We strive for our future. For our children's future."

They were happy to see the king; they respected him, and that was something that made me smile.

"For our protection and safety, I have asked Her Presidency, the minister of Earth, Manali Clinton, for a permanent military presence to help protect my people and to help train my police officers and civilians for military duty, if they so wish it. We will not be slaves. We will be ready if the PFS come back. But I request for a high officer to take on the responsibility of guarding this planet and training her troops and police officers. We are willing to set aside a base to house these troops. In regard to the base, we request a seat on the Federation for a show of loyalty. That is all. Thank you all for your help; my people are in debt to you."

When the press left and the king was out of my jurisdiction for the evening, it was time to prepare for the officer ceremony.

As I was the first to successfully land, an invitation was extended to me and another person of my choosing to the castle celebration. The king personally gave me a room in the castle and said it was mine forever. The clean bedding and soft look made it a place I could stay indefinitely. Evelyn had prepared for me a dress uniform of black and olive green that was neatly folded along with my cap and sword. Now the question of who would accompany to the dance were either my sister, the sniper, or Olivia? Was that even a joke?

The rumor was not that the princess and I were together; it was that she owed me a favor for saving her. Ignorance was bliss. No one knew the struggles we had; no one knew how she was in my head and understood me. Not even she knew I had read her entire diary about me.

However, she probably had seen me reading from my wrist tablet earlier, since the following question made my heart skip a few beats.

"So what have you been reading lately that keeps you from looking up?"

Luckily, I had planned this out with a prepared response.

"You had a story that I downloaded. The one about

a man being punished by having an angel live with him for a year because of a crime he will commit in heaven."

"That's an old book. I didn't think it would interest you."

Holding her hand while we danced was a feeling that was new to me. We moved with a slow grace that soon made everyone forget us. I asked her if she could hold me tighter.

"I'm a lazy dancer," I said. We both smiled at that.

The music was so melancholic and easy that the castle seemed to join in on the mood. Olivia's blue-and-black dress left onlookers with a sense of awe. I hadn't attended prom, because I'd had no one to go with. I could not imagine what would happen if I had done so and my future had changed.

We had so much privacy in such a crowded room. No one saw Olivia planting little kisses on my cheek.

"What happened to Demi and Finn?" Olivia asked, her eyebrows raised.

"The reports indicate that they were badly wounded and are recovering on Earth. They made it in the end—something I can't say the same about regarding the rest of Ghost Battalion."

In the end, when the dance was over, I returned Olivia to her room, with her getting a piggyback from me. The room that had been given to me stood empty, aside from me. It heard my crying and felt the tears fall down. On the message screen of my holographic projector, there was one projection from the damn tyrant who was my leader.

"Please consider taking this position. Your experience fighting the Protectorate will be considerably useful. You have no ties to this planet, so why would you stay here and be its defender, as the king has asked of you? Major, this is an honorable position. I expect your acceptance tomorrow at the same time. Over and out."

In the morning, I sat in an office that had been temporarily given to me. *A position to protect this planet—now that is tempting.* I thought. *I like defense; it's a lot more fun than offense.* My lie was bitter even myself.

I laid my Hornet on the desk and sat down on the spinning chair. I like spinning chairs. When I thought about it, I realized I didn't have to stay with Olivia; I could leave with the fleet, rendezvous on one of the outer planets, and begin assaulting the PFS planet after planet, until we found Ortyra. But all that I had made for me and Olivia, what about that? I had survived numerous conflicts, never doubting myself, only to end up in an emotional conflict, doubting every decision I had to make.

I kept spinning and spinning on the chair, thinking and thinking. A green light flashed on the desk. I pressed a button, and the communication device beeped to a start.

"Major Grey, this is Admiral Beckett. May I have a word?" His image appeared on the window overlooking the city.

"Of course."

"I think you should know that before I became involved in the navy, I was a student in psychology. Would have gotten my master's, but that was a long time ago."

"I'm not sure where this is going, sir," I said, glancing at my rifle as I considered whether I should stay or not.

That was when I noticed the scope on my rifle. It showed a different picture than the one it should have. I picked up the weapon and looked through scope. There I saw debris, fire, smoke, and a destroyed room. It took me a while to notice that it was this room. I stood up straight and looked around through the scope. All around me, the scope made it look as if the room were destroyed, as if a great battle had happened and the whole world had been burned. The admiral was still speaking, but I paid no attention to him. When I put my rifle down, I decided to stay on the planet to see a doctor. At that moment, the view through the scope turned back to normal.

"You and the princess have something, no?" That was the only thing the admiral said that my ears registered.

"How do you know?" I blurted without meaning to.

"I saw it in your expression and in your eyes, man."

I aimed the rifle out of the window; the city still remained the same. I considered that what I had seen earlier might have been an illusion. Maybe I didn't need a doctor; maybe I was able to leave with the fleet. That was when the sight changed again. I dropped the rifle with a yelp.

"You don't have to leave her. You can stay. There is more honor in loyalty to your fellow humans than to your government."

"Where did you learn that?" I asked him, picking up my rifle.

"When I decided to stop fighting for a warlike cause. When I decided to leave the Protectorate to save them."

The rifle no longer held my attention; it was now on the admiral.

"You're Ortyran?"

"No, I was born on their colonies, which is how I know where it is. No place like home, but I like Quebec.

That is my new home. I love the cold. Sometimes it reminds me of my child ... oh, never mind that. Stay with her, protect her. That will make you more of a man, and is it more honorable an action than leading millions to die. Admiral out." With that, he left me in a small office with a rifle that was acting very strangely.

No, not strangely. I looked at the sight and remembered what it was made of—Promethean tears. Crystallized Promethean tears. And as cliché as it sounded, I was looking into a different dimension. Into time. If I stayed, the planet would remain the same. If I left, there would be genocide and destruction. Or maybe it was the other way around.

I laid the rifle down on the desk again and took out my data compressor. It had a picture of Olivia on the background. She had her hand on her hair and was looking up; I had taken it while she wasn't paying attention. She had smiled and asked me to delete it. Later on, while I was talking to a platoon leader, she took a picture of me. I pulled my pistol out and told her to erase it—in a humorous way. We laughed, and she used it as her screensaver.

Something still made me uneasy. I connected the rifle with my helmet, and my visor covered my eyes and audio began to play.

"Now we're here in a hellhole." The voice sounded foreign to me.

The next voice sounded vaguely familiar. "You think you lost so much? Tell me, honestly, do you think you lost so much?"

"You damn well know how much I lost."

"However much you think you lost, the major has lost even more."

Seeing nothing but the smoking ruins, I moved to the corner, where six people took cover behind the debris. Beyond the ruins lay a razed city. Carriers from the Protectorate faction claimed the skies.

"Look at him. Poor guy lost the one he cared about. Never should have left her in the protection of others."

"What about the sniper?"

"She helped our asses; trained most of us. If they catch her, they'll execute her."

"We've got to get to the extraction point."

I was staring at myself—something not many can say. Behind a boulder of rubble, a female figure stood over me. She could not cover my eyes, could not hold on to me; her hands kept getting slapped away by mine. She kept trying to comfort me, but I kept rejecting it.

Her green uniform threw me off. She was familiar. She held a knife similar to the one that had tried to kill me near a car, the same one she tried to use when I was on the Goliath's body. That future was not something I could handle. I threw off my helmet. When the instrument landed, the future changed.

The voice I was willing to give life up for spoke. "When can we tell everyone?"

"Whenever you want."

"Tomorrow?"

"Are you in such a hurry to have a nice wedding?"

I threw myself to the floor, and I almost dropped the rifle in my rush to put on the helmet.

Through the scope, I saw Olivia sitting on my desk

with me, ignoring my work for her. There was a holographic design of an antiorbital cannon on the desk, but I didn't appear to be interested in it in the least.

"Tomorrow," I promised as she pressed her lips against mine.

Back in reality as I knew it, I threw my compressor down and called Ryan. I asked him to meet me in the king's control post. I was ready to talk to both of them. I stood up and admired the city for what would possibly be the last time. The sight changed as quickly as I changed my mind. A thought came to my head. I called the head of management for PFS prisoners and requested to talk to one of them—the sniper.

"Hello handsome," she said hesitantly. "Seems like you can't get away from me."

"Well, I kinda need you, if you're willing to help me." I sounded like such a flirt with her—something I wanted to avoid.

"If it means I can stop fighting, live with ya, or get out of this prison, I'll do anything."

"All right, put the man back on; you're coming with me then."

"You really are a good man. I like that, you bad boy." She giggled.

"You know, I never got your name," I said, putting on a serious face.

"Thrope, Miss Ann Thrope." She laughed.

She even took her crystal dog tags out and showed me her name. Even in her projected form, I could still see them.

"I really love your name." I chuckled and blushed.

"Really? Everyone thinks it's stupid, but you're the first to tell me anything nice about it."

"Well, beautiful name. I can't lie; it's true."

"And what's your name, handsome?" Her grin was as sweet as her tone.

"Gerald. Major Gerald Grey. But you can just call me Gerald."

Her smile melted away, and the weight of regret shone in her eyes.

"I feel so awful; you're being so nice to me, even after I hurt you. Why?" She was holding her arm under her breast, which, had I died on the Goliath, would have been one of the last images in my mind. It made me uncomfortable to be staring at … okay, you know, if I'm going to be her friend and colleague I might as well admit it. The reason her chest armor piece had bulged out was because she had an enormous pair of breasts. Now that that has been mentioned, it will never be touched again. As in subject-wise. Erm... you know what I mean.

"Why not? Why should I have a reason to be nice? Kindness saves lives." I smiled at her. "Besides, I forgive you."

She hesitated. "I'm sorry. I can't say I didn't mean to shoot you, but I can't say I wanted to, but do you mean it?"

Nearly every person that has shot at me has ended up dead. Did I really mean it? On any windy day my answer would have been a simple no, and a piece of lead being shot to my facing direction. But she could help me train troops. And she had been following orders from her superiors. However, regarding the kiss, I would not forgive her because of that. I owed her either way. I had killed her teacher, maybe her only friend.

"Hey, it's fine. I forgive you, and I mean it. Besides, I'm fine." I opened my shirt to show her that the wound she made was no longer there—somehow, thanks to Olivia.

"Sir?" the head of the POWs looked puzzled as he again appeared.

"Oh yes, as clearance level ten, I am authorized to ask for female prisoner number ... the one I was just speaking to ... to be escorted to the castle. That's an order."

"Yes, sir." His expression matched the tone of his voice.

The other prisoners sounded their discontent as she was released to me. She was called a harlot, a whore, and a traitorous bitch. I had no interest in the rest of the prisoners; another officer would be in charge of them

I stood up, stretched, and readied myself to go talk to the king and Ryan. However, I still didn't know what I was going to decide. The image in the scope kept changing, and I was still filled with indecision. Train an army here, or train them on carriers.

The parade of the liberation of the city was taking place. The troops marched into the streets, singing and cheering without a worry in the world. As I sat down with a glass of water, the cheers of the people turned my frown upside down. Some music came from my compressor, and it vibrated. I had received a message from Olivia saying she would see me later at lunch.

They wanted to cut my hair if I joined. They would cut my pay if my acceptance of command was not sent off to the prime minister later on. I was stalling for time.

Stalling to maybe make the right decision. Three ships flew overhead and passed the castle. I thought maybe a walk would clear my head. The sun was something I needed, and I hoped the walk would ease my troubled mind. I stood by the door and stared at the scope, which was lying on the desk. It again changed to the razed environment. *What if that is what happens if I stay? The other one could be the future if I leave to fight. Or it could be the other way.* I smiled and shut the door before stealing one last glimpse at the scope. It changed and changed and changed, always between those two scenarios.

I would either stay and defend Olivia or go and fight for Olivia's safety. Either way, my choice would be for her. I heard my boots echo down the hallway. As I moved down it with the other soldiers, who were going about their business on their own paths, I moved toward my own destiny, my own path, something I controlled.